YEAR 14

Published by Barrelhouse Books
Baltimore, MD

www.barrelhousemag.com

Published in the United States of America

ISBN 13: 978-0-9889945-5-3

First Edition

Cover design & illustration: Shanna Compton, shannacompton.com
Page design: Adam Robinson, goodbookdevelopers.com

YEAR 14

Michael Konik

Barrelhouse Books 2017

Other Books by Michael Konik

Report from the Street: Voices of the Homeless
How the Revolution Started
The Termite Squad
Making It
Becoming Bobby
Reefer Gladness
The Smart Money
Ella in Europe
In Search of Burningbush
Telling Lies and Getting Paid
Nice Shot, Mr. Nicklaus
The Man with the $100,000 Breasts

For Joseph Astrud Pineda,
who inspires me to view the world with his wonder and delight.

CHAPTER ONE

I understand that writing this down on paper without first obtaining the proper license is not permitted.

I will be dealt with appropriately. You could say this report will be my suicide note.

But at the risk of displaying what might seem like a horrible lack of appreciation, I feel a strange responsibility, a civic duty you might say, to record what happened here in my sacred Homeland.

After I am gone, and after everyone else who was here is gone, I would like people to be informed. Not just my fellow citizens. I would like everyone—allies and enemies, natives and neighbors alike—to have an eyewitness account from a professional who was on the scene. Even those who profess disdain for my sacred Homeland and our exalted way of life, they should know what happened.

I would like the whole world to know the truth.

Yes, of course, this concept of "the truth" is a subjective construct created by outsiders whose secret wish is to colonize my people. A good citizen does not muse upon this unhelpful notion, this abstract concept of "the truth," and he certainly does not raise the subject in polite conversation. Or write it down on paper without first obtaining the proper license!

I am ashamed to confess that I am not a good citizen. I am a bad one, probably an evil one, and I probably deserve the punishment that awaits me.

So I apologize in advance for causing offense of any kind. I am truly very sorry. All who know me well—my family and my colleagues at *Perriodocko* and my local community team of Dedicated Servants—they must have expected better of someone like me, someone who was given every opportunity to fulfill his potential. To all of you, then, I ask a thousand pardons. Please try to understand that I cannot help myself. What I saw, what I experienced, what we *all* experienced—well, I do not think there has been anything like it.

As I write these words by candlelight, in a location I cannot mention, I do not fear for my future. I understand that I have no future. My only fear is that what happened here will one day be forgotten.

Let me tell you.

CHAPTER TWO

Maybe it is best to start at the beginning. Except I am no longer sure if what I once understood to be the beginning—what I and every other person here is taught from a young age to be the beginning—is the real beginning, or if it is just the Official Version.

Ah bolah, I have surprised myself.

Ah bolah, or, "Oh, my goodness," you might say in English or another unauthorized language. *Ah bolah*! I am sorry for writing down something so rude.

Please accept my previous apology.

And perhaps to save time and space you will forgive me in advance for other terrible things I am about to write? And for writing it all without obtaining the necessary permission?

It happened this year. For us, Year 14.

We measure the passing of time a little differently than in other places, since we no longer recognize false calendars created by the Jews or the Christians or the Muslims, or any other degenerates who would attempt to impose their debased values on us. Our History Book shows that these people once occupied our sacred Homeland, and so did the British and Americans at various points. And the Spanish, for a time. And so did others, it has been rumored, although you cannot find confirmation of this in the Guiding Text.

Much of what occurred here before the Caring Leaders rescued us is probably misunderstood and slightly mixed up. If you were not here at that exact moment, it is easy to be confused by hearsay repeated and enhanced by very old comrades who possibly have drunk *bolo* beyond their ration and started imagining unhappy thoughts.

However, I was here in Year 1, when everything was switched: the calendar, the flag, the anthem, the money, the policies. Everything.

We cleansed ourselves of all that was not working.

Ah bolah, it was rather confusing in Year 1.

Many of my acquaintances mysteriously disappeared, simply vanishing overnight. Others I saw with my own eyes being taken away by uniformed National Heroes.

Some of my acquaintances were attached to the failed old ways. They were so brainwashed that they broke the new rules *intentionally*, as I am doing now. And some broke the rules by so-called "honest mistake," which we all quickly learned was not a valid excuse. It was a confusing time, I must say.

I was still in my twenties then, in Year 1. A young man.

Before the changeover, I was even younger. A boy. Forgive me, please, for displaying *meowkaleet* (too much pride) when I report that I was a serious student with top marks in all disciplines, including the important ones such as Chemistry, Agriculture, and Homeland History, and also frivolous ones that are no longer taught, such as unauthorized languages, European Art, and International History. Because I had performed with honorable distinction at my university studies, I was given every opportunity to be a Dedicated Servant of the people, and, it was understood, I might eventually learn to be a Caring Leader.

Unfortunately, I was not able to fulfill my destiny.

Before the changeover, serving in the military was not yet mandatory. But even back then the law was clear: one could not be a lifelong Dedicated Servant without first volunteering to be a National Hero for five years. One of the two great tragedies in my life, please allow me to say, was being disqualified from joining the National Heroes because of my condition.

My right leg is two *plongi* (maybe a centimeter or so?) shorter than the left, which causes me to walk with a very slight limp, which almost none of my fellow citizens notice or comment upon, except naughty children. It is not a serious condition. But, apparently, serious enough to exclude me from proudly serving.

Although I quietly accepted the examiner's decision at the time, and I never said so out loud, to this day I remain convinced that I could have been an exemplary National Hero, despite my imperfections. To my great dismay, I was not permitted the honor.

Because I had demonstrated advanced academic abilities and significant promise, upon graduation at age 21 I was assigned to the excellent position of Junior Assistant, specializing in Information Gathering at our highly respected National News Service, where I was trained in the approved methods of keeping my fellow citizens educated, motivated, and committed to the future.

I did important work there, gathering information. My superiors went so far as to characterize my work as heroic. But I did not feel this way.

Except on *Tink*, our weekly Day of Reflection, when the electricity is turned off, every day I saw National Heroes parading past my office, high on the 3rd floor of the imposing National News Building. I could not march with them. This, I confess, hurt me, like the slap your teacher administers when you are not concentrating properly. Although I understood I would never wear the handsome green uniform or carry a weapon, I consoled myself with the knowledge that I was not altogether worthless. In my position of unusual privilege, working in a room with air conditioning and given free drinking water and *uchaana* (our version of cigarettes, but without tobacco), I could do my small part for the National Heroes by helping prepare informative and inspiring articles about them.

My boss at the time, whose name I prefer not to invoke, since he has been discredited (and has since vanished), was the Deputy Supervisor responsible for organizing all the news stories about our Heroes. We were expected to produce as many as eight or nine articles a day, although the average at that time was closer to four, since a certain amount of editorial space was expected to be set aside for other Dedicated Servants and Caring Leaders—and also for *scrachi*, our national sport, which involves stones and tethered birds and is badly misunderstood by those who were not lucky enough to be born here.

When I started out at the National News Service, our sacred Homeland still had many tabloids and magazines. Back then, there were four daily broadsheets in addition to the official newspaper, *Perriodocko*. Published proudly by the National News Service, *Perriodocko* has never contained advertising or commercial interests, and is therefore the only newspaper that can be trusted. The other newspapers, the "alternative" publications, which we later learned were financed and controlled by foreigners and internal subversives, were at one time quite popular among the uneducated members of our society. These second-rank papers published numerous photos of our beloved singing stars, the most celebrated entertainers in our sacred Homeland. As well as extensive *scrachi* coverage, of course.

If the unofficial publications had simply conducted themselves responsibly, with proper ethics and etiquette, there is a chance they would still be around today, printing their colorful concert pictures and exclusive backstage interviews with beautiful recording artists. *Chu-chu*, we call this kind of thing, the *chu-chu* world of show business. Silly, perhaps, but harmless. *Ah bolah,* we are crazy for our *chu-chu.* Some say we are a nation of *chu-chu* maniacs, and they mean that as a compliment.

But the other "news outlets" were not happy giving the citizens what they wanted. Instead, the unofficial papers got into the regrettable habit of printing the most revolting slander, making rude accusations about respected and influential citizens. Senators, even.

The syndrome started out small, as these things usually do. An anonymous tip. An impertinent question. A so-called "investigation." And then everything went out of control. Common decency was sacrificed for the sake of scandal. *Ah bolah,* reputations were destroyed, just like that!

They even wrote that our most revered Agriculture Minister, who came from a very good family and needed nothing, was diverting public funds that were meant for purchasing seeds and fertilizer. Can you imagine?

The entertaining *chu-chu* reporting gradually diminished, and the lies increased, primarily among the top columnists. It later came out that these writers were being manipulated by unscrupulous handlers, who plied them with *bolo* and drugs, and sometimes immoral women, and, in one case, it was rumored, peasant boys from the provinces.

This was indeed a dark and challenging time, this period right before Year 1. You couldn't pick up a newspaper – except *Perriodoko,* of course – without finding some wild accusation of corruption and deceit. *Ah bolah,* the so-called Opinion Section, where the most reckless "journalists" could say anything that came to their head without fear of consequences: I tell you, it was criminal without being technically criminal, and a big embarrassment to those of us at the National News Service, where dedicated Information Gatherers conscientiously reported the real news and advocated for the betterment of the common man.

But these newspapers, these dirty rags, worthless except for wrapping fishmeal cakes, got into vulnerable minds, like trash in the river, infecting them with dangerous and unhelpful ideas. All you heard was problems. Problems, problems, problems! Never solutions.

If it is possible for an entire country to be depressed, to feel that there is no hope for a better future, we experienced that kind of suffering. It is a very sad way to live.

Fortunately, several of our Senators—this was, as I say, just before the changeover, back when we still had Senators—devised a clever solution. They concocted and unanimously passed a new law, popularly known as BABA (an easy-to-remember acronym), whose official title is difficult to translate directly but which means, more or less, "Legal Right to Reply, Retort, and Refute Anything That Is Said Against You."

If one of the scandal mongers wrote something negative about you or your family, you were legally entitled to BABA: to reply, retort, and refute the accusation in the newspaper that started the trouble. By law, the offending publication was required to give equal space to anyone who had been insulted. The newspaper was also required to print the BABA in the identical place as the accusation. If something rude about a Senator was written on the front page above the fold, that was where he was entitled to have his BABA. If a malicious column appeared in the so-called Opinion Section, where much of the most irresponsible dirt was flung about, like monkeys playing with their droppings, then the next day's column would be authored by the offended party, who would be granted equal space to clear his good name.

It was very fair.

Predictably, the worst violators, the publications that caused all the turmoil in the first place, complained and whined like spoiled children, claiming that their precious editorial space, which really ought to have been dedicated to stories about *chuchu* and *scrachi*, would be monopolized by back-and-forth bickering between their writers and the people whose reputations were being wantonly damaged.

For a very brief time, there was talk of all the newspapers in our sacred Homeland banding together in a kind of cartel and organizing an anti-BABA crusade. But the Chief Editor of *Perriodoko* at the time, a great and humble man, reminded us all of what really matters. The Chief Editor, who to this day still permits every citizen, important or not, to call him by his informal nickname Junior, or Jun, even though he is now Minister of Information and one of our most beloved Caring Leaders—he made a very interesting point. Chief Editor Junior said that there is no amount of newsprint and no amount of ink that should be spared in the pursuit of fairness. That was the most important thing, Chief Editor Junior told us. Fairness.

Perriodoko flourished during the BABA era, because our newspaper was the fairest. We enlightened our fellow citizens *and* showed respect to Dedicated Servants who had pledged their lives to helping the public. We were polite.

Do not assume we shirked our national duty to thoroughly investigate and report our findings to our fellow citizens. At the risk of exposing my tendency for *meowkaleet*, I must brag a little and note that we won many, many awards for our valuable work. We were the only publication in our sacred Homeland to be multi-awarded by the most respected awarding organizations. Our record spoke for itself.

The other newspapers, with their disgusting stories and interminable disagreements, could not match our determination to do things the right way. They rapidly faded into oblivion. People lost interest in reading two grown men shouting at each other in print.

We at *Perriodoko* were not insensitive to the needs of our readers. We expanded our *chu-chu* and *scrachi* coverage. If you asked any educated citizen, they would tell you they were happy to have one completely reliable and trustworthy newspaper.

It was certainly more convenient.

CHAPTER THREE

For the next three years, almost four, I performed acceptably in the eyes of my superiors, and I was gradually promoted to positions of increased responsibilities: 2nd Senior Assistant, 1st Senior Assistant, and, eventually, Assistant to the Deputy Supervisor.

Finally, when my boss, who reported directly to Chief Editor Junior, was courteously asked to retire after some embarrassing episodes, I was named Deputy Supervisor, Information Gathering.

I mean no immodesty when I note that I was the youngest person to hold the position.

Concurrent with the elevation in title, I received generous salary raises and an elite double ration of *bolo,* which was considered a prestigious and valuable benefit reserved only for Dedicated Servants and the most productive regular citizens. I felt somewhat guilty accepting the bonus, I confess, because I do not drink wine!

Ah bolah, it was an uncomfortable situation. Here I was surrounded by fellow workers at the National News Service, many of them lifelong *bolo* enthusiasts, and, except for our bosses, almost none of whom were permitted the extra jug afforded me.

To refuse the honor of a double *bolo* ration would have been an insult to my team captains, who, I knew, had pulled invisible strings and redeemed long-held favors to procure the fermented reward for me, a regular citizen.

So I accepted the sweet-and-sour juice, which always made my throat feel burnt. I took it home to my family's apartment—I was not yet married and living in the next door apartment—and I gave it to my brother, Boy, who said the wine helped him with his pain. Boy lost most of his right arm in a training accident that happened less than a week after he joined the National Heroes. He feels strange, imaginary shocks in the area where his elbow would be if he still had it. The *bolo* helps with this condition, although nothing, it seems, can make it entirely disappear. *Ah bolah*. My brother.

What happened to Boy was a shame. But he found consolation in the knowledge that he had upheld our family honor in a way that I was not able, and whether he wore the beautiful green uniform or a soiled white t-shirt, whether he protected our borders or stayed at home watching NTV-4 and listening to *chu-chu*, he would always be a National Hero

All of us were very proud of him, of course. I just found myself occasionally wishing that Boy still had all of his arm and didn't have to drink himself to sleep, only to awake to another day of interminable agony.

Naturally, I did not say this to him, nor to anyone else. I did not want to lower his morale. The *bolo* was my way of saying it.

CHAPTER FOUR

I was 26 in Year 1, when the changeover happened.

I had settled into my duties as the Deputy Supervisor, Information Gathering at *Perriodocko*; I drew wages and benefits in line with an official Dedicated Servant, although I was not one; I had my brother, Boy, and my father (mother having died when I was young, from a water illness) and all my cousins; I had plenty of professional acquaintances among the National Heroes, top ranking officers who talked to me with a familiarity usually reserved for lifelong friends; and I had my great-grandfather's wristwatch, a beautiful old timepiece, I must say, which still functioned and needed winding only once a week.

My life was good.

But one cannot be always selfish. We have a saying: *Bebudew op en beberoo kap.* "You are never alone, you only feel alone."

My life was good. But my sacred Homeland, not so good.

I would prefer to not dwell on the negative, for that accomplishes nothing. I shall simply say that we had some areas of our society that were broken and had to be fixed. Certain challenges vexed us, no matter what solution was proposed, and you could say we were the victim of too much of one thing and not enough of another.

Something drastic was required.

The History Book has the entire story of the Glorious Citizen Power Revolution, so I will not repeat what is already well known. Every schoolchild can tell you.

Even with experienced Generals overseeing the transition, there was some minor chaos at first. Such confusion was to be expected, of course. Change is never easy.

And change does not come without sacrifice. For my family, it meant taking in a cousin, Gurly, from the provinces, whose home and field were needed by a National Hero. Like many regular citizens, she could not immediately find work in our Capital City, even with my assistance. I tried, but she did not understand the urban ways. Without an officially recognized job, Gurly could not obtain the proper coupons for rations, and so we gave her what we could to eat, which often seemed like not quite enough.

Even worse than chronic hunger, which one learns to endure and outwit, most regular citizens struggled to absorb and understand the new regulations designed to improve life for all of us.

New and innovative rules for the benefit of society were announced almost every day in Year 1. I was aware of each of them, and not only because I could read—which a number of regular citizens in our sacred Homeland cannot do, including most of my cousins from the provinces. I was fully aware because I was an employee of the NNS. In fact, I was good friends with another Deputy Supervisor at *Perriodocko.* He was responsible for publishing the directives, making certain they contained proper spelling and punctuation.

My friend went on to become a Dedicated Servant at the Department of Information. He had toiled admirably as a National Hero before joining the National News Service. He was supremely well-qualified.

When we still worked together, my friend would sometimes show me the latest proclamations as soon as they were set in type.

I therefore knew that my bicycle had to be properly registered with both my local council *and* the newly formed National Transportation Commission.

I knew about the need to obtain the proper permit from a Dedicated Servant at the Office of Creation before commencing with a group theater or dance production—not that I would be a candidate for such a thing!

I knew that our traditional *compastee*, small bits of arable land in our crowded Capital City, patches of dirt that old women liked to use as miniature gardens, could be claimed for the public good and developed into Beautification and Celebration projects, so long as a detailed proposal for the intended project had been properly registered with all appropriate offices (the six of them).

I knew that lawlessness would not be tolerated, and that violators, whether native or interlopers, would face appropriate consequences.

Many others, at first, claimed they did not know about the rules, because they could not read, or at least not well enough to fully understand the necessary requirements.

This was not really a credible excuse. Our MATAA buses, the most popular and inexpensive form of transport—*hahnkers* is the slang term for them—could not be missed. They are plentiful and loud. *Ah bolah.* Very noisy. These *hahnkers*, the motorized vans and trucks that traverse our city from sun-up to sun-down every day except *Tink*, were outfitted with loudspeakers, generously provided by our Caring Leaders. In calmer times, it was understood, these speakers could be programmed to play patriotic *chu-chu* music, or deliver inspiring greetings.

But during the changeover they were best used to announce the new regulations. So even if you could not read—which, I note, can indeed be a problem for some unlucky people—you could still listen to the messages from the *hahnkers*. You simply had to pay attention.

Some citizens, apparently, found this difficult. Or they were unwilling to understand. They were a problem.

The vast majority, however, were able to learn rapidly. They paid attention. The ones that did not—well, we have a saying. *Nevaa lahang en nini warmung.* "You cannot educate a goat."

Eventually, order and understanding took hold. Once the most troublesome offenders were dealt with, the vast majority of citizens behaved according to the rules. They followed the necessary steps, and almost everything in our sacred Homeland became calmer.

There was certainly less crime. *Ah bolah*, that was obvious from the start. And the statistics only improved. Our streets were usually very safe. People here had respect for the laws, which, after all, were created simply to make life better for everyone.

It did not take long—maybe six months—before all citizens, even the illiterate, understood the new ways. Ignorance was transformed into splendid knowledge. Everyone helped his neighbor become an improved citizen. I myself on multiple occasions patiently explained to my father the crucial difference between a license and a permit, a simple concept that he had trouble grasping.

He was an older man without a formal education, a simple man, and he did not understand that a permit is valid only for a one-time use—although, in most cases, if it is properly endorsed by the relevant authority it may be renewed up to three times.

A license, on the other hand, is good for a full year, superseding the need for an individual permit.

For example, I told him once: I, your youngest son, have a *license* to write news stories at *Perriodocko*, as well as a *license* for my bicycle, and another one to carry a tape recorder on my person (so long as it is used in my official capacity as an Information Gatherer for the National News Service). If, however, for some unknown reason I had the strange impulse to write a non-factual book, such as what they call a novel, I would be required to obtain the proper *permit* from the Office of Creation, which oversees this type of activity.

Father said he could not imagine me wanting to write something made up, so I gave him a different example: If, for some unknown reason, I wanted to leave the wonderful NNS and become, say, a common *hahnker* driver, I would need the proper *license* to secure a route. But if I wanted to paint my new *hahnker* a brighter shade of orange or improve it with an encouraging message emblazoned on the side, I would need a *permit* from both my local council and the national commission.

My father said he thought he understood. Yet for several months he was cited for various permit violations—including one for unauthorized flower planting in the dusty strip of dirt beside our apartment building—and he was compelled to pay modest but necessary penalties. I helped him with the funds. My father eventually caught on. All of us did.

It was somewhat funny: During Year 1, before a new regulation was announced that forbade such impertinence, regular citizens liked to say that they were living in a "fine country," because there was always an appropriate fine for not following the ordinances correctly. Do you get the joke? It maybe does not translate perfectly.

I do not consider it unchecked *meowkaleet* to mention that I myself was never fined. I report this fact not because I think I was a better citizen than others around me but because I do not think it is fair to suggest, as some have, that knowing the right way to do things, the right way to do everything, was somehow impossible, or that it required an exceptional memory. That is nonsense. Anyone can be law-abiding and polite. You simply must use common sense. Rather than assume that something does not require the proper permit, it is merely commonsensical to assume that it does. When one is uncertain, one simply asks the relevant authority. Being a Dedicated Servant of the people, he will want to help you.

During Year 1, it was sometimes said that Dedicated Servants were more inclined to help you if you helped them in some way. *Bolo* tickets, and such. This situation was soon corrected, and besides, after a regulation was announced prohibiting the discussion of certain unpleasant topics, including this particular one, almost nobody cared to focus on the matter.

Our sacred Homeland made tremendous and admirable progress. No, we were not perfect in Year 1. But we seemed to be headed in that direction.

CHAPTER FIVE

The decade following the changeover was a period of prosperity for our sacred Homeland.

Food and drinking water were often more plentiful, and safer to consume.

We built the magnificent Kulla River Dam and the FFA Memorial Reactor.

We increased national productivity by impressive percentages.

We upgraded our roads, our telephone system, and our broadcasting capabilities. Nearly every household had a radio. Many had a telephone.

We even sent our national football team, the Brave Warriors, to a Planetary Cup qualifying tournament, although I am not certain how that concluded.

Our crime rate continued to drop, consistently, allowing some of our former prisons and interrogation centers to be used for other important projects. There is a misguided school of thought that claims the death penalty is not a deterrent. I would strongly disagree. Indeed, studies done by researchers at National University have shown that it is even more effective when applied against a wide array of offenses, not simply murder or treason. Thieving, smuggling, assaulting: all these crimes can be lessened when potential culprits know that they will pay the ultimate price.

I would like to point out that composing an Unauthorized Report is not punishable by execution. The penalty is twelve years of hard labor. Unauthorized Reports that undermine national goals, however, are treated differently, more like treason, and with the same mortal consequences.

But I am going to finish this anyway. If I may make a joke: Maybe those who say the death penalty does not function as an effective deterrent have a point in my case. *Ah bolah, bolah, bolah.*

It is said that all of us bring unpleasantness into our life because of the choices we make. We have a folk saying, which mothers in the provinces tell their children, and which I will translate: "If you kiss a snake, expect to be bitten." One cannot act with impunity. Every action has an opposite and equal reaction. That has been proven by our sacred Homeland's best scientists.

The lesson was made clear to me and to all my fellow citizens when, in Year 6, two female enemy spies were captured while attempting to sneak across our borders. Some of my colleagues at *Perriodocko* felt the criminals should be shown some level of mercy because of their sex, as if their biology was a valid explanation for breaking our sovereign laws. I was in the camp that believed you do not kiss a snake unless you are prepared to be bitten.

We all bring things upon ourselves. That is clear.

I am not so filled with *meowkaleet* to imagine that my good fortune in the happy years was solely a product of my determination and fortitude. No, I was looked after. I was given every opportunity to distinguish myself, and I was treated with respect and appreciation commensurate with my position as Deputy

Supervisor, Information Gathering at our sacred Homeland's newspaper.

I do not mean to suggest I lived extravagantly. None of us did.

Yet, under the guidance and benevolence of our Caring Leaders, I had enough to eat, and often enough to share with the less fortunate members of my clan. I was given a new bicycle in Year 7, and a cellular telephone in Year 8. And in Year 9, when I was almost 35, I was given the most precious gift: a wife.

She was quite agreeable, and not at all unintelligent. She had been born and raised in the city and had attended finishing school. I came to enjoy chatting with her about various subjects after I returned home from the news office, although regulations did not permit me to discuss the inner workings of the NNS. I grew to like her very much, and, if I may be blunt, I eventually became accustomed to being addressed as "Dear Husband." You could say I grew fond of hearing her say those words. I cannot explain why.

She was also quite a good cook, an expert soup-maker. That cannot be overlooked.

When I received notification that I would be married, my father panicked. He was concerned we would not have enough space in our apartment, what with him, Boy, Gurly and me already occupying two of the three rooms and the kitchen commanding the other. To his delight, and to my surprise, the apartment next door was made available for my wife and me. The previous occupants, a seller of dried fruits, his seamstress wife, and their four children (two of whom I knew to be unauthorized), were relocated.

Having a wife was quite awkward at first, I confess. *Ah bolah*, I did not know what to do. I had not been with a woman before.

We were both embarrassed. But we figured it out.

Although my wife was no *chu-chu* star, she was not bad looking, and she had the bone structure of one who would be predisposed to delivering healthy babies. I was, therefore, quite sad when, in Year 10 and Year 11, she suffered two consecutive miscarriages shortly after undergoing the initial tests confirming her pregnancy.

We did not talk about hypothetical situations. But I recall one rainy evening in our apartment. Through the walls I could hear the muffled shouts of my brother, who could have been arguing with my father about something, or who might have been drunk. The radio in our apartment was playing an uplifting song by one of our very finest singers. While sitting at the table, sipping *vurben,* a kind of homemade tea, my wife got emotional, as women will, and she confessed that she wondered what her daughters might have been like. Would they have been beautiful? Or smart? Would they have been *chu-chu* stars? She cried.

I comforted her as best I could, although I do not have a natural talent for that kind of thing. I told my wife that we could always try again, and with the correct astrological positioning it was even possible that next time we would produce boys.

Unfortunately, her tubes had been damaged during the second operation, which we only discovered after a series of fully-authorized supplementary examinations.

Once my wife accepted that she could not bear children, we did not talk about it again, preferring to concentrate on the positive initiatives launched by our Caring Leaders, and sometimes the weather and other pleasant topics. As I say, I found my wife rather likable. I always have.

Life did not stop for our personal disappointment.

Our sacred Homeland continued to prosper, always improving. "More power!" ("*Grabvey!*") we would say to our fellow citizens. *Grabvey! Grabvey!* "More power!" Gains were made. New challenges were identified and met. We became better and better, more modern and advanced, but also more aware of our proud national roots, established only a decade previous.

Everything for me—my job, my family, my health—everything was adequate. We have a saying: *A bili en creneckulo.* "I cannot complain."

Having not been blessed with children, my life proceeded without complications or undue concerns. Year 11 was satisfactory. Year 12 was also satisfactory. Year 13 seemed to be, as well.

And then, around harvest time of that year, something unexpected happened, something that no one could have predicted. TupTup came into my life.

CHAPTER SIX

I had been working at my desk, reviewing a story that one of my team members was preparing about a National Hero who had discovered an unauthorized Website page on the computer at his barracks. According to our thoroughly researched article, the soldier had stumbled accidentally upon the filthy Internet content and subsequently made all the correct reports to his superiors. Even though this National Hero modestly claimed he was only doing what was required of a good citizen, he was rewarded with his photo in *Perriodocko*, guaranteeing he would forever be remembered as an admirable example to others confronted with dangerous breaches of the law.

As I was vetting this uplifting article, Mr. K, Administrative Assistant to the Chief Editor, appeared before me, bearing a small note card. He nodded politely and handed it to me.

I had been summoned to the office of our boss, Chief Editor Pops. He had replaced Chief Editor Junior when our former inspiration and guide was deservedly elevated to the Ministership and officially declared a Caring Leader. I was to come immediately to the 4th Floor.

Chief Editor Pops was known to everyone at *Perriodocko* as an exceptionally fair and decent man who treated all of us, no matter our rank, with respect and courtesy. These were the qualities that allowed him to be an exemplary journalist, a man who could be trusted with sensitive information and sensitive feelings. He was, I would like to say, something of a living legend at *Perriodocko*. A role model.

Because of his excellent reputation, and because he had personally complimented my work three days earlier, I was not unduly nervous about our meeting. But I *was* curious. Could it possibly be? Might this be the day I would be notified that I had been approved as a candidate for promotion? Might I be elevated to full Supervisor status? My department's production, forgive my *meowkaleet* tendencies, had been highly praised. And I was nearing almost 20 years of experience. I knew how everything worked. Was it really such a far-fetched fantasy?

I dashed up the stairs, perhaps a bit too quickly. Breathless, I took a few moments to compose myself. Then I walked to the end of the hallway to the Chief Editor's office and announced myself.

One of his secretaries told me to wait. He was on a phone call.

In all my years at the National News Service, I had never been inside the Chief Editor's office. The prospect was quite exciting.

I sat in the anteroom outside his suite, gazing admiringly at the impressive gallery of photographs lining the walls. The pictures represented a sort of Tribute of Honor, you might say, a series of portraits of our greatest citizens, our most powerful Caring Leaders and our biggest stars—and there beside them, in every photo, was Chief Editor Pops, smiling contentedly. He looked very happy, I thought. And why not? He was friendly with the people who really mattered in our sacred Homeland. Indeed, he was one of them.

I felt a tickle in my belly, because I allowed myself to imagine that I was on the cusp of also being one of those rare achievers.

Ah bolah, I had allowed myself to get carried away by foolish daydreams.

About ten minutes later, when I was finally admitted to the office of Chief Editor Pops, he smiled a little at my salute and invited me to sit in the empty chair in front his desk. Mr. K appeared with a cool glass of water and offered me an *uchaana* and matches, which I declined. I wanted to be focused.

"Starting tomorrow morning, we have a new man joining our team," Chief Editor Pops said, looking down at me across the polished wood expanse, empty except for a modern push-button telephone and a miniature national flag in a smart plastic holder. "Because you are considered one of the most reliable Deputies in the entire building, I have decided that the new man should be integrated into the system with your guidance. He will be given the title of Special Assistant, and he will report to you directly. You will be his boss."

Chief Editor Pops paused, but he looked as though he wished to say more, so I did not respond.

"Do you understand?" he asked pleasantly.

"Yes, sir," I answered. Training a new staffer was not unfamiliar work to me.

Then Chief Editor Pops mentioned the name of a very important person, a Caring Leader, one of the most powerful people in our sacred Homeland. "You are familiar with this great individual," Chief Editor Pops said. It was not a question.

I nodded appreciatively. "Yes, sir, Chief Editor. I am personally grateful to him for all he has done at the Bureau of Industry. He has made life better for all of us."

"Yes," Chief Editor Pops said. "Anyway, the new man is his son."

"*Ah bolah!*" I exclaimed, perhaps a bit too forcefully.

"Yes. So you understand." Chief Editor Pops fixed his gaze upon me, and I felt the solemnity of the moment.

"It is a great honor," I said.

"Yes. Now I must inform you that I myself have not yet had the good fortune to meet this young man in person. But I am told that the son—well, he is a bit of a *vernando*," Chief Editor Pops said, chuckling, using the slang term for what you might call "a joker," someone with a tendency to be unserious.

I nodded. "I understand."

Chief Editor Pops frowned slightly, the way people sometimes do after a sip of *bolo*. "I do not foresee any problems."

"No, sir," I said. "There certainly will not be."

"Very good," Chief Editor Pops said. "You are an excellent team member, and it will continue to be noted as such in your file."

I stopped myself from smiling too broadly. "Thank you, Chief Editor," I said, as humbly as I could.

"I would look after him myself if I had the time," Chief Editor Pops declared. "But, *ah bolah*, there are other matters requiring my attention."

It was true. Chief Editor Pops was a terribly busy man, with enormous responsibilities. I was privileged to be chosen to assist him, especially since the assignment involved a member of one of our most revered families.

"Here," Chief Editor Pops said, reaching into an unseen drawer behind his desk. "You may review this." He handed me a folder embossed with the official seal of the National News Service. "It is not to be copied or distributed."

"No, sir," I said, accepting the folder, which felt surprisingly light, as though it were empty.

"Some background information," Chief Editor Pops said, wagging his hand. "Nothing unusual. Just to help you be prepared."

"Yes, sir. Of course."

"Yes. Very good." Chief Editor Pops nodded and raised his eyebrows twice. I understood that our meeting had concluded.

"Thank you, sir, for the opportunity. I will handle everything with the proper respect," I said, making a salute. Then I rose with the skinny folder and departed the Chief Editor's grand surroundings, leaving the glass of water untouched.

The moment I was back downstairs at my small office, I informed my assistants and secretaries that I should not be interrupted until further notice. Then I sat at my desk and opened the folder.

Inside was a single sheet of paper.

Beneath the familiar NNS letterhead printed across the top, someone had typed in bold capital letters the new man's name—a long one, befitting his family's stature, with three middle names honoring his ancestors. And right below it: "Prefers to be addressed as *TupTup*".

This was not unusual, even for a very important person. We are quite fond of our informal nicknames. What was unusual was the name itself: If you spelled it and said it just a little differently, "TupTup" sounded like another word in our language that most educated people would consider somewhat vulgar and demeaning.

I made a mental note to take care in my pronunciation.

Aside from a few mentions about his illustrious family, the file contained a limited amount of biographical information: his home address (at one of our Capital City's finest private communities, I noted) and his birth-date, which indicated that my new colleague, this TupTup, was nearly 30.

I found this remarkable, since accomplished and important citizens of our sacred Homeland typically begin entry-level jobs, such as the one being offered him at *Perriodocko*, closer to age 21, after completing university or National Hero duty. Also, the single photo, a standard identification bust, about four *plongi* square, did not appear to show the face of an adult. By the looks of the photo, which, I surmised, must have been quite out-of-date, I would have thought he was a teenaged boy.

You could tell that what Chief Editor Pops had suggested was accurate. With his crooked smile, boxy haircut, and mischievous eyes, TupTup certainly looked like a real *vernando* -- a *vernando* laughing at his own private joke. I made another mental note to discourage unproductive workplace behavior while still demonstrating the respect all important people deserve.

At the bottom of the page, which, I noticed, lacked the signature or identification number of whoever had prepared the file, there was a brief citation entitled "Supplemental Note."

It said: *Specially gifted but requires constant supervision. Main area of interest:* chu-chu. *Wishes to work at* Perriodocko.

For some unknown reason, I felt a little wave of *meowkaleet* pass through me. Although he surely could have picked any occupation he fancied, Mr. TupTup, it seemed, wanted to be one of us.

I closed the file and put it in the top drawer of my desk. I looked out my window at the street below, and I saw what I always saw at that time of day, marching past.

And I remember thinking that it was quite wonderful how, for some worthy people, every dream comes true.

CHAPTER SEVEN

"**H**e is here!"

My 2nd Assistant turned away from my office window, wide-eyed and obviously nervous.

I was, too. But I refused to betray my jitters in front of my subordinates. They looked to me for leadership. "Very well," I replied, curtly. "Now compose yourself."

My 2nd Assistant seemed not to have heard me. "He just arrived, just got out of a *blecky*, a very shiny one, with an escort!"

These private sedans, made abroad and imported at unthinkable cost, were reserved for the most elite Dedicated Servants and Caring Leaders. Not even Chief Editor Pops had one—only the very, very top people. Each *blecky* bore a license plate number of 999 or less. The lower the number, the more important the occupant, although you seldom saw who was inside, since the windows were usually darkened.

"What a beautiful automobile!" my 2nd Assistant gushed. "Impressive."

"Yes, they are quite fine vehicles, you silly goat," I said. "Of course he travels by *blecky*. What do you expect? For him to commute by *hahnker*, like a common peasant? Now return to your post and prepare for the proper introductions."

"Yes, sir," my 2nd Assistant said, unable to hide his grin as he shuffled out of my office.

When he was gone, I went to the window. There was no sign of our esteemed visitor, and the *blecky* was just pulling away into the morning traffic, engulfed by bicycles and *hahnkers*, professional charity collectors and *uchaana* hawkers. I could not see the license plate.

Suddenly I felt very thirsty, and hot.

Looking back now, almost a year later, I must laugh at my initial anxiety prior to meeting TupTup. *Ah bolah,* I spent the previous night badgering my poor wife with imaginary concerns: "What if this important man is unwilling to take direction?"

"Should I mention my admiration for his father?"

"Does he expect immediate promotion?"

"What if he is unpleasant to my Assistants?"

My wife, sensing that I did not seek answers, only a forum to air my worries, said nothing. She did, however, knit her brow and bite her lower lip.

"It is a very delicate situation," I concluded. "I must be careful."

She nodded. And quietly, almost apologetically, she said, "They tell you he is a *vernando*. That kind of person is usually not difficult. You must only laugh at his jokes."

"Yes," I agreed. "I shall."

In the morning, after a restless night made worse by the disturbing sound of wild dogs fighting over a bitch in heat, I left home almost two hours earlier than usual, just after dawn. None of my family was awake, except my father, who liked to walk at sunrise. Riding my bicycle on the not-yet-crowded streets and avenues of our beautiful Capital City, a place normally bursting with energy and industriousness, nearly empty *hahnkers,* broadcasting important messages to all citizens, rolled past me, their windows down, allowing bits of radio music to seep into the sticky air of daybreak.

I recognized the songs, simple melodies that everyone knows. Some of the *hahnker* drivers, I noticed, hummed along with the radio, oblivious to my presence.

For safety reasons, such listening and humming while driving a public conveyance is not permitted. But my mind was elsewhere, so I said nothing and made no report to the appropriate authority. I pedaled on, envisioning all the ways my life might change once a man as influential and powerful as Mr. TupTup joined our team.

A few blocks from the National News Building, I took a shortcut through an alleyway. There I saw a very old woman, hunched and toothless, tending to a quaint *compastee*, picking out weeds with her fingers. We call these elderly matriarchs *flona*. It is a term of respect. Anyone could tell by the absence of a sign or fencing that her little plot of soil was not properly permitted. As I passed, the *flona* winked at me, as if to say, "This is just between us; I know I can trust you to make no report." I did not respond. But for some unknown reason her gesture cheered me.

So did the sight of three grime-covered children, barefoot urchins with laughing eyes and giant smiles, using a beetle they had caught to improvise an imaginary game of *scrachi*,

So did the crisp salute I received from the bicycle minder at the parking area behind the NNS.

My mood was bright. I welcomed whatever challenges awaited me, and I knew that with determination and a positive attitude I could accomplish whatever goals my superiors set for me.

I passed through security and arrived at my office much earlier than I had planned, nearly an hour before the rest of my staff.

I had instructed them to be ready for a team meeting thirty minutes prior to 8:00 a.m., the usual beginning of our workday. I wanted everyone properly briefed on how to conduct themselves around our newest employee.

Alone in my office, without any Assistants to distract me, I paged through *Perriodocko*, the noble messenger of all that matters in our sacred Homeland. Throughout the night, while citizens slept and animals prowled, our highly respected newspaper was being printed and distributed to every city, village, and township. And now, in the morning, millions of my comrades, elite and regular alike, were reading words that I had written, re-written, or approved.

Call it rampant *meowkaleet*, or call it wishful thinking, but I supposed that even as I sat at my desk, watching our Capital City come to life, somewhere someplace our Caring Leaders were quite possibly enjoying my work. Maybe, I allowed myself to think, even TupTup's father at the Bureau of Industry.

The great man would be pleased to discover the brief story on page 7, the one our team had hastily assembled and submitted just before the evening deadline:

Celebrated Son Joins Perriodocko *Staff*

Chief Editor Pops had provided an appropriate and memorable quote: "We are honored and humbled to welcome such a distinguished man, the offspring of an equally distinguished man, to our humble enterprise."

And now he was finally here.

I checked the buttons on my shirt and combed my hair with my fingers. I organized the already-organized papers on my desk. I glanced at my great-grandfather's wristwatch: 8:00 a.m., exactly.

I could hear murmuring outside my office, and footsteps. I could hear a group congregating in the hallway. Then, with a crisp knock, my 1st Assistant was standing in my doorway.

"Good morning, sir," he said. "Please allow me to introduce the newest member of our glorious team."

Everyone in the hallway fell silent.

A head slowly appeared, peeking around the doorjamb. First hair, then a wide forehead, then eyebrows and nose and a mouth bursting with teeth. Then a weak chin and long neck. No body; just a large head.

The head swiveled and looked at me, flashing what I presumed to be a smile, although the expression on his face would not be inappropriate to someone discovering a mouse floating in his soup.

"Mr. TupTup?" I said.

"Yes. Obviously," he said, suddenly emerging from behind the wall, standing in the doorway beside my 1st Assistant. "I am here. Yes. It is me. Obviously." He tittered and made a peculiar humming sound. "Hee-heh-ah. Hmmmm.Yes."

We all laughed. He was indeed quite the *vernando*.

I stood to greet him, but he crossed his arms around himself and walked right past my desk to the bookshelf against the wall.

"You are most welcome," I announced to his back.

"Hmmmm. Alphabetical, obviously," he said, tracing the binding of each volume with his finger.

"Yes," I said, laughing again.

An older man I did not recognize stepped into my office. "I am his uncle," he said, removing his rare and expensive sunglasses. He sighed softly. "TupTup, this man is your boss."

Without turning away from the books, TupTup offered a limp hand in my direction, which I shook. It felt somewhat moist. "Hello, Boss!" he said, staring at the books. "Hello! Hello! I would like to ask you a question."

"Yes, of course," I replied.

"What month were you born?"

I told him, "June."

He turned to me, his eyes wild. "Ah, yes. June. You are most likely a Gemini, although it is also possible that you are also— did you know, the mega-star Miss Angel Lee Diamond, who was born in January, is one of my top five girlfriends, although she is not a Gemini. Now, Miss Princess Cookie the Elegant Songbird, is also technically not a Gemini even though she was born in the month of June like you, and she is also one of my top five girlfriends, along with Miss Baby Sweets the People's Star, obviously, who is set to begin a new recording project of national folk songs after her current touring schedule is completed. Miss Baby Sweets the People's Star, well, she is also—but this is obvious. I would like to ask you another question."

The uncle stepped in. "That is enough questions, TupTup." He turned to me. "I am sorry."

"Oh, no," I said. "We are—"

"Let me ask you something. Do you know that Miss Baby Sweets the People's Star, was first discovered by Hitmaker to the Stars Boss Bo, the legendary head of the prestigious Galaxy Records label? Hitmaker to the Stars Boss Bo discovered her when she was singing on a bus! Hah! This is well known, obviously."

"Yes. I believe I have heard this," I said, unsure where his joke was leading.

"Yes!" TupTup said, smiling broadly, displaying all his teeth. "Hello, Boss!" he said, extending his hand, which I shook again. "Hello!"

He went to all my Assistants and ceremoniously shook their hands, too. "Hello! Hello! Hello! Hmmmm. Hello!"

We all chuckled uncomfortably, including the uncle, who sighed again and said, "*Ah bolah*. Well, now you have met."

"What is your birthday?" TupTup asked my 2nd Assistant.

"No more birthdays, TupTup," the uncle interrupted. "Time to work."

"Ah. Yes. Hmmmm. Where are you working, Uncle?" he asked. "At the newspaper?"

"No," Uncle said. "I will be waiting outside."

"Ah. Yes. Hmmmm. In the *blecky?*"

"No. But the car will come back for us at six, or whenever your new boss says you are permitted to leave." Uncle winked at me.

"Ah! Hmmmm." TupTup blinked several times and began mumbling to himself, not loud enough for me to make out what he was saying, although I thought I picked out the familiar name of Miss Baby Sweets, one of our greatest *chu-chu* singers.

"OK?" asked Uncle.

Tup Tup did not reply. He just continued mumbling to himself, and wagging his head, which I took to be an affirmative.

So did Uncle. "OK, then. Thank you all, comrades" he said, nodding at me and my staff, all of whom smiled and bowed slightly, their faces frozen in a combination of surprise and confusion. "Oh," Uncle said, handing me a card. "Here is my number. Do not hesitate to call if I may be of any assistance."

"Thank you, sir," I said, pocketing his card. "Everything should be fine. We will make sure of that, I can promise you." I looked at TupTup, who continued to mumble and seemed to be counting his fingers, making certain all ten were still there.

"Hey, TupTup," Uncle said. "Do not worry. *Bebudew op en beberoo kap.*"

"Yes," TupTup said, looking at his fingers. "Of course. Yes. You are never alone, you only feel alone. Obviously."

"We are a large team here," I added, helpfully, I thought. "We will all work together to make your transition happy and successful."

TupTup looked at me as though he did not understand.

"Everyone," I stammered. "Here. Helping."

We all stood in uncomfortable silence. Finally, Uncle said, "Well, good! Very good! Call me…" He saluted and bowed and nodded and turned to leave. My 2nd Assistant escorted him out, ensuring he would have no complications with the stairs, or security.

As soon as their footsteps could no longer be heard, TupTup seemed to relax. The crazy smile was back. "Let me ask you a question," he said. "Would you like to see my girlfriends?"

"Well, actually, Mr. TupTup," I said, attempting to find the perfect balance between politeness and firmness, "my First Assistant is now going to escort you to your work station, which is just down the hall, with the other junior Information Gatherers."

"Ah! Yes. Hmmmm," he said, pulling a worn black wallet from his trousers. "I have five top girlfriends, but I am considering adding some more."

Before I could stop him, he was pulling out ragged papers stuffed between banknotes and laminated identification cards. These papers were folded multiple times, into neat squares and rectangles. I could see that the papers were photos clipped from the *chu-chu* pages of *Perriodocko*.

As TupTup unfolded them, he seemed to fall into some sort of trance, oblivious to me or anyone else in the room. "Now," he declared, "obviously everyone knows that Miss Baby Sweets the People's Star is always—well, she is the People's Star. Obviously!

Hmmmm. Hah! But let me ask you something: Are you familiar with Miss Princess Cookie the Elegant Songbird? Yes. Well. She is often considered a leading candidate for a possible Miss Cosmos crown, however she is now busy making a TV program on NTV-4 and it is certain to be a big success, obviously. Hmmmm. Now. So let me ask you something else. Hmmmm. Are you familiar—and of course, by the way, I like Miss Princess Cookie the Elegant Songbird very much, and she will be in my top five. For now! For now! Ah. Hmmmm. Therefore I would like to ask you: Have you seen the mega-star Miss Angel Lee Diamond? That is a different story altogether. Ah! Hee-heh. Ah. Very nice. Very, very nice. But this is obvious. Yes. Hmmmm."

I didn't know what to say. So I shrugged and heard myself involuntarily agreeing. "Obviously."

TupTup raised his pointer finger to the ceiling. "Yes."

We all stood silently again, uncertain of what was supposed to happen next. I briefly made eye contact with my 1st Assistant, who subtly shrugged and looked away. TupTup's sense of humor was difficult for us to understand.

Finally, speaking to no one in particular, I repeated the plan: "My First Assistant is now going to escort you to your work station, which is just down the hall, with the other junior Information Gatherers."

Tup Tup wheeled toward me, his eyes moist and shiny as a just-washed *blecky*. "OK!" he said, with great enthusiasm. "However, I would like to ask you something. I would like to see where the *chu-chu* stars have their pictures taken. That is a top priority. Because—yes."

"You mean you would like to attend a photo shoot?" I asked politely.

"Yes. Hmmmm. Yes!"

"I am certain that can be arranged, Mr. TupTup," I assured him, "perhaps as early as next week."

TupTup squinted his eyes, as though he were riding a bicycle behind a belching *hahnker*—an indignity, of course, such an elite citizen would never have to endure. He scratched his forehead, rather forcefully. "Ah. Hmmmm. Well. But let me ask you something. I would like to see that today. The photo-making. With the mega-star Miss Angel Lee Diamond. Or also Miss Baby Sweets, who is the People's Star. Obviously. Or even—Well! Today. Hmmmm. Yes."

I felt extremely distressed, unsure of how to say no without appearing rude to our very important colleague. "Mr. TupTup," I said, "it most certainly can be arranged. It is just that we were not prepared properly today, for which I must take responsibility. Please accept my apology, Mr. TupTup."

"Hmmmm. Yes. Hmmmm. Let me ask you something else," he said, no longer smiling. "Does the megastar Miss Angel Lee Diamond not work here?"

"Work here?" I asked.

"Yes. Does the megastar Miss Angel Lee Diamond work here? Every day, but not on *Tink*, obviously. That would be ridiculous! At the newspaper. The mega-star Miss Angel Lee Diamond, getting her picture taken!"

I burst out laughing. I could not stop myself. He was a *vernando* unlike any other I had seen.

My staff joined me, giggling and repeating his humorous comment. And TupTup tittered with us.

I shook my head and grabbed my chest. "Quite a *vernando*, this one!"

We did not understand that Mr. TupTup was not joking.

CHAPTER EIGHT

Although, I confess, Mr. TupTup could be somewhat confusing to those who did not understand his jester's way of looking at the world, he was not unintelligent. This I discovered immediately, during his first week at *Perriodocko*.

TupTup had the most astonishing memory of anyone I have ever met. He was able to recall facts and figures and dates with startling accuracy, as though he had a complete National Library in his large head. His ability to remember information became a kind of amusement among the staff, an entertaining trick that delighted my Assistants, who spent far too much time dreaming up questions to stump him.

"What was the name of the first album recorded by Miss Butterfly Rose in Year Two?"

"For what song was Miss Sugar Pie Sunshine awarded her first National Service Medal? And, by the way, how many does she have in total?"

"How many individual artists and groups have recorded the number one hit song, 'Time is Forever?' And can you name the composer?"

His answer was always, "Yes. Obviously."

After a few days, TupTup's reputation had spread throughout the entire department. I had to reprimand my subordinates. "Mr. TupTup is not a proper substitute for old-fashioned research. When you have a question of fact, do not rely on him. Look it up."

I do not mean to suggest that our newest employee was, to be quite blunt, a model Information Gatherer, or even a superior one. His extraordinary powers were only useful when applied toward subjects that personally interested him. And there were not many of those. Some sports: boxing, football, basketball, but not *scrachi*. Annual amounts of precipitation in our sacred Homeland. The fluctuating price of baked bread, which seemed to somehow be tied to the size of the allowance he was given (I did not pry). Sometimes, he seemed to know many fine details about certain Caring Leaders he had met through his father.

But, as his file had indicated, Mr. TupTup's primary interest was *chu-chu*. I do not intend any rudeness when I say that his focus on the glamorous world of musical stardom often seemed to border on what you might unkindly call an obsession.

I quickly learned to not mention the subject unless I was prepared for the impassioned monologue that would inevitably follow. He was clever, though. No matter how diligently I limited my conversation around him to National Heroes— which, after all, was our department's area of expertise—TupTup somehow found a way to return the discussion to his preferred topic.

I would say, "I have just now been informed by Chief Editor Pops that an award ceremony will be taking place tomorrow to honor a platoon of National Heroes. They have volunteered to help repair a broken well in the Greenleaf Hills District. I shall assign a Senior Information Gatherer and Photographer to document this proud occasion."

TupTup would flash his crooked smile and look off somewhere distant. "Yes. Hmmmm. Very good. Yes. But let me ask you something. The Greenleaf Hills district is home to the Greenleaf Municipal Auditorium, where the greatest stars have all performed, including, in Year Seven if I am not mistaken, yes, Year Seven it was. Yes. Well. Miss Jasmine Joy the Concert Queen, performed all her greatest hits for a special broadcast on NTV-4. That program—hah!—that program was the most popular program of the week, higher rated than the Piko Juice Box *Scrachi* Tournament, and a big success for Galaxy Records. Obviously, when the album was made available at music stores everywhere, the Chairman of Galaxy Records, the legendary Boss Bo, Hitmaker to the Stars, was very pleased to announce that the record was going to number one in the first week. Miss Jasmine Joy the Concert Queen was featured on the cover of several publications that are no longer available. But this is obvious. Hmmmm. Yes. Miss Jasmine Joy the Concert Queen is one of the top beauties, obviously. Which reminds me! Would you like to see my top five girlfriends?"

TupTup's first week at *Perriodocko*, I must say, was very tiring.

When Mr. K appeared at my desk, summoning me once more to the office of Chief Editor Pops, I was not surprised. I knew that he would be taking a special interest in such an important individual working in our midst and would want to be fully briefed by me, the lucky Deputy Supervisor given the prestigious assignment. But even as I climbed the stairs to the 4th Floor, I cannot say I was fully prepared to answer the Chief Editor's questions. *Ah bolah,* perhaps there was no correct way. I had not previously handled an employee like TupTup.

Chief Editor Pops was on an important telephone call when I arrived, so I had additional time to compose my thoughts in the anteroom, where, I noticed, a new photo had been added since my last visit, a week ago. There was Chief Editor Pops, smiling, with his arm draped around the newest starlet on the Galaxy Records label, a girl whose name was not yet familiar to me. She was quite beautiful, as all our *chu-chu* stars are. I intend no vulgarity when I mention that I found it difficult to take my eyes away from her.

Looking at the photo brought my mind back to TupTup. I had not figured out what to say. How should I describe his first week to my superior? It would not be appreciated if I used words such as "frustrating," "challenging," or "baffling." Yet it would also not be appreciated if I deliberately failed to make a complete disclosure. That kind of reckless behavior was grounds for a demerit in my file, not to mention all sorts of other trouble that I and my family did not need.

Before I could figure out the most perfect and polite way to describe TupTup's initial performance, I was summoned in to see Chief Editor Pops, who seemed to be distracted and in a hurry.

"Sit down, sit down," he said. "And tell me."

"Well, sir," I began.

He interjected. "No incidents, am I correct? Nothing worth noting in his file?"

I was going to mention something, an embarrassing moment that had occurred during a department meeting about the proper volume of celebrity photos within our pages. Without provocation, TupTup had declared to the entire group that his all-time favorite newspaper for *chu-chu* pictures was, in fact, the defunct *De Zipper*. But since it was no longer around he was glad to work at his *third* choice: our publication. *Ah bolah.*

I also considered mentioning the encounter with my 2nd Assistant, who was attempting to teach TupTup how to use our modern electronic filing system. Although it is not a complicated procedure, apparently TupTup was not catching on immediately, or not adequately interested. My 2nd Assistant had come to my office quite agitated. Indeed, to explain his frustration, he said to me, "Sir, you know what they say: *Nevaa lahang en nini war-mung* ("You cannot educate a goat")." I had to reprimand him severely and remind him that such impolite language was never again to be used when describing our VIP employee.

For some unknown reason—maybe because of the way Chief Editor Pops was looking at me—I stopped myself. I do not know if I was trying to protect myself, or TupTup, or all of us. Instead of mentioning anything, I said to my boss, "Nothing to report, sir."

Chief Editor Pops nodded. "Very good. No trouble from the minder? You know—" he snapped his fingers three times. "The man. The uncle. Uncle What's-His-Name."

"Ah, yes," I said. "No trouble, sir."

I did not mention that on the first day, when the *blecky* arrived to retrieve TupTup after work, I could see from the window in my office that Uncle was not happy with his nephew. Although I was unable to hear what was said, I could tell by the way Uncle guided TupTup into the back seat of the sedan that they were not enjoying the usual courtesies shared between family members. I also did not mention that a very good friend of mine, a trusted source at National Heroes Headquarters, told me he had heard of this Uncle of TupTup's, and that he was, according to my friend, "extremely connected to all the important Caring Leaders." I assumed Chief Editor Pops knew this part, anyway.

I nodded solemnly and repeated, "No trouble."

"Very good," said Chief Editor Pops, half-smiling, half-frowning. "That is very good." He fingered some papers on his desk. "Very good. Thank you for your excellent service, which shall be duly noted."

I understood that our meeting was finished, so I rose and thanked my boss for the opportunity to please him. And then I was shown out.

Halfway down the stairs, I had a powerful impulse to turn around and return to Chief Editor Pops and make a full confession. I would simply say, "I mean no disrespect or insolence whatsoever. But I feel obligated to tell you that despite his obvious talents and potential for positive contributions, Mr. TupTup is perhaps not well-equipped to be a Special Assistant Information Gatherer for the following reasons..." And then I would calmly enumerate them, starting with his infernal fondness for *chu-chu,* all the time, all the time, all the time.

You are aware, perhaps, how people are sometimes said to have key moments in their lives, when two different paths present themselves, each one leading to a different conclusion. As I look back now, the light growing dimmer and my wrist growing weary, I realize this may have been my moment.

If I had simply done the correct thing, maybe the rest would not have happened and I would still have some good years ahead of me.

But I didn't. I kept walking. I never turned around.

CHAPTER NINE

Looking back on what I have written, I feel that I should make clear: I do not mean to give the impression that anyone is to blame. I take full responsibility.

Permit me, however, to mention that some individuals, such as Mr. TupTup, had a powerful effect on me, almost as powerful as the guiding influence of our Caring Leaders, Chief Editors Junior and Pops, and the many National Heroes whose spirit of sacrifice and service inspires us all. *Ah bolah*, I understand that this is a terrible thing to admit, and I apologize once more for what could be perceived as grotesque impertinence. It is not intended that way. I am merely attempting to make a valid report. I hope you will understand.

So, even though it is me and me alone who must deal with the consequences, looking back I can see how my outlook was swayed. It can happen, believe me. For example, have you ever become an expert on a certain subject without ever intending to know a thing about it? It is a very strange phenomenon. All your life you have nothing more than a vague interest in a particular specialty—honeybees, foreign aircraft, chess, it can be anything—and then one day you wake up and realize you have managed to learn almost everything there is to learn about your new specialty, and you didn't even try!

On a winter night in Year 13, after supper and before bedtime, my wife and I were listening to the radio, enjoying one of the most popular variety shows in our sacred Homeland, a program called *Star Time*. They have a mix of entertainers on this delightful program, including comedians, *telastooricks* (reciters of national folk tales), and famous singers. After a stirring performance of the great romance ballad, "My Endless Sorrow," sung by one of my favorites, Miss Sparkles Rainbow, I made a casual comment about how many versions of this fine song had cracked the Top-10 on the national charts—three of them, in fact—including a rare all-instrumental version done in Year 5 by the Capital City Ballroom Dancing Orchestra.

My wife said, "Dear Husband, you have become quite the master of *chu-chu* knowledge. Just kidding. I am only joking."

She was right, actually. Forgive my gross *meowkaleet*, but I have always had a talent for learning things quickly.

Without meaning to, I had soaked up all sorts of useless knowledge, like a dry sponge placed upon a puddle of spilled *bolo*. The source of my involuntary expertise, of course, was Mr. TupTup, whose workplace pronouncements were my daily background noise, a constant stream of facts, opinions, and predictions that seeped into my brain, no matter how much I tried not to listen.

I must confess that more than a few times I had the impulse to shout out, "Stop it, you silly goat! Enough already!" Thankfully, I drew upon reservoirs of discipline and instead said something much more appropriate, such as, "Thank you, my valuable colleague, for your insights on this fascinating matter. Now, shall we concentrate on gathering information about the new missile test?"

Even if I never read *Perriodocko*—which, of course, I did daily, with great pleasure—simply going to work six days a week, where I inevitably encountered our special employee, was enough to keep me abreast of all the relevant *chu-chu* developments, as well as all the irrelevant ones.

This was how I came to know that aside from the Hitmaker to the Stars Boss Bo and his friendly rival at Republic Records, Boss Mike, the most important people in the industry worked not at the recording studios and pressing plants, but at the Office of Creation. Without the proper license, an aspiring musician could not obtain all the necessary permits to make a record album. There were 22 required in all; in Year 12 there had been 19, but a few new ones were added to ensure higher quality products. Naturally, to get the overall license, you had to demonstrate good moral character, a clear understanding of national values, and the proper admiration of the relevant Dedicated Servants.

The average citizen enjoying his favorite song on the radio probably did not know how many concerned authorities were involved, how much hard work was required, to make the process go so smoothly. TupTup, though, was not the average citizen. He was extremely well-informed.

This was how I came to know that Miss Baby Sweets the People's Star was having a bitter feud with Miss Cookie Princess the Elegant Songbird. The official explanation given to the Media was that their disagreement was simply a minor misunderstanding about who should receive top billing at an upcoming free concert in the famous National Park Amphitheatre, a beautiful band shell where many important events have occurred. But knowledgeable observers suspected the real source of their friction was actually a handsome man. A *married* handsome man. I do not mean to instigate scandal. This is only what I was told by a very reputable source.

This was how I knew that, despite her impressive track record, dear Miss Sparkles Rainbow was personally experiencing the lyrics of "My Endless Sorrow." According to an insider of my acquaintance, her latest project was being held up for permitting because she obstinately insisted on using an electronic foreign instrument—my insider acquaintance called it a *mook*, but I could find no record of such a thing—an instrument that was once common on our recordings but, after the changeover, was no longer considered helpful in promoting the musical traditions of our sacred Homeland.

This was also how I became aware of the secret (but widely rumored) drinking problem that sidetracked Miss Butterfly Rose for a number of unhappy and artistically barren years.

And it was how I was first introduced to the most important musical artist our sacred Homeland has ever produced, the woman known as Miss Mae Love.

CHAPTER TEN

In the later months of Year 13, when the official opening of the annual National Song Competition was announced on the front of the *chu-chu* section of *Perriodocko*, my colleague TupTup was, predictably, full of opinions.

We have a saying, "No one likes to be judged." There is much wisdom in that phrase. Opinions, as we are all taught from a young age, can often be quite troublesome, since they are what tend to cause misunderstandings and unnecessary controversies. But TupTup, for some unknown reason, did not worry about such matters. Maybe because he knew his great father would never allow anything bad to happen to him. Or maybe because, against all reason, he cared too much about things most people considered insignificant.

Ah bolah. I do not know.

The day the National Song Competition was in the newspaper, he knocked on the doorframe of my office, and slowly poked his head into view, as was his custom. I came to think of this maneuver as the TupTup Turtle. Do you get my joke?

Clutching the morning copy of *Perriodocko* like a bouquet of flowers, he said, "This National Song Competition. Hmmmm. If you would like to know, I can tell you who must be the top five people who you must be considering as potential champions. Yes. Hmmmm. Let me ask you something. It is well known that Miss Sugar Pie Sunshine has been multi-awarded for her memorable compositions. Hah! Obviously, Yes. But let me ask you something else! Did you know, are you aware—well, this is obvious. My top five candidates for the National Song Competition are different than my top five girlfriends. But this is obvious. Yes. Hmmmm."

By now, several months into his tenure, I had learned how to handle TupTup's outbursts. I barked at him, just as Uncle did: "No more questions, TupTup."

Uncle, I noticed, simply declared that there would be no more questions, and, as if struck by dark magic, TupTup would cease his monologue and grow momentarily taciturn, if not altogether silent. It did not matter whether Tup Tup was really asking questions or simply showing off his vast repository of *chu-chu* knowledge. Uncle's command always worked.

Soon it began to work for me, too.

Except on this day. I declared, "No more questions, Tup-Tup." But for some unknown reason, TupTup was so excited about the National Song Competition that he could not stop himself. "Hmmmm. Yes. But let me ask you something. Now, in Year 14, the voting will be done as it has always been done, by a distinguished panel of judges. These distinguished judges include Mr. Boss Bo Hitmaker to the Stars of Galaxy Records, his schoolboy friend and very friendly competitor in the recording business, Mr. Boss Mike of Republic Records, and, of course, the esteemed and very honorable Director of the Office of Creation. But this is obvious. Hmmmm. Ah! But let me ask you something else! This time, in Year 14, something is going to be different than in the previous seven years of the National Song Competition. This you know. Obviously. You know this. The National Song Competition was inaugurated in Year 6. Recognizing the very best musical minds in our sacred Homeland! Yes.

Hmmmm. I can tell you the Top Five winners, but this is a different story. But. Hmmmm. Ah! This year there is something different, because this year for the first time, the public is going to be invited to observe the competition. Yes. If you would like you can read all about it in the newspaper!"

He held *Perriodocko* above his head, like a ceremonial torch. "The public is invited!"

"Yes. This is true," I agreed.

"This has never happened before. Obviously."

I nodded. "Yes. This is true."

"Ah! So you understand. But let me ask you something. I want to be in the public. To watch. Yes. Hmmmm. The National Song Competition! Recognizing the very best musical minds! And I want to be in the public! Yes. Let me ask you something. You can make the arrangements."

I knew that TupTup could gain entry to any event he wished to see. His family, his father—anything was possible for him. He did not need me. "I'm sure you can get a ticket. Perhaps your father?"

"No, no, no, no, no," he said, agitated. "No, no, no. Hmmmm. I do not want a ticket. I want to go for the paper. Obviously. To make an Authorized Report. The National Song Competition! Recognizing the very best musical minds! For the newspaper. Yes."

He looked at me expectantly, with that crazy crooked grin of his. "For the newspaper!" he repeated.

I did not know what to say. So, without thinking, I said, "Yes. All right."

Before I could retract my foolish acquiescence, TupTup startled me. I thought he meant to kill me in some unorthodox way. He sprang before me, inches from my face, and wrapped both of his arms around me, squeezing hard, pinning my arms against my side and forcing the breath out of my lungs. Just as I was going to cry out for help, he loosened his grip and pressed his lips against my right cheek. I suppose you would technically call it a kiss, although I assure you and all the relevant authorities that there was no immorality connected to this male-to-male contact. It was really more like a child honoring his parent, that is all.

Then, without a word, he released me and dashed from my office. To where I did not know.

The spot on my face where he had brushed against me was cool and moist. I peered out my doorway to make certain none of my Assistants had witnessed TupTup's antics. Everyone was at his desk, being productive.

I turned and looked out my window, as if someone might have been looking in from the sky. My eyes were drawn to the street below, where a brilliant brigade of National Heroes completed its morning march. Seeing them inspired me. I knew I should not have approved my subordinate's absurd request without doing a proper evaluation of the situation and consulting with my superiors. I knew I had made a mistake. But I also knew that I could do something glorious for our sacred Homeland, just as a celebrated National Hero would.

I could please a Caring Leader. All I had to do was please his son.

I had long ago determined that TupTup had no aptitude for traditional Information Gathering. Accomplished as he was as a reader, he lacked the concentration and discipline to do proper writing, laying out the facts in an easy-to-understand and logical manner. He could gather information, but he could not properly share it—at least not without numerous tangents and digressions and boasts about his beautiful girlfriends. There was no way I could permit him to represent *Perriodocko* at the National Song Competition. Besides, he didn't even yet have a license to compose news stories!

I could, however, arrange impressive-looking credentials for him, which he could wear around his neck and display to the security forces. Meanwhile, two of our regular and most trusted Information Gatherers on the *chu-chu* beat would attend, as usual, and file the anticipated report and photos. TupTup would be made to feel important—which he was, of course—and our glorious newspaper's commitment to serving our sacred Homeland would be upheld.

It was not impossible, I told myself: TupTup might even contribute an interesting fact that somehow might elude our multi-awarded team.

Just as I was settling into my desk chair to review my tasks for the day, TupTup burst back into my office. "Thank you," he said. "Yes. Hmmmm. Thank you." He dashed off again before I could reply.

Then he was back. "But let me ask you something. We can meet the lady who should win. Yes!"

"That should not be a problem," I replied. "An interview would be appropriate."

"Yes. Obviously. But let me ask you something else. I do not want an interview, I want her to be one of my girlfriends! It is a very exclusive list, obviously. This list includes Miss Angel Lee Diamond and Miss Baby Sweets. It also includes—well, this is obvious."

"I am afraid I do not have the ability to make the winner of the National Song Competition your girlfriend," I said dryly. "But I am most delighted to make sure an official interview is arranged."

"Yes! This is very good news. Then I am going to interview Miss Mae Love!"

"Who?" I asked.

"Miss Mae Love, who does not yet have an honorary nickname. But I can tell you that I propose the nickname 'the Next Great One.' Yes! Hmmmm. Miss Mae Love the Next Great One. Obviously, this is not yet official. Hmmmm."

I was confused. I assumed TupTup had gotten mixed up. "Ah. You must mean Miss Mae Angel. Or perhaps Miss Mae Baby."

"No, no, no, no, no," TupTup cried, shaking his head violently. "This is not what I mean. No. The other one. Miss Mae Love!"

As you have probably surmised, this name, Mae, is popular among our *chu-chu* stars. There are actually three Maes who are famous in our sacred Homeland. They are affectionately known as the ABCs. It is a little joke.

"Here," I said, pointing to the copy of *Perriodocko* on my desk. "Right here. It is written in the only trusted newspaper in the land. Read it for yourself. I direct you to the paragraph that begins, 'All three of the ABCs, Miss Mae Angel, Miss Mae Baby and Miss Mae Cookie, are expected to be contenders.' So, Mr. TupTup, I am not understanding your agitation."

Hunched over my desk, TupTup examined the relevant part of the story, humming and talking quietly to himself. I could not make out what he was saying, other than "yes, yes," and sometimes "*bolah.*"

Standing up straight, pushing aside the paper, he declared, "Well, this is not a complete report. Obviously."

Now I was somewhat annoyed. "Mr. TupTup, sir, allow me to mention, please, that this story was prepared by two of our most senior and respected Information Gatherers, who together have a combined experience of more than twenty-four years on the *chu-chu* beat. I assure you that all relevant facts were included in this excellent report."

He squinted. "Let me ask you something. I have read this report on the National Song Competition. Recognizing the very best musical minds! Yes. Hmmmm. And I have seen the pictures also, obviously. They include many of the leading contenders. I can tell you the Top Five. Well, this is obvious. But let me ask you something. There is no mention of Miss Mae Love. She is very nice!"

"Which of the ABCs do you mean, sir?" I pressed, attempting to muffle my mounting exasperation.

"Hah! None of them! Obviously!" TupTup made a laughing sound, as though clearing his throat.

I pointed at their photos in the newspaper—rather lovely photos, I would like to note. "None of these?"

"Nooooo!" TupTup replied, laughing and growling more.

"Not this one?" I demanded, pointing to Miss Mae Cookie.

"Noooooooooooo!" he said, nearly hysterical with amusement.

I had grown tired of his game. "Well, then, who?"

"This one!" he said, pulling his wallet from his pants pocket. He extracted a folded piece of paper stuffed beside the other folded pieces of paper, and placed it on my desk. "Her!" he said, smiling like a lunatic. "Miss Mae Love. The Next Great One."

For a moment I felt as though I had stopped breathing. I recognized this lady. And I recognized the photograph. She was quite beautiful, and strangely magnetic, just as she was when I first gazed upon her face, up on the 4th floor.

But this time she was standing alone, without the arm of Chief Editor Pops draped around her.

CHAPTER ELEVEN

On a normal day, when my work is done, I bicycle directly home, look in on Boy, Gurly, and my father next door, and join my wife for supper. We begin, of course, with soup. My wife has a famous recipe—well, famous in our family—for Bone Soup with Garden Vegetables. The *filolo* (a type of cabbage, I believe) and *sensas* (onions) come from a small plot behind our building for which I was able to obtain the necessary permit. She boils everything all afternoon and keeps it on a low simmer right up until the moment we give thanks and commence to eat.

She is very conscientious, my wife. Somehow, even when I am detained by *Perriodocko*-related matters, she manages to have food on the table and ready for my arrival, as if she knew the exact moment I would be walking through the door.

I thought of this on the night I stayed out longer than I ever had before. I knew she would be concerned that the fishmeal cakes would go cold—or become dry from overcooking. But I told myself that I had important business to attend to, and she would surely understand.

Also, if I may be blunt, I was enjoying myself on this particular night—and not because I was engaged in immoral activity. *Ah bolah,* no. I suppose it was because I was doing something new and different, a novelty for me.

For the first time in my life, I was spending an evening after work at what is called a *U-House*, a place where they serve a variety of *uchaana* and drinks, and where guests with the necessary permit may sing along to a recording of their favorite song, but with the *chu-chu* star's voice taken out.

*U-House*s were once quite popular with foreign visitors, before the changeover. Now, mostly younger people, of university age, attend. The *U-House*s have a reputation in our sacred Homeland for being a good place to meet like-minded friends.

I was not at the *Go Paja* ("Big Winner") *U-House* to meet anyone, or even to smoke *uchaana*, as it tends to make me light-headed and unsteady on my bicycle. I was there to gather information.

A very reliable source in my office had suggested to me that this particular *U-House* was where I might encounter informants who once knew Miss Mae Love. Some of them, he thought, might even still know her, although what with her various upcoming recording projects and the National Song Competition looming she probably didn't have time for idle frivolity. (These were not his exact words, but I understood his point.)

My source explained that scouts from Galaxy and Republic Records were said to show up unannounced at the *U-House*s, looking for the next big voice. According to my source, like many other budding *chu-chu* stars, Miss Mae Love got her start at the *Go Paja U-House*, copying the style of older, more famous artists. Her talent and looks made a very strong impression. He said this was obvious.

In the week following the announcement of the National Song Competition, I attempted to gather as much information as I could about Miss Mae Love. Do not mistakenly think I had any dishonorable intentions. Quite the contrary. Miss Mae Love had been identified by our resident *chu-chu* expert as a leading contender in the National Song Competition, and members of my staff confirmed his opinion. She was an important subject in an unfolding story of great interest to our readers. Therefore, we had a professional responsibility to familiarize ourselves and our loyal audience with her work.

I briefly considered assigning a subordinate to this crucial research task but decided that the project required a higher level of experience and expertise. So I assigned myself.

Did I notify my superiors of this decision? I cannot recall at this time. I may have mentioned it in passing during my daily briefing.

According to TupTup—and according to a couple of reports I was able to retrieve from the archives—Miss Mae Love had released but one record, a single, on a second-tier label. But that recording, a stirring version of "Dedicated to Victory!"—originally made famous by Miss Annie Queen—had catapulted her to the attention of Boss Bo, who offered her a contract on his prestigious Galaxy Records. Miss Mae Love's first Galaxy release was scheduled early in Year 14, one week after the public finals of the National Song Competition.

Important people had taken an interest in her.

When I arrived at what I had been told was the location of the *Go Paja U-House,* an easy 15-minute bike ride to the east of the National News Building, in an old part of the Central District, I supposed I had gone to the wrong street. There was no sign. There was no picture window with the all of the establishment's necessary licenses proudly on display. The doorway, down a couple of steps, did not even bear a proper address, just a small **U** carved into the wood.

But I could hear the faint sound of laughter and conversation, and the low thump of a beat vibrating through the weathered timber walls.

I tried the door. It was open.

I stepped inside. The familiar scent of *uchaana* smoke, spicy and sweet, greeted my arrival. It filled the room, a long rectangular space with a low ceiling and a few dim lights hanging on cords. At the front of the room, near the doorway, two girls wearing unmatched uniforms stood behind a counter, where they poured drinks and distributed cigarettes. At the back of the room, there was a small stage, which I assumed was eight *plongi* high or less, since anything taller required a special license (for Theatrical Performance, I believe) that was known to be difficult to obtain.

Although I did not make reports to the relevant authorities at the time, looking back now I can say that I suspect the *Go Paja U-House* was operating without any number of necessary licenses and permits.

This probably explains why I felt a change in the smoky air when I walked into the room. The customers, about 20 of them, seemed to stiffen in my presence. Their voices became softer, and even the girl on the stage, a pretty and talented lady singing "Triumphant"—a song made famous by Miss Princess Cookie, I had recently been reminded—missed a word or two, losing her place for a moment.

Also, I was clearly the oldest person in the *U-House,* by at least 10 or 15 years, and you know how youngsters can be.

Some of the customers might have even mistaken me for a *Kapaa*, the highly trained and elite security force of the National Heroes. They are what you call plainclothes. A *Kapaa* does not sport the green uniform of a National Hero, or any sort of consistent color, although many of them like to wear certain brands of sunglasses, since they work outside often, I think.

Not only was I not wearing such sunglasses, I do not even own any, as they are a bit too expensive and I spend most of my time working indoors. But because I was not dressed like the younger patrons, they viewed me with mistrust and caution, as you would any interloper. I was in my proper office attire and they were wearing short pants and shirts with random words and phrases upon them, including one that said *a bili en creneckulo* and another that simply said *Permitted?*

Ah bolah, I do not pretend to understand the fashion sense of our younger generation.

Feeling the kind of tension that is caused by misunderstanding and ignorance, I retrieved from my shirt pocket my National News Service Information Gathering license and my official *Perriodocko* identification card. I placed them on the counter and smiled at the drink girls, who seemed to be the only employees on the premises.

"Good evening," I said to them. "How are you, my fellow citizens?"

"*A bili en creneckulo,* sir," said the shorter of the two, looking down at a glass she was drying with a soiled cloth. The other girl, the taller one, nodded in agreement.

"Now that I have met you, I cannot complain, either," I said. "Just kidding!" We all laughed together, as was customary. "I am here to gather information for a report," I said, finding myself shouting to be heard above the volume of the singing, which had continued with full enthusiasm.

"A report, sir?" the first girl asked.

"Yes, for *Perriodocko,*" I said. This got their attention. Everyone is interested in our sacred Homeland's newspaper.

"Oh, yes, sir" they both said, nodding. I felt they were trying to mask their excitement at talking with a fully authorized Information Gatherer. This was not unusual. I was accustomed to such nervousness.

I retrieved my credentials. "I have been told by a reliable source that the rising *chu-chu* star, Miss Mae Love, may have gotten her start here at your *U-House*, right here on this very stage," I said, gesturing toward the back. "I am interested in interviewing anyone who might have known her, who might have a personal story to share, something the many readers of *Perriodocko* would appreciate knowing." I smiled—rather nicely, I thought. "That is why I am here."

The girls looked at each other and looked at me. They said nothing. They sort of shrugged, sort of shook their head. It was all quite difficult to understand.

"Miss Mae Love? The singer?" I repeated.

"Yes, sir," the shorter girl said. "We are aware of her. But would you excuse me for a moment, please, sir?" She looked toward the stage. "I apologize, I must announce, sir."

She picked up a microphone from the counter and said, "That was Miss Mae W doing 'Triumphant.' Let us make a nice applause for her!"

Almost everyone put down their *uchaana* cigarettes and clapped. The singer returned to her table, where her friends made gestures of adulation in her direction. She was indeed quite good.

"All right! Mae W… Now, fellow citizens, let us keep it going for Sunny! Miss Sunny!" A lady rose from another table, flashed her singing license to both sides of the room, and stepped upon the stage. The taller girl behind the counter, the one without the microphone, turned to a console behind her and moved some dials and pushed some buttons. Then the familiar strains of "All Together"—Miss Jasmine Joy, Year 10, nearly four months on the charts—filled the fragrant air. But instead of hearing Miss Jasmine Joy's dulcet voice, we were treated to the girl on stage, Miss Sunny, I presume, belting out the opening lines, which translate roughly as:

> *There is nothing impossible*
> *For every noble heart*
> *When we work together*
> *All together!*

She was also quite good, I thought. Very much like Miss Jasmine Joy.

I must say that I felt a quiver of sentiment in my chest. My brother Boy, I remembered, sometimes played this song at night, during a *bolo* stupor. These immortal words have always given him comfort and inspiration, and for some unknown reason hearing a young person sing them so proudly and with so much conviction made me feel as though the sacrifices and turmoil we have endured, all of us in our sacred Homeland, was leading to something great and lasting.

But I was not here at the *Go Paja U-House* to watch a show or get caught up in selfish thoughts. I was on official business.

"Very nice," I said to the girls behind the counter. "So, tell me, is it true that Miss Mae Love once sang upon that very stage?"

They looked at each other wordlessly. The shorter one said, "I think so, sir."

"Well, did you ever witness this yourself?"

"Maybe, sir," she said, looking down at the counter. She straightened a pile of tissues upon which I could see written various numbers next to the names of famous songs, and also the names of people, none of them famous as far as I could tell.

"Maybe?" I was growing confused.

She nodded. "It is possible, sir." The other girl busied herself with the control console. I noticed some of the customers looking toward us furtively, careful to avoid staring and impoliteness. The shorter girl forced a smile. "I am very sorry, sir. Would you please excuse me? I must bring some drinks to our guests. Of course, sir, you are most welcome to sit down wherever you like. I shall bring you *uchaana* with our compliments. You are most welcome, sir." She began arranging glasses upon a tray.

I was perplexed. Most regular citizens are quite eager to be interviewed by a *Perriodocko* Information Gatherer. It is considered an honor.

"Yes. Well. Fine," I said. "If you have no objection, I shall have a look around."

"Yes," she said, gathering up her tray. "Of course, sir."

As she went off to serve, I investigated the wall running from the front of the room to the back. It was adorned with numerous framed photographs of aspiring *chu-chu* singers, some smiling, some appearing pensive, all clutching a microphone. I did not recognize any of the people, although I do confess that they were all rather nice to look at.

Some of the photographs were signed with cheerful greetings. "*Thank you to Go Paja,*" one said. "*The best* U-House *in Capital City!*"

As I made my way along the wall, inching toward the stage, I made sure to give a polite salutation to each couple or group I passed, although many of the young patrons, I noticed, avoided my gaze. I told myself to be unbothered by their rudeness. It is well known that too much *uchaana* can make people somewhat oblivious of their surroundings. Indeed, with all the smoke swirl-ing around, I was starting to feel a bit dizzy, and for a moment I forgot why I had come here.

Then Miss Sunshine, the girl onstage, hit a long, piercing, high note, and I recalled my purpose. This was also when I thought about my wife and the possibility of my absence caus-ing concern. But, as I say, this was all new and different to me, a pleasant fascination. I decided to stay a minute.

The other listeners did not seem to be paying full attention to Miss Sunshine's touching performance. They seemed to be concentrating on paper booklets. Each table had one.

I examined one of these booklets sitting upon an empty tabletop. The front cover said:

SONGS 4 U

Inside, there was an alphabetical list of our sacred Homeland's most beloved tunes, and near the back of the booklet another alphabetical list of our sacred Homeland's most beloved *chu-chu* stars and the songs that had made them famous. *Ah bolah,* it was quite extensive. Possibly not even the remarkable Mr. TupTup could name them all.

I made a mental note to ask the girls in charge if I might take a copy of their booklet for my research.

As I proceeded closer to the stage, I encountered a young man sitting by himself at a small table near the wall. He wore an amusing black shirt that had written upon it in white letters the word *vernando*, with some of the letters facing the wrong way and off-center, as though they were tipsy. To my surprise, as I passed he looked directly into my eyes and smiled at me.

I smiled back, and to my further surprise he invited me to join him. "Please sit down, my comrade," he said, indicating the empty chair. "I am Z. My dear older brother is also a *Kapaa*, and I have much respect for the valuable service you provide for our sacred Homeland."

I shook my head and chuckled softly. "Thank you for your kindness, Mr. Z, my fellow citizen. But you are mistaken. I am not *Kapaa*. I am an Information Gatherer from the National News Service!" I produced my documents from my shirt pocket and placed them on the table.

"Well, then, my comrade, it is certainly a great honor and privilege," Z said, without carefully reading my credentials. Holding up a handful of brown coupons bearing the official stamp, he said, "May I buy you an *uchaana*?"

"Thank you again for your kindness," I replied. "But I really should not smoke *uchaana* while attending to my duties."

"My accomplished comrade," he said, smirking, "you certainly are much better informed than a mere student such as myself. However, unless the policy has been changed since this morning, when last I checked, I assure you that enjoying an *uchaana* is permitted. You are in violation of nothing."

He was correct. Selling and distributing *uchaana*, of course, required a rather expensive license controlled by the Bureau of Industry. But buying and consuming it did not. Like *bolo*, *uchaana* is readily available with the proper tickets, which are as plentiful and easy to obtain as raindrops on a stormy day. Our Caring Leaders have recognized that, like *bolo, uchaana* makes regular citizens quite happy—including, it seemed, this affable fellow.

I explained to him the nature of my business, and the need to stay focused. Then I asked him, "Can you, my new friend, tell me anything about Miss Mae Love?"

His face darkened. "Has she done something?"

I laughed. "Yes, she has! She is being named a finalist in the National Song Competition!"

He held his smoldering *uchaana* aloft. "Wow, wow, wow. Here is to Miss Mae Love!"

"So you know her?" I inquired.

Z giggled. He nodded. He rubbed his face. He puffed his cigarette. And without saying a word, he looked over his shoulder and jerked his head.

I followed his eyes to the wall behind us. I pointed to it and raised my eyebrows.

He grinned and nodded.

"Please excuse me," I said, rising from my chair. Z nodded again and took a puff.

I went to the wall, just as Miss Sunshine poured her entire lung power into the sensational climax of "All Together." She reached the famous final note, the long one on the word *ontongull* ("together"). The audience began to applaud enthusiastically, even before the song was finished. I joined them because, yes, she was really quite good. And then, as the cymbals swelled and the final chord went right to the center of my heart, one of the photographs on the wall drew my eye, like it was a string and I was a fish on a hook.

There was Miss Mae Love.

The photograph, shot in color, looked old and slightly faded. But I had no doubt what I was seeing, despite the dim and hazy light. There she was: Miss Mae Love, standing on the low stage of the *Go Paja U-House,* surrounded by a large group of what appeared to be friends and comrades. She was smiling broadly. Her eyes sparkled, and her teeth were very white.

I must report as a matter of fact that she looked quite beautiful.

"Let us give it up for Miss Sunshine! Miss Sunshine, everybody!" The counter girl was back on the microphone, stirring up the crowd. They clapped and hooted. I felt terribly sentimental. The song had united us, brought us closer to our common goals. *Ontongull.*

"And now, dear friends," I heard the counter girl announcing, "we have a very special guest who has come here to bring honor to our *U-House* and everything that we stand for. He is from the National News Service! He is from *Perridocko*! Let us all make him feel completely welcome!"

The entire room burst into applause. Now, let me tell you, I have never had a large audience clap for me, and it was quite embarrassing. I stood against the wall, looking out at the crowd. It was almost as though they were TV cameras and I was an accomplished *telastoorick* reciting his tales, or an important Dedicated Servant – or even a *chu-chu* star. Very strange. I was energized yet paralyzed. Really, very strange, I tell you.

I smiled and waved and nodded dumbly, unsure of what I was supposed to do next. It seemed as though the audience would never stop cheering.

Then I felt a hand on my shoulder. It was the counter girl. "Here, sir," she said, forcing the microphone on me. "This will make it easier to hear you."

Before I could protest, she was gone, and I was holding the microphone in my palms, unsure of how one uses such a thing properly. The room was eerily quiet. As I examined the appliance, I recalled the technique employed by people like Miss Sparkles Rainbow and Miss Butterfly Rose, and, in fact, the nice ladies singing at *Go Paja*. I raised the bulb end of the stick to my mouth and took care to avoid brushing my lips against the spongy cap. "Hello," I whispered. "Hello."

I heard my voice. It was much louder than I had ever heard it. I tried again. "Hello, my fellow citizens. Good evening."

Almost in unison, but not quite, the audience responded, "Good evening, sir."

I did not know what to say next. Time seemed to be passing very slowly.

Mr. Z, the nice young man I had just met, the one with the *vernando* shirt, was closest to me. He broke the silence. "*Tock!*" he shouted. "*Tock, tock!*" ("Speech, speech!")

Soon, many others in the audience joined his call, taking care to not shout simultaneously, lest they be unintentionally guilty of an Unauthorized Group Pronouncement.

"Well, now. OK," I said, feeling my voice grow steadier. "I thank you, my fellow citizens, for your warm welcome…Thank you for your kindness." I nodded for emphasis. Some of the people nodded back. Others made puffs.

"It is true what you have been told by our kind hostess," I continued. "I am indeed a Senior Information Gatherer at *Perriodocko*, our sacred Homeland's newspaper. And so, you see, in preparation for the big National Song Competition, I am here to gather information about one of the leading contenders, Miss Mae Love."

When I said her name, there was more applause, and even whistling!

I had the strangest sensation: For a moment, I felt as though I was floating outside my body and observing what was happening a split-second after it was actually happening. Do I make sense? Forgive me if I do not explain this properly; I had never felt this way previously and I have not since. It was as though I had been placed under some kind of spell. The voice projecting into the microphone and out of the loudspeakers was mine, but someone or something else was controlling what the voice was saying, not me. I am sorry if this sounds like an unexplainable dream, but that is how it was, I assure you.

I heard myself saying, "I suppose I could make a private visit with each of you to gather your recollections of Miss Mae Love, a fellow citizen who is worthy of pride. However, I am feeling so happy tonight for some unknown reason, and I would like to say that maybe it is the spirit and the energy of you, our younger generation, that has caused this happiness in me. And, therefore, although it is technically not permitted to have a News Conference in an establishment such as this, I have a thought. Let me tell you. Since it is *I*, the individual, who is asking the questions and *you*, the group, providing the answers, I am confident that I am in violation of no laws when I say to you, my fellow citizens, that we shall all *share* our stories about Miss Mae Love! *Ontongull.*"

Feeling like what it must be like to be a *chu-chu* star, completely in charge of the moment, I punctuated my declaration with a smooth—and rather dramatic, I must say—flourish of my right hand. I reached inside my coat pocket and, with an exclamation of, "Hah!" produced my tape recorder!

I heard gasps.

"Do not worry," I announced. "I am fully licensed to use this on official NNS business! You are in no danger, my fellow citizens and new friends."

The light was dim and smoky, and everything seemed a little blurry, so it was difficult for me to make out the faces of the audience, to gauge their enthusiasm for my fun idea. But no one clapped or shouted out encouragement.

"Here," I said, holding up the recorder in front of me. "*Ontongull.*" Then I pushed the red *record* button.

The room was silent.

I cleared my throat. "I shall start. Hello. Yes. We are here at the *Go Paja U-House* in the historic Central District. This is where the emerging star Miss Mae Love got her start. We are gathering information from patrons of the *U-House* who may have seen her perform upon this very stage. Or maybe knew her. So…I ask: Who would like to be the first to share a recollection?"

The room remained silent.

"Anyone? Please, my friends, do not be shy. I'm no *Kapaa*. Just kidding!" I laughed at my joke, as is the custom. But no one else did.

"Has no one a story?" I heard myself pleading. "Is there nothing to say?"

The room stayed silent. I thought I could hear the gears of my recorder turning, wasting perfectly good tape. Crestfallen, I asked once more, "Nothing?"

Nothing.

But then Z, the *vernando,* called out, "She is different."

I heard murmuring and whispering.

"That is really all that needs to be said," he declared. "Miss Mae Love is different. That is all that needs to be said."

I heard other voices in the dark saying "yes," and "that is right."

I tried to think of an appropriate follow-up question. I tried to figure out what he meant. But my brain, as I say, seemed to be working on a delay. And before I could probe further, someone shouted out, "Song!"

"Song! Song!" someone else chanted.

People laughed. People howled. Someone else yelled out, "Song! Song! Song!"

And then, from every corner of the room, very nearly in unison, they shouted a chorus of "Song! Song! Song! ... Song! Song! Song!"

"No, no," I said. "That is not possible." But they kept chanting, and they got louder.

"I ... No, really. I am—well, I cannot," I stammered. I was trying to explain what a bad idea this all had been, but before I could get the words out, the music started.

Everyone recognized it instantly: "Dedicated to Victory!" As performed by Miss Mae Love.

I heard an enormous roar, and for a moment I was not sure if it was them or if it was me.

Then the room became silent again, and all you could hear was the music, the familiar introduction, the beautiful chords that move all of us to keep trying and to keep believing. I could hear the spot where Miss Mae Love would begin to sing, but her voice had been taken out, of course, and it was up to me to supply the melody.

I felt myself inhaling deeply, filling my lungs, getting ready to let loose what was welling inside me. And then, in a providential moment of clarity and wisdom, I found my voice. "My dear fellow citizens," I heard myself intoning through the microphone, "I thank you for your kindness. But we must show respect for ourselves by showing respect for our laws. I do not have a license or permit to sing songs in public, or upon a stage. Being unauthorized for such an activity, I must decline your warm invitation."

The music continued. I must say it sounded particularly good, perhaps better than any recording I had ever heard. I cannot explain why. Perhaps because I was listening more closely than ever before. I do not know.

I felt something in my chest, something else I also cannot explain. It was like a throbbing, but it was not painful, only insistent. I felt myself swallowing repeatedly, to keep this thing down and not let it escape.

When it seemed as though I would not speak more—the truth is I *could* not speak more—the audience began chanting again. "Song! Song! Song! ... Song! Song! Song!"

They got louder, almost as loud as the music. But I had the microphone. "Now, please. No, no. Thank you, but no."

They would not cease. "Song! Song! Song!"

"No!" I shouted. "Now stop it! That is all!"

I felt myself dropping the microphone to the ground, gathering up my credentials, and storming past the counter, the triumphant strains of "Dedicated to Victory!" filling my head.

Outside, the air was cool. It was quiet. The *hahnkers* had parked for the night, and most regular people were home in their kitchens, eating soup. Soon I would be, too.

As I went to unlock my bicycle, I heard a familiar click. The batteries on my recorder had expired. I put it back in my coat and instinctively considered discarding the tape. But when I thought about what had just happened, I was not frightened or concerned. I had done the right thing.

Yet I must confess that I felt the strangest impulse, something I could not understand then, something I had not done since well before the changeover, a long, long time ago, when I was informed that I had lost my mother. For some unknown reason, I felt as though I might cry.

I got on my bicycle and pedaled especially hard, and, eventually, the feeling passed.

CHAPTER TWELVE

The next morning, at 7:54 a.m., I observed from my 3rd-floor window a *blecky* pulling up to the National News Building. I saw two familiar figures emerge from the back seats. At precisely 8:00 a.m., according to my great-grandfather's trusty timepiece, TupTup appeared in my office.

"Hello! Hello, boss. Hello!" His eyes were wide, expectant. He bore that crazy grin of his, a mask of glee and terror.

"Good morning, Mr. TupTup," I greeted him.

He hummed but said nothing, rocking from side to side, like a metronome.

I knew what he wanted. "I suppose you are interested in the information I have gathered from my fact-finding mission to the *Go Paja U-House*."

"Yes!" he exploded, pointing toward the ceiling. "The *Go Paja U-House* is the particular *U-House* where the next great one, Miss Mae Love, is rumored to have gotten her start. But this is obvious."

"Yes," I agreed. "This is indeed obvious."

"Yes," TupTup said. "But let me ask you something. Hah! Hmmmm." He produced from the back pocket of his pants an official Information Gatherer's notebook and an official *Perriodocko* pencil. Following the guidance of several influential advisors, I had allowed him these prized tools even though he was, of course, not properly licensed.

I looked at him quizzically. "Yes?"

"Yes. Well. Obviously, I am ready!"

"Thank you, Mr. TupTup, for your preparedness, which I and every member of the staff deeply appreciate. You are a fine example to other Special Assistants and junior Information Gatherers."

"Yes!" He stared at me, his pencil poised above his notebook.

I did not know what to say. "I am sorry, Mr. TupTup. I must apologize for what is surely a misunderstanding caused by me and me alone, for which I must take full responsibility. But I have no further instructions for you at this time."

"No, no, no," he yelped. "Obviously, you are going to tell me what Miss Mae Love the Next Great One said to you. But first let me ask you something. You can tell me what she was wearing. But let me ask you something else. Usually she is very well known for dressing in black. But this is very well known, obviously. Ah! Yes. Hmmmm. Well! Do not believe me. Hmmmm. You can believe the official photograph released by the organizers of the National Song Competition." He set down the notebook and pencil on my desk and fished his wallet from his pants. "But do not listen to me. Hah! I am well prepared, obviously."

He retrieved a folded paper from his collection of folded papers and peeled it open. "Miss Mae Love is very well known for dressing in black. But this is obvious." He held up her photo, which I recognized from the *chu-chu* section of the previous day's edition of our sacred Homeland's newspaper. She was in fact wearing a black dress, with silver highlights. It was, I am compelled to report, a very pretty dress.

Perhaps intending to imbue the morning with his singular brand of humor, TupTup fell into one of his *vernando* trances, cataloguing everything he felt I needed to know about Miss Mae Love. *Ah bolah*, I assure you I was already quite well aware of all the relevant information. I was not surprised to learn that she was being given careful consideration for a spot among TupTup's top five girlfriends.

Up late from the night before, I suppose I did not have the energy or will to interrupt my esteemed colleague. Anyway, I knew he would eventually run out of juice, like my tape recorder.

But before I could explain the unpleasantness that had transpired at the *Go Paja U-House*—before TupTup was finished with his presentation, in fact—a loud noise stopped him. It sounded like a cannon.

We both dashed to my office window. On the street below, regular citizens were scurrying everywhere. Hundreds, maybe thousands, of National Heroes were filling Central Avenue. But on this morning they were not marching. They were dashing, running, streaming out of personnel carriers, wearing protective gas masks, swarming like emerald bees. I could hear agitated shouting, but I could not make out what was being said. When I saw all traffic pulling to the side of the avenue, and bystanders of all classification assuming the Safety Position—squatting in place, arms hugging the legs, face down on the knees—I understood that our sacred Homeland was undergoing a Security Emergency.

I heard another distant explosion, and then the official recording coming from *hahnker* loudspeakers: "Warning: Assume the Safety Position! Warning: Assume the Safety Position!"

Acting on decades of Information Gathering experience, I turned and sprinted for the stairs. I did not have time to apologize to Mr. TupTup for my rudeness.

Running down, I was met by several members of my staff, none of whom required instruction. All properly trained Information Gatherers at the National News Service know what to do in the case of an unfolding Security Emergency: exit the building, avoid dangerous confrontations, and assume the Safety Position as soon as possible.

Despite the calamity surrounding us, I was terribly proud to note that none of my people wasted energy on needless chatter or unhelpful speculation. Not one. They were true professionals.

When I got outside, my eyes and nose immediately began to burn. The air smelled rotten, and each inhalation felt like being pricked with a million sewing needles. But I understood that I had to plunge onward into the foul air, that if I wished to survive a Security Emergency I had to get far enough away from tall buildings to avoid being crushed in the case of a structural collapse.

Before I could assume the Safety Position, another explosion, this one much closer, it seemed, split my ears, and I could hear nothing but the faint sounds of repeated *hahnker* warnings and urgent shouting of brave National Heroes: "Get down!" "Hurry!" "Over here!"

We were under some sort of vicious attack, but I was unarmed and could do nothing but cower. All of my advanced education and elite credentials were suddenly useless. *I* was utterly useless. At that moment, I must confess, I did not care if I lived or if I died.

I turned to look back across the plaza at the National News Building, our sacred Homeland's enduring symbol of fairness. It was not aflame, nor crumbling. Outwardly, it appeared undamaged, without a single broken window.

I was relieved but concerned. Others around me in the flee-
ing crowd looked back, too, calculating their distance from the
towering façade, should it fall. Judging themselves far enough
removed from the potential hazard, many of my fellow citizens
dropped to the ground and assumed the Safety Position.

I was about to join them. As I began to squat, a lone figure
emerged from the front entrance, beside the suddenly vacant
security lobby, lurching forward then stopping, then lurching
forward again. My eyes stung badly, and I could barely keep
them open. But I knew it was TupTup.

A bolt of terror jolted me, worse than any mortar shell. I
was his superior. I was responsible for him. Yet I had allowed
myself to be overcome with fear and cowardice. His illustrious
father, Chief Editor Pops, Uncle—I knew they would say I had
abandoned him when he most required my leadership, and a
large part of me understood that this was true.

For some unknown reason, I thought of my brother, and I
knew what I must do.

Violating the excellent training that everyone in our sacred
Homeland gets from the start, the training that every schoolchild
receives, I did not assume the Safety Position when directed. I
knew that this was wrong and a big mistake. But I also knew
that leaving TupTup alone was a big mistake.

As I ran back to the National News Building, I heard a stern
order: "Get down! Now! Get down!" A squadron of National
Heroes was occupying the plaza, coming to our rescue. They
were screaming at me, "Safety Position! Safety Position! Now!"

I did not have time to thank them, or to explain. How does
one explain a man like TupTup to those who do not know his
full story? All I could do was yell out, "He is very important!"
and keep running.

"Get down!" I heard. And then something hard, like a cricket bat, struck my back, between my shoulders. I could see nothing but the pavement rushing toward my face. For a moment I thought I had been shot. When I caught my breath and opened my eyes, I was in the care of two National Heroes, who stood over me, ensuring my well-being. "Safety Position!" they yelled. Apparently, I was not bleeding.

"Yes, yes," I said frantically. "I shall. But, you see, that man over there, the one—"

"Safety Position! Now!" I felt the urgency in his voice. There was no time to talk. I did what I was told, although it was difficult to hug my legs, since something felt broken in my left shoulder. Whatever had hit me had dislocated something, and my socket did not move correctly.

The National Heroes helped me get situated properly. Understandably, they were rushed, facing terrible challenges, and I must have cried out when they assisted me a bit too roughly. They were facing unimaginable pressure. I do not blame them for replying to my exclamation with a vulgar word.

"Over there!" someone yelled. "We got them!" The two National Heroes attending to me ran off, and I was left in a somewhat modified Safety Position, not quite fully tucked together, and with my head aloft rather than with eyes facing down. Nearby fellow citizens, I noticed with pride, were all positioned perfectly, like a field of mushrooms.

My eyes were excessively watery, and I was having trouble keeping them open against the burning air, but I could make out Mr. TupTup wandering away from the National News Building, toward the avenue, where the awful disturbance seemed to be centered. As I say, my vision was not good. But I thought I could see something in his hands.

I was able to focus for a second. No, I was not imagining. For some unknown reason, as he walked directly into the conflict, TupTup was writing in his notebook. Unlicensed and untrained, he could justifiably be cited and detained for making an Unauthorized Report.

I tell you, I did not know what to do. I understood that unless he got into Safety Position immediately, TupTup could be shot and hurt, or worse. He was an easy target.

I tried to rise. I swear I tried. But my injuries did not allow it—or maybe it was merely my stupid short leg and stupid lack of courage. I do not know. All I know is that the *meowkaleet* had been drained from my big head and replaced with shame.

A squad of National Heroes, perhaps six of them, ran to TupTup with their weapons drawn. I could make out furious gesticulations, which I knew meant that he was in grave danger of attack. TupTup apparently did not understand what was happening, and a National Hero pointed his gun directly at TupTup's chest, to illustrate.

Instead of immediately getting safe, TupTup dropped his notebook and pencil to the ground and pulled out his wallet. I held my breath and prayed to all our Caring Leaders that he was not showing the National Heroes his top five girlfriends.

One National Hero grabbed the wallet and ripped something out, throwing the rest on the ground. TupTup seemed to be talking and the National Heroes seemed to be screaming, and I could feel that something awful was going to happen—all because of my personal failings.

Somehow I found the strength and balance to rise. I knew I would probably be hit by whatever was causing this Security Emergency—religious insurgents and hostile foreigners crossed my mind—but I no longer cared about my welfare. I knew I had to intercede before something happened to TupTup.

I stumbled in their direction, the pain in my shoulder spreading through my torso like electricity. I may have even cried out. But nothing I uttered was as loud as the roar I heard next, louder even than the screaming National Heroes and blaring *hahnker* speakers. "STOP!!!"

I tell you, the sound was chilling. Everyone clustered on the plaza, everyone who had been talking or gesturing, suddenly froze.

Only one person moved: it was Uncle.

"STOP!!!" he repeated. Holding some sort of paper in his upraised hand, his eyes partially protected by dark glasses and his mouth by a cloth mask, he dashed into the middle of the squad of National Heroes, putting himself between TupTup and their weapons. He made a big show of what he was holding, jabbing it in front of each National Hero's face. One of them, the one who had grabbed TupTup's wallet, also grabbed Uncle's paper and seemed to be examining it closely. I could not make out what was being said, of course, but I could tell that Uncle was extraordinarily upset, pointing at people and placing his nose very close to theirs. The look on TupTup's face was hard to discern: he could have been terrified or amused. It was always impossible to tell with a *vernando* like him.

The National Heroes lowered their weapons and moved away from TupTup and Uncle, who scooped up his nephew's belongings from the ground and shoved them into TupTup's arms. I continued shuffling toward the two, as fast as I could, which was not very fast. Wiping my eyes and nose and mouth with my untucked shirt, I discovered, gave some temporary relief from the itching, and I could see somewhat better.

So could TupTup. When he saw me, finally, he shouted, "Hello! Hello, boss!"

Tup Tup started walking toward me, that crazy, toothsome smile in place. Before he could make three steps, though, Uncle grabbed him by the collar of his shirt and yanked him backwards. The National Heroes pointed guns at me and yelled, "Get down! Get down!"

"That is his boss!" I heard Uncle screaming. "Hold fire! Do not shoot!" Then he beckoned me with his free hand, urging me to join the safety of their group.

"Hello, boss!" TupTup chirped, his eyes reddened and his nose dripping fluid. "Hello!"

"Mr. TupTup! I am so very happy that you are unhurt! We are very lucky. *Ah bolah,* we have been saved by these brave men. A thousand thanks." I bowed as much as I could to all of the National Heroes, and Uncle. "We are so grateful."

Uncle grunted his acknowledgment and shook his head with what seemed like disgust, or dismay. I did not blame him for his anger. It was I who had put us all in this dangerous position.

"I will handle this," Uncle said, dragging TupTup by his neck and motioning for me to follow. "Back in the office."

I knew returning prematurely was a violation of protocol, but I was in no condition to protest. Also, aside from TupTup, who maintained a cheerful front, I could feel that everyone was still quite upset and on full alert for threats. This was not a good time to discuss regulations.

We three trudged back toward the front entrance of the National News Building. The air seemed to be getting fresher, and it appeared as though entire platoons of National Heroes were getting back in their vehicles and driving away to their barracks. Whatever calamity had confronted us, I deduced, must have been neutralized successfully, although the *hahnkers* continued to encourage regular citizens to remain safe.

"Let me tell you something else," TupTup said to me, breathlessly. "I have made preparations for an Authorized Report!"

"You shut up," Uncle snapped. "Not another word, *DipDip*."

I understood that Uncle was extremely tense. But, still, I was stunned to hear him address his nephew with this slang term, which I hesitate to translate. It is a very rude way to describe people who cannot learn properly because of the way they were born.

I said nothing, of course. We three, and all my fellow citizens, had already survived an awful, but preventable, incident. I did not want to be the cause of additional turmoil.

CHAPTER THIRTEEN

By the middle of the day, everything was completely back to normal. Aside from some sniffling and persistent irritation of the tear ducts, our magnificent team was perfectly fine, as though nothing had happened.

This was somehow appropriate, almost poetically appropriate, I must say, since, if you looked out my window any time after noon, you could not tell there had been a disturbance. It was just like any other day, absolutely calm and organized. Adversity, you see, has never conquered our sacred Homeland's legendary resilience.

With all the activity of the morning, my brief but unforgivable lapse in judgment was forgotten, or at least postponed. Uncle had deposited me and his nephew back on the 3rd floor, announcing, "I will deal with you later." I was not certain who he was addressing. He seemed to be in a great hurry, already making calls on a fancy phone with a screen before he was out of my office.

After a comprehensive personnel review—no one missing, no one seriously hurt (except me)—we all returned to work. And, *ah bolah*, we had much to do.

The entire staff of *Perriodocko*, including our peerless Chief Editor, worked long past sundown, right up to Final Deadline, taking great care to assemble the official account of what had transpired in our sacred Homeland's Capital City. We compiled inspiring quotes from the relevant Dedicated Servants and Caring Leaders. "Lack of belief in our laws, or the wrong beliefs, always leads to havoc," the Minister of Unity declared. "To improve our sacred Homeland requires cohesion and team confidence, not discord."

The Information Liaison for the National Heroes—a longtime friend and trusted colleague—provided superb photographs of our courageous protectors in action.

The dangerous incident, we soon learned, was probably caused by a small but determined group of radicals, funded by outside agents who despise our sense of compassion and justice. Technically speaking, the troublemakers were residents of our sacred Homeland, but because they acted on the advice of malicious manipulators, you couldn't really call them citizens. They were traitors.

According to our exhaustive Information Gathering, these heartless terrorists had assaulted morning commuters with clubs, and possibly knives. Some reports coming from National Heroes headquarters indicated that a particularly brutal gang may have brandished pistols at a *hahnker* filled with women and children. One expert issued a chilling analysis that proved the terrorists had set off several small explosive devices, several of which I heard with my own ears. Miraculously, not a single regular citizen was seriously harmed, and the National Heroes suffered no casualties.

Throughout the day, TupTup was uncharacteristically silent. Every time I passed his station, he was hunched over his desk, deep in concentration – probably focused on some starlet's photo. We have an expression about not disturbing sleeping goats, and I chose to follow this folksy wisdom. Better, I thought, to leave him to his special interests than encourage a detailed—and no doubt lengthy—recapitulation of how he did this, and how he did that, and then what happened next.

Besides, Uncle had been rather harsh with him—for good reason, of course. One does not flaunt the regulations, no matter who one's father is. TupTup seemed to have learned his lesson. Sitting there in his cubicle, with no one paying him any attention, he seemed chastened and reflective. I did not want to disturb a rare moment of solitary meditation, when he could figure out for himself what he could have done differently and better.

If I may be blunt, I determined that our crucial labor would be executed most efficiently without Mr. TupTup's unique contributions. With all due respect to him, his great father, and his great and powerful family, I did not think our published report suffered from his exclusion.

Our coverage, beginning on the front page and extending for seven additional pages, all the way up to the *scrachi* section, was some of our finest work. Although I make it a practice to avoid doing anything that might encourage complacency among my subordinates, when we had put the paper "to bed," as we like to say, I convened my entire staff: Information Gatherers, Assistants, everyone. "Gentlemen," I began, speaking softly, since it was still difficult for me to breathe properly, "you have approached greatness today. I do not think it is unwarranted *meowkaleet* to suggest that tomorrow's edition of *Perriodocko* will win many awards from the appropriate award-giving bodies. Thank you for your commitment to the National News Service, and to our sacred Homeland."

I pulled from my desk a bunch of tickets I had been saving for an occasion such as this. "Now," I said, distributing them to my appreciative colleagues, "please go home and enjoy a glass of *bolo*. You have earned it."

Everybody exclaimed, *"Grabvey, Grabvey,"* saluted each other, and filed out, exhausted but satisfied.

Everybody but TupTup.

He stood to the side of my desk, rocking from side to side, saying nothing. His eyes faced toward the floor. I could detect him humming faintly.

I did not know what to say. "Mr. TupTup," I tried. "You are unusually quiet today. I understand that the events of the morning must have been a big shock to you, as they were to all of us."

He continued rocking, saying nothing.

"I suppose I should have offered you an apology much sooner. But I became involved with my important official duties. Please, sir, I ask you to forgive me."

He did not reply.

I bowed my head deferentially and repeated my apology. "I am sorry."

When I looked up, TupTup's face was screwed into an inscrutable mask that might have been horror or glee. He had his hand outstretched toward me. In it was a sheet of paper, the color and size of which I recognized from his personal notebook—the one I had bequeathed him.

"What is this?" I said, taking the paper.

"Top five list," he blurted, wheeling around and dashing out my door.

I shook my head and chuckled. You could always count on our office *vernando* to lighten the mood, even on the most stressful and challenging days. Knowing TupTup for some time at this point, I remained amused and strangely entertained by his dynamic collection of glamorous girlfriends. I admit I was fascinated that he could devote unwavering attention to his social affairs even as everyone around him worked diligently to compose the Authorized Report of the day's dramatic news.

I was very tired, exhausted really, and I almost put his rankings aside for the next morning. But something caught my eye.

Across the top, in big block letters, he had written:

TOP FIVE THINGS I SEE TODAY

Below it, in smaller block letters, it said.

NATIONAL HEROES TAKING THEM
BIG TRUCK WITH BARS AND NO ESCAPING
GUNS!!! SMOKE AND BOMB
UNCLE HELPING
MANY OLD WOMAN CRYING

As with much of my illustrious colleague's communications, his list didn't make complete sense to me. But I could tell Tup-Tup had labored over this thing with great care and concern. There were numerous erasure marks and words crossed out and re-written. Two whole lines had been scribbled over so forcefully and repeatedly that he had made small tears in the paper, and the excess graphite on the page left a shadowy mark on my thumb. Whatever items he had elided, I surmised, apparently had not been Top Five material.

Too tired to devote another second of thought to his authorial output, I left TupTup's list on my desk, gathered my belongings, and headed out the door for home, where I knew a nice bowl of soup would be waiting for me.

CHAPTER FOURTEEN

The next morning, I found it difficult to rise from bed at my usual time. My injured back was terribly stiff and tender, and I had not slept well.

Actually, I had hardly slept at all. When I went to bed, my body felt completely spent, but my mind would not stop thinking, and I passed most of the night staring at the ceiling trying various tricks to make myself rest. None of them worked. I would drift off and come back, drift off and come back. I even considered my brother's *bolo* method, but I was too weary to drag myself to the kitchen.

We have a saying: *Ju na-mee pevra klot.* "Do not go to bed angry." I had not been angry, exactly. No, that is not the right way to describe my condition. I was, I suppose, slightly annoyed, and maybe a little disappointed—with my family.

How should I say this? I do not want to portray them as ignorant, for that is not accurate. Perhaps *misinformed* is a better way to put it. Or, better yet: not fully informed.

You may accuse me of *meowkaleet* if you must, but I do not think it is unduly proud to note that I am in a unique position to be better informed than the average citizen on the happenings in our sacred Homeland. Perhaps this is why I found my family's general attitude somewhat irksome and perplexing.

First, my wife, who is normally patient and understanding, did not even smile when I returned home from *Perriodocko*. No.

Instead, when I came through the door, she greeted me coolly, with a little nod, and said, "Hello, Dear Husband. It is very late. But I recognize that this is becoming your usual arrival time."

I pointed out to her that, in fact, I had been engaged with extremely important National News Service business, and I reminded her that two evenings out of thousands did not constitute a habit or a trend, but, rather, a coincidence.

"I understand," she said. But I suspected that she really did not. Of course, I did not mention my suspicion. I did not want to argue.

We did not speak to each other throughout supper, other than when I requested she fetch some ice to place upon my injured shoulder. She went next door to my father's apartment, where Boy kept a supply of cubes for his drinks.

When she came back, she told me that Gurly and father were having a heated discussion with my brother, who was in one of his moods. I had repeatedly told my family that the best thing to do when Boy gets in such a state is to leave him alone, to not talk with him until the unpleasantness subsides. But on this night they must have thought they knew better than I, because when my wife returned I could hear the yelling through the door—and it was not just Boy's usual wine-induced ranting. I detected father's voice, too, and a higher-pitched sound, which must have been Gurly's keening.

"What is happening there?" I asked my wife, who was clutching a lumpy plastic bag.

She placed it behind my shoulder. "I have told you, Dear Husband," my wife replied with a hint of exasperation in her voice that I did not appreciate. "They are having an unpleasant discussion."

"Yes, that is clear," I said. I turned my head sideways and looked expectantly at my wife. She said nothing. "Very well," I declared. "I shall investigate." With some effort, I pulled my chair away from the table and rose to go. My back was starting to stiffen.

"Dear Husband, permit me to say: I do not think you should get involved. Perhaps you should let them be."

She had a point. It is always better to avoid meddling in someone else's concerns. But I did not like my relatives to be upset with each other, especially since Boy endlessly endured the kind of physical torture that eventually affects the mind. Arguing with my brother was useless, and it only made his missing arm feel worse.

"This shouting is inappropriate," I announced, and left my wife standing beside the table, with the bag of ice in her hands, looking into her unfinished bowl of soup.

Their door was closed but unlocked. I let myself in without knocking. The radio was on and tuned to the nightly National News broadcast. An important National Hero commander was being interviewed, stressing that our sacred Homeland was safer than ever—and would remain so if all citizens would simply obey our laws, not just the ones they liked. Boy was sprawled in his chair, gesticulating with his good hand. Gurly was standing near him with her arms crossed. Father was sitting at the table, with old copies of *Perriodocko* strewn haphazardly. Each was talking loudly to the others, with nobody listening. It was all quite rude.

All three looked at me when I entered the apartment, but they did not cease their bickering. I could pick out words and phrases—"the law," "*compastee*," "Heroes"—and it seemed as though father and Gurly were teaming up against Boy, who, naturally, I wished to protect. Had he not he suffered enough?

"Excuse me," I interrupted. "You have a visitor."

"Ask him!" Boy snapped. "Ask him. He can tell you."

"Tell you what?" I inquired, immediately determining that he had been drinking. My brother always got a certain sound in his voice when he was on a *bolo* binge, as though his voice was coming through his nose.

"Yes," my father said. "My son is a valued member of the National News Service. He is the one who can say—not you with your wild rumors!" I had not seen my father so upset since a Dedicated Servant, an officer from the Department of Building Safety, had determined (correctly) that the unregistered potted plants father kept on his windowsill, jade and mint I think, were a potential danger to innocent citizens walking beneath them, and were subject to immediate confiscation.

"He doesn't know," Boy said, scowling, dismissing my father with an impolite wave.

"What is the meaning of all this commotion?" I demanded. "This has been a long and challenging day for me. I have not had the luxury of staying home listening to *chu-chu*. I have been busy working." The moment I said this I felt bad. It was true, of course. But I did not need to point out the obvious.

Boy narrowed his eyes and shook his head.

I felt his disgust, and I shared it. "Dear brother," I said, humbly. "Please forgive me. I should not have said that. You are a hero, a National Hero, and you deserve much greater respect than I have shown. I beg a thousand pardons."

Boy said nothing. He reached for a glass near his feet and drank deeply.

"This was a difficult day," father said.

"Yes," Gurly agreed. "Very difficult."

"Yes," said father.

I sighed loudly. "*Ah bolah*," I said, smiling. "Much has happened. But now I am with my dear family. *A bili en creneckulo*."

"Of course you cannot complain," my brother roared. "If you did, you would lose your precious job, and your pension."

"And extra *bolo* tickets," Gurly interjected.

Boy glared at her, and she walked away, sitting beside my father.

"We are all tired. Let us talk in the morning," I proposed. "Perhaps then whatever is bothering you will have passed."

Boy laughed bitterly, more like spitting than chortling. "Yes. That is a fine idea in our fine country with a fine newspaper. Just wait. It will be better later. Yes, that is a fine idea. Let us talk in the morning, when *Perriodocko* appears and all our questions will be answered and no one will care about yesterday. Yes, let us talk then, dear brother. Maybe I will have forgotten everything when the sun rises. Most excellent. A most excellent idea!"

"You are drunk," I said. Turning to father and Gurly, I shrugged. "He is drunk."

"Yes," they agreed.

"So?" Boy complained. "Yes? So? Therefore?"

Gurly looked at me desperately. "Dear cousin, I fear your brother will get us all in trouble with his raving."

"Trouble?" Boy howled. "Trouble? You do not know what trouble is, you peasant."

"Now stop this!" I ordered. "Stop it. All of you."

"You see?" Gurly said. "He is dangerous."

I did see. I saw my dear brother possessed by demons and plagued by circumstances he did not choose. He was piteous.

"Believe what you want," Boy said. "But I know people. I talk to people who know. People who know the people that make the decisions. OK? You can believe what you want, but I *know*." He snorted and waved us all away.

"We have all experienced various difficulties today," I said, with a conciliatory tone. "But we have survived. We have triumphed. That is what is important. Let us keep things in perspective."

"You really believe what you are saying?" my brother shot back.

"I do, dear brother. No attack, no matter how vicious, can break our spirit, if we remain together. *Ontongull*."

Boy held his head with his hand and waved his stump about wildly. "There was no attack. It was a crackdown. A roundup of harmless citizens just trying to grow some food."

"What?" I thought I had misheard him.

He looked at me with revulsion, as though I were an injured *scrachi* bird. "A crackdown. A show of force. An example."

My brother was terribly drunk, and obviously disoriented. I looked to my father, sitting silently, as in meditation. He took a great inhalation and held his breath, as though he were preparing to dive for clams in the bay. Finally, he murmured, "I have also heard this."

I could have misunderstood. "What?"

"Yes. That is what was said on the street," father said softly, nodding.

"Ah!" exclaimed Boy. "Someone had the audacity to repeat it to someone else without getting the proper permit! How scandalous!"

I looked at my father. He was a man who did not seek trouble, although, since the changeover, trouble had a way of

somehow finding him. He was not a bad citizen, just forget-
ful sometimes. Father preferred to avoid controversy, to be left
alone with his little plants and such. "Is this what was said to
you, father?" I asked.

"Yes. This is what was said," my father whispered. "But unlike
your brother, I do not think such nonsense should be repeated,
and I will not have insolence in my home." His voice rising,
father said, "I will not have my son, or anyone else, putting us in
danger. I will not have it. No. No, no. I will not."

Other than the time he was refused a travel visa for reasons
that were difficult for him to understand, I had seldom seen my
father so vexed. He was normally a quiet man, and calm. This
night he was trembling with frustration, and maybe fear.

"Look," I said, holding out my hands, palms down, "all of us
should calm down. Stress can make us say and do things that we
do not mean, things we later regret. Let us all relax. We will feel
better in the morning."

"Easy for you to say," Boy sneered.

"Perhaps you have had enough *bolo* for one night," I told
him.

"You do not understand," he said, his words slurry and slow.
"You never have."

I failed to control my temper. "You are right," I said. "You are
so right. I know nothing. I am stupid. I do not talk to supremely
knowledgeable sources like you. My contacts are trivial people,
like the Information Liaison for the National Heroes. Like the
Chief Editor of *Perriodocko*. I am a simpleminded goat. You
could try to teach me, dear brother. But that would be pointless.
Nevaa lahang en nini warmung. I foolishly wished to bring har-
mony to our family. But that is a challenge beyond my meager

capabilities. Please forgive me. I am very sorry for wasting your time."

Then I left, closing the door perhaps a bit too firmly, my brother yelling his delusions at my increasingly sore back.

"Is everything OK, Dear Husband?" my wife greeted me.

I told her it was. "You know how Boy becomes."

"Yes." She looked at the floor and remained silent.

"What is it?"

"Nothing, Dear Husband," she said, forcing a momentary smile.

"You are very quiet."

Usually, my wife would reply to my observation by saying something like, "I am a bit tired," or "I prefer to hear you talk," or something polite. She is quite conscientious about avoiding controversy whenever possible, knowing that minimizing unnecessary offense is the best way to get through life. Like me, my wife does not drink *bolo*. As long as I have known her, she has smoked *uchaana* only once and deemed it unpleasant. She is careful with her words, which I have always found to be one of her best qualities.

I was therefore taken aback when I repeated my query, "Wife, you are very quiet. I ask you again: Is everything OK?" and she said to me: "No, Dear Husband. It is not."

"No? Are you sick again? With female problems?"

She shook her head.

I searched my brain. "Because I have rudely forgotten to properly demonstrate my appreciation for your excellent soup?"

She shook her head.

"Because of Boy's outburst?"

She looked at the floor.

"Ah, I see. Do not let this trouble you. You know how he gets."

"Yes, I know," she replied. "But I am concerned, Dear Husband."

I was touched. "Because you care for him, even though he is not your own blood."

She looked up. "Because ... well, what he said out loud."

"Yes. That was rather irresponsible. But do not worry. In the morning, he will probably have forgotten everything."

"I am frightened, Dear Husband."

She stepped near to me, put her lips against my ear, and whispered, "I heard the same thing."

CHAPTER FIFTEEN

My back hurt.

I was annoyed by my family.

And it started to drizzle on me as I pedaled to work through my shortcut alley, where no one gave me an encouraging wink. No one was there attending to their *compastee*. The streets felt drained, and so did I.

Although these are not valid excuses to be impolite, perhaps it is understandable to you that I was not in a cheerful mood when I arrived at work. Indeed, if I did not have such a large responsibility to my subordinates, my superiors, and my sacred Homeland, I confess I would have liked to have stayed at home, sleeping and forgetting.

Every little thing seemed to rankle me: the unidentifiable speck of something floating in my water; the scuff on my shoe, which must have occurred during the previous day's chaos; the slight but perceptible humidity in my office.

It was not a good morning to be entertained by TupTup's antics.

He did the TupTup Turtle minutes after I settled into my desk chair. Before I could stop him, he was in my office, grinning. "Hello! Hello, boss."

He was clutching the morning edition of the newspaper. I simply did not have the energy to listen to one of his monologues—especially since I knew Chief Editor Pops would have learned by now of my dereliction of duty during the terrorist attack. I needed to be prepared, to find the correct words to explain myself without sounding as though I thought what I had done was right. Chief Editor Pops was a supremely fair man. This was well known. But, clearly, one could not oversee an enterprise as vast and important as *Perriodocko* without a firm hand and clear directives. I knew that consequences were possible and fully warranted.

"Good morning, Mr. TupTup," I said, hurriedly, careful to avoid pausing long enough to allow him to get started. "I am eager to talk with you about many different subjects, including our adventure yesterday, but at this time I am quite busy with pressing matters that require my attention, so I ask for your patience and understanding when I tell you that I cannot really talk with you at this very moment. I hope you understand. Thank you, sir."

I nodded at him and directed my gaze at the papers upon my desk.

"Ah. Yes. Hmmmm. But let me ask you something."

"Mr. TupTup," I said, perhaps a bit too sternly, "I have just told you that I do not have time for questions, answers, or anything else. I am very sorry, sir. But please excuse me for now. Thank you."

"Yes. Hmmmm."

"Thank you for your understanding."

He did not reply. But he did not leave, either. Instead, Tup-Tup stood there, rocking slightly, mumbling incomprehensibly to himself.

I could not work like this. "Mr. TupTup? Please return to your station. Please."

He looked at me in a way that I could not decipher. For a fleeting second I thought he wanted to kill me, and then the next second I felt he was scared I might kill him, and then I thought that maybe this all was one of his big jokes. Then he laughed, half moaning, half gargling. It was a strange, mirthless laugh that reminded me how unfunny I presently found him.

Then he blurted, "I am going to make my report."

I did not know what he was talking about, but I did not care. *Ah bolah,* anything to be left alone! "Good," I said. "You do that."

"Yes. But let me ask you something: Can I have my top five list back? Which I need. For my report. Obviously."

"What? Your list? Oh, yes." I remembered. "Yes, of course." I reached to one of the stacks of paper on my desk, where I had left his peculiar "notes."

I could not find it.

TupTup stood there grinning, waiting. I riffled through the mess, looking for his unmistakable handwriting among the official typed documents. But I could not locate it. "I am very sorry, Mr. TupTup, I seem to have misplaced your, your—I cannot find it at this time, I am afraid."

He continued grinning, saying nothing.

"When I do—and it must be here, of course, where I keep all my important documents—I promise you, sir, I shall have my 2nd Assistant bring it to you directly. At your station." I nodded strenuously. "I promise. You have my word."

He made another of those strange laughing sounds and without saying a thing skipped out of my office, mumbling happily.

We are taught from an early age that a man has nothing if he loses his honor. You are perhaps aware of our most popular *telastoorick* tale, *Kenki Kaanki Koorki* ("Tall, Taller, Tallest") about the farmer with a magic bean? This tale is a perfect illustration: What are riches and prestige if a man has lost his honor?

Perhaps it is faithful adherence to this guiding principle that makes our sacred Homeland so very wondrous, so unlike any other place on Earth.

This is why I found myself becoming increasingly upset throughout the morning. I was not able to fulfill my promise, to keep my word and uphold my honor.

Several times I looked through everything on my desk, which, admittedly, can sometimes be a bit messier than I would prefer. Several times I touched every piece of paper with my fingers and flipped over each one, making sure nothing was stuck to the back. I checked my drawers, and I even checked my shelves, even though I was absolutely certain I had not placed TupTup's list there.

It had vanished.

I reminded myself that I had much more important things to worry about and resolved to put TupTup's silly scribbling out of my mind.

He never mentioned it again. Indeed, I did not see TupTup for the rest of the day.

Nor did I see Chief Editor Pops. I was surprised and, I confess, more than a little relieved, that I was never summoned to his office. Perhaps, I told myself, everything had blown over and would soon be forgotten. My superiors certainly had more vital things on their minds than my stupid mistakes.

Late afternoon, after our group water break, my 1st Assistant commented on the upcoming National Song Competition— only two weeks away; Miss Angel Lee Diamond the Megastar said to be the early favorite in public sentiment; excitement building—and asked if it was too early to begin Information

Gathering for a special commemorative section *Perriodocko* always published on the eve of the event.

I made some humorous comment—"Perhaps you should consult Mr. TupTup," I think I said—and my 1st Assistant looked at me with shock. "Were you not told?" he asked.

"Told? About what?"

"Please accept my apology, sir," he said. "A message was supposed to have been relayed to you. I shall investigate why it was not delivered."

"A message? I received no such thing," I said, growing irritable.

"I am sorry, sir," my 1st Assistant said. "Mr. TupTup was taken away this morning."

I felt a mix of nausea and dread envelop me, like I was on a boat in high seas.

My 1st Assistant immediately understood my misapprehension. "Oh, no, sir. Not *that* kind of taken away. Uncle came to fetch him."

"Ah," I said, nodding, careful to not display my profound relief. My subordinates looked to me for leadership and guidance. I could not afford to appear weak, or they would lose trust. But really, I felt an inexplicable joy coursing through me, like when you hear Miss Princess Cookie the Elegant Songbird singing "Our Sacred Homeland," or when a battalion of National Heroes marches down Central Avenue in perfect formation.

"Yes," my 1st Assistant continued, "around nine this morning. He—Uncle, I mean—he came bursting into the junior area and told Mr. TupTup they had to go, right away. Some kind of emergency. At home, maybe? I am not certain. But, anyway, yes. They left quite quickly."

"At nine, you say?"

My 1st Assistant nodded. "Yes, sir."

"But TupTup only arrived an hour earlier. At eight. His usual time." I looked at my great-grandfather's watch. It was a little past four in the afternoon.

"That is correct, sir."

I shrugged. "Very well," I said. "This certainly does not affect our ability to gather information."

My 1st Assistant looked as though he wanted to laugh or make a clever comment, but I could tell he was not sure if I was joking.

I was not. "This office runs perfectly well without Mr. Tup-Tup's unique contributions."

"Yes, sir."

"Let us strive to gather information with newfound commitment," I declared. "And let us compile an Authorized Report on the National Song Competition that is as compelling and useful to our fellow citizens as our exemplary coverage of yesterday's terrorist attack."

"Yes, sir. We shall."

"Yes. Good," I said. "Very good."

Break time was over. Everyone returned to his station.

Back in my office, at my desk, I attempted to complete the various tasks that are a Deputy Supervisor's usual responsibilities, tasks I have executed a thousand times, tasks that have become for me a matter of habit. But I could not concentrate properly. I found my gaze rising from my desk to my doorway. For some unknown reason, I kept expecting to see a familiar shock of black hair poking into view.

It never came.

Was I relieved to be rid of an unnecessary burden? I suppose I was. My office would certainly be quieter, and I knew that I would be able to devote my attention to things that really matter in our sacred Homeland, not the romantic whims of deeply admired *chu-chu* singers.

But still, I confess, I suppose I had grown accustomed to being interrupted and quizzed and entertained. I had never known a *vernando* like TupTup. Oh, he could be taxing on one's patience. That I do not dispute. Yet not until he was gone did I realize how much I had come to like the young man. Or how empty the 3rd floor would feel without him.

For some unknown reason, I suddenly felt as though I did not want to go home and face my wife, and my brother, and my cousin and father. But also, for some unknown reason, I had the strongest desire to be around people, fellow citizens, my comrades. During the workday, I was surrounded by dozens of colleagues at the National News Service, yet as I sat at my desk, silent, I felt a powerful sense of solitude.

Bebudew op en beberoo kap, I told myself. "You are never alone, you only feel alone."

Even though I knew this was always accurate, it did not make me feel less lonely.

I must admit that I wished TupTup might come bounding into my office at that moment, a photo of his latest girlfriend proudly on display.

He did not. Obviously.

Normally, at the end of the day I re-read all the Authorized Reports my department has produced, giving them a last look-over before sending them onto Chief Editor Pops for his approval—which he always grants. *Ah bolah*, I do not think he has time to actually read all the articles we produce. He is a terribly busy man with important relationships to maintain with all the greatest and most powerful people in our sacred Homeland.

But as a courtesy he gives our work some personal attention. I know this because many of the page proofs bear his initials.

On this particular day, I did not seem able to muster the strength or willpower to read five more stories about National Heroes. The Information Gathering was first-class, as usual, and the spelling and punctuation were good. But for some unknown reason I found myself staring at the pages, unable to begin.

TupTup was gone. I was alone in my quiet office. But I felt more distracted than ever. I cannot explain why.

To calm myself and find focus, I hummed one of my favorite songs under my breath. Doing so out loud, I understood, was not permitted without the proper license, not since Year 2, when the law was changed. Originally, audible humming *was* allowed, and certain scofflaws took advantage of that fact. They would engage in illegal public singing, potentially annoying passersby and possibly communicating with destructive elements in a kind of musical code. Then, when detained, they would claim that, in fact, they had not been singing at all, they had merely been humming loudly! To limit confusion, the Caring Leaders simply outlawed any sort of musical utterance without the proper license. These could be troublesome to obtain, so most people found it easier to just stop humming out loud.

The more I hummed, loud enough that only I could hear, the more, I confess, I thought about the National Song Competition, and Miss Mae Love. And the *Go Paja U-House*. And TupTup. And suddenly I realized that I had been humming "Dedicated to Victory" at my desk, as though it were stuck in my brain and I was trying to let it out.

Call it *meowkaleet* if you must, but I have to acknowledge that what I heard in my head sounded pretty good. Do not laugh, please, when I admit that there have been times in my life when I sang a song in the shower—not loudly, of course, but loudly enough I could hear my own voice—and at those times it also did not sound too terribly bad, either.

Ah bolah, I cannot explain what came over me that late-afternoon. Maybe it was too many things happening at once. Maybe it was something else. I do not know. Maybe it was merely further evidence that I really did not deserve my position at *Perriodocko*, or anywhere in a nation that gives so much to an irrelevant man like me and asks so little in return.

I do not know. I will allow others to be the judge.

All I can say for certain is that I decided right then and there that I would go back to the *Go Paja U-House*, and maybe, possibly—and I had not really made up my mind at that point—maybe I would go back on that modest stage and maybe this time I would do something really crazy.

I felt my heart beating rapidly, and my neck tickled. My mouth felt strangely dry, though water break had been less than an hour ago.

Perhaps it is fair to say I was excited, although about what, exactly, I was unsure. Meeting new friends? Smoking *uchaana*? Possibly perhaps performing? I cannot say. I found myself straightening and re-straightening piles of papers on my desk. I organized my pencils by height—*kenki, kaanki, koorki.* I even performed another comprehensive search of my desk for TupT-up's lost list.

Running out of constructive tasks, I remembered that my tape recorder needed new batteries. I retrieved it from the desk drawer on the left where I keep it. Now, I confess, my state of mind was not entirely reliable at this moment, and I fully admit that I could have been imagining it, but when I opened the back of my recorder to remove the old, dead batteries, I could see plainly that the batteries were new and shiny, and slightly cold. And when I pushed the "play" button, the red power light on top immediately illuminated.

But no sound came out. I checked the volume control; no sound. I held the device to my ear: nothing.

Then I looked inside the machine, and I found a perfectly reasonable explanation for the silence: There was no tape inside. It must have dropped out somewhere in my apartment, or maybe when I transferred the device into the desk drawer.

I told myself not to fret. I did not really need it. Depending on how you looked at it, maybe it was for the best.

When I looked at my great-grandfather's watch again, it was almost time to go. My staff filed in, one-by-one, for their end-of-day review, and I sent each one home with an encouraging "*Grabvey!*," which each person echoed. Everybody was in good spirits.

Tomorrow would be *Tink*, our day off, when the newspaper is not published—which works out just fine, since usually nothing happened in our sacred Homeland when the electricity was not working. We have an expression about this: "No news on *Tink* is good news." Pleasantries were exchanged and plans announced. My Junior Assistant said he would be taking his wife and children—he had a fully authorized girl, as well as a boy—to National Park, our splendid public strolling area in the very heart of the city, where you can see statues of our most important Caring Leaders and visit our informative and clever National Museum. It is famous for telling the inspiring story of our sacred Homeland in a thrilling multi-media production, which includes a slideshow and patriotic music. The museum has its own generator, of course.

When he asked what I was planning on doing during *Tink,* I told him I did not know. "Maybe I shall sleep all day," I said, laughing. "Just kidding! I am joking."

My Junior Assistant laughed, too. But when he left I thought maybe it was not such a bad idea.

CHAPTER SIXTEEN

After work, riding my bicycle from the National News Service to the *Go Paja U-House,* I was hearing my city as I had not heard it previously. It was remarkably quiet. Traffic still clogged the avenues, and thousands of people—hundreds of thousands, it sometimes seemed—were getting from work to home, or to another job, or maybe to a night of relaxation at their favorite *U-House.* But I heard fewer exclamations, less beeping from the *hahnkers,* more natural ambience.

There seemed to be fewer people than usual on the sidewalks. Even in the alleyways, where one could usually count on witnessing some kind of unpermitted activity, I saw almost no one: no children kicking about rocks; no elderly matriarchs—the *flona*—gossiping with their neighbors about whose turnips would turn out larger.

I was in a cheerful mood, but I had no one to wink at.

The relative calm all around me allowed the sound of my bicycle to become clearly audible. Until this evening, I had never noticed the way the chain spinning around the sprockets gave off a distinct rhythm as it scraped and pulled. It had a sort of recognizable beat, I suppose. A tune, almost. And the tires made a sound, too, a pleasant peeling as the rubber retreated and returned to the road. I found I could even change the sound—such as what they call the "pitch"—when I turned.

I mention these things only to explain why I found myself humming out loud as I pedaled. I am not trying to defend my unauthorized behavior. I am merely pointing out that I did not consciously decide to disobey the regulations. Granted, a stronger and better man would have resisted. Me? I could not help myself from humming along to the accompaniment of my creaky bicycle.

Bebudew op en beberoo kap ... bebudew op en beberoo kap ... bebudew op en beberoo kap.

For some unknown reason, my impromptu "song," or whatever you call this kind of thing, made me pedal faster, which produced an accelerated, higher version of the melody.

Bebudew op en beberoo kap—bebudew op en beberoo kap— bebudew op en beberoo kap.

For one crazy moment, I allowed myself to imagine that I was being chased by people wishing to detain me, and I went even faster!

Bebudew op en beberoo kap bebudew op en beberoo kap.

I was flying down the narrow alleyways like a rocket on wheels. I could hear my bicycle and my breath and some small part of my voice. I felt like—well, I do not know what the word is for this feeling.

Was it pleasant? I am not sure.

I *am* sure, however, that it was dangerous. Moments after I reached my very top speed, hurtling down the street like a carousel horse ripped from its moorings and shot out into the night, I nearly crashed into a *flona* who did not see me coming. Luckily for her, and I suppose also for me, I was able to squeeze my brakes and swerve just enough to slide past her, missing a collision by no more than a few *plongi.*

As I skidded to a stop and glanced back to make sure she was all right, the old lady looked at me in horror, as though she had just seen death. "*Ah bolah!* she cried out.

"I am very sorry, *flona*," I called to her, catching my breath. "Are you OK?"

She nodded quickly and hunched over herself, trying to hide what was in her hands. But I could see anyway that she was carrying a small basket of illegally harvested *filolo* cabbages, which no doubt she intended on throwing into a pot instead of donating to the local Council of Dedicated Servants.

"Do not worry, *flona*," I assured her. "I am not *Kapaa*. Indeed, it is my fault. Completely my fault. I was cycling much too fast, and I was not concentrating properly, and I was the one breaking the rules. So I will not report you, if you will not report me." I smiled and raised my eyebrows twice.

She did the same, and without another word she shuffled off into a dark doorway and disappeared.

It was that peculiar time between day and night when the lights of the city have not yet come on but the sun is ducking behind the horizon. At this time of year, approaching winter, it can get very black very quickly. I silently reprimanded myself for my recklessness and lack of discipline, and I resolved to henceforth pilot my bicycle like an educated person with some level of self-respect.

For the rest of my journey to the *Go Paja*, I did not make a sound and I did not collide with anyone—which would have been difficult, I admit, since I saw almost nobody. Nonetheless, my correct behavior should be noted for the record.

The street where the *Go Paja* was located had previously struck me as rather desolate. This night it was even more so, if that is possible. I saw no one. Not even a dog scratching itself.

The air was still, and the squealing of my brakes seemed especially noisy as I rolled to a stop before the familiar **U** carving. I suppose it did not occur to me that the thumping pulse which usually emanated from behind the door was absent. I became aware of the silence only after I parked my bicycle and tried the door. It was locked.

I knocked.

I knocked again, a little harder.

I waited for some time, and I knocked again, this time in the same rhythm as the chain on my bicycle: *Bebudew op en beberoo kap.* Nobody answered.

I looked around the street to find someone who might explain why the *Go Paja U-House* was not yet open on the night before *Tink*, when most regular citizens in our sacred Homeland choose to socialize, and attend *scrachi* matches and *chu-chu* concerts and the like. There was no one to ask.

The *Go Paja* had no windows. I tried to peer through a crack in the doorframe, but all I could see was blackness.

As I pressed my ear against the door, a great mechanical roar exploded behind me. I thought it was a tank filled with National Heroes! Or a helicopter somehow making an impossible landing on this narrow lane. It was loud!

I wheeled around and saw the source of the noise barreling toward me: it was a speeding *blecky*.

The beautiful sedan screeched to a halt beside me. It emanated heat and low rumbling vibrations, as though it were an angry bull catching its breath. I could not see through the darkened windows, but I could see the license plate: #602, a very low number. Although I understood intellectually that the *blecky* could have belonged to a very important Caring Leader, for some unknown reason I knew instinctively that the automobile's occupant was Miss Mae Love. It *had* to be Miss Mae Love.

She was making a triumphant return to the place that had launched her into *chu-chu* stardom. And here I was!

I did not have time to think about what I would say to her. The back door cracked open, and a head emerged.

"Uncle?" I cried out. "What a surprise! What are you doing here?" I made a salute and extended my arm for the traditional embrace.

He did not offer his hand. "Get in," he said.

"Thank you, Uncle," I said, genuinely honored to be offered a ride in a *blecky*. "But I have my bicycle,"

He did not smile. "Leave it there and get in."

CHAPTER SEVENTEEN

The inside of a *blecky*, I can report, smells very nice, much better than a *hahnker*. The seats are leather, I think, and there are petite carpets for your feet. Also, the air is cool and fresh as it comes out of miniature vents that you can aim in various directions. The interior is so *clean*. No stains anywhere. Forgive my *meowkaleet*, but it would take a far more humble man than I to not feel quite important being driven about in such a magnificent vehicle.

And that is what happened. The car pulled away from *Go Paja,* accelerating so rapidly I felt like a butterfly pinned to the seat. Then we were gliding, like on a train, but much smoother. A silent chauffeur, who I did not have the pleasure of meeting formally, a large man wearing a smart suit and expensive cologne of foreign heritage, I would guess, drove me and Uncle while we talked.

The ride was so comfortable. I swear to you I could envision exactly what it must feel like to be a Caring Leader: you can concentrate on important matters while others attend to mundane tasks and ensure you are not distracted. There was even a small box between the front and back seats containing chilly bottles of purified water. I did not take any of them, of course. But I could certainly imagine driving around the city all day, never experiencing a moment's thirst.

"*Ah bolah,* you have a very nice car," I commented. "Thank you, Uncle, for inviting me inside."

Uncle said something charmingly modest about the *blecky* belonging to every citizen of our sacred Homeland, that he was merely an honored passenger, but that, yes, it was a nice car. "Anyway, you are probably wondering where we are going," he said. "It is a fair question."

Actually, I had not had time to wonder about this. I was overwhelmed, I must say, by the newness of the experience, and I was still trying to understand the amazing coincidence of Uncle and his *blecky* being on the same street as me and my bicycle.

My bicycle: I worried that it would be vulnerable to law-breakers. "Oh, yes, Uncle, I am eager to learn more about this great surprise," I said cheerfully. "But before we get too far away, I am concerned about leaving my bicycle unattended for too long."

"Do not worry about your bicycle," he said flatly. "It will be taken care of."

Although he did not speak hurriedly, Uncle seemed to be slightly impatient and busy, so I did not pursue the matter further. I still did not understand about my bicycle, but I did not want to be impolite. "Oh, I see," I said. "Thank you."

"You are most welcome," he replied. "Now, look, this job, or whatever you want to call it. The position that has been created for the son. Your little pal. Mr. Di—" he stopped himself and made himself smile for a flash —"Mr. TupTup. The job at the newspaper. Look, it is not..." he perched his sunglasses upon his crown and looked away from me, out his window, through which I could see familiar buildings and civic landmarks. We seemed to be driving out of the center of the city. He sighed. "It is not working the way that it was envisioned."

I understood. "I am very sorry," I said. "All criticism is welcomed and appreciated."

"I guess the situation was not made clear to you, although, I must say that I thought it was very clear." He stared at me and leaned forward for emphasis. "The kid likes *chu-chu.*"

I nodded in complete agreement. "Oh, yes. He does."

"We tried to find him a position at Galaxy or Republic. Several places, actually. But I will tell you a secret. He does not even care about the music. It bores him after five minutes. That is not his interest."

I did not interrupt Uncle. But from the skeptical look on my face, he must have understood that his story was hard to believe.

"No. Seriously. That is what I am trying to tell you. He does not really care about the songs or the singing, or any of that stuff."

"Oh, Uncle, I do not mean to contradict you, sir. But it is well known that Mr. TupTup has devoted a large portion of his life to this passionate interest."

"Yes, that would be putting it lightly," he said, laughing through his nose in a series of short exhalations. I was not certain if I was supposed to join in the mirth, so I remained silent.

Uncle continued, "TupTup does not care about the music. He cares about the *stories.* The *chu-chu* stars—they're like characters to him. You know: what adversity they are overcoming, or what awards they are getting ... or who they are feuding with. Or the romance aspect. You know, who they are—" Here Uncle used a vulgar word that I do not wish to repeat. "These are his concerns."

The way Uncle was looking at me, I sensed he expected a reply. "That did not occur to me," I said.

"The point is, it is best to keep him occupied with *chu-chu* tasks. Stories. Interviews. Pictures. *Chu-chu* and nothing else. Do you understand?"

"Yes, Uncle, I do," I said. "And I ask you to forgive whatever mistakes I may have made in the past. I will endeavor to improve in this area."

As I offered my apology, the words sounded right to me. But the more I thought about the TupTup situation, the more I realized there was some sort of misunderstanding, some sort of mistake. I could not recall a single conversation with Mr. TupTup about anything other than *chu-chu*. I could not recall a single comment offered or sought about National Hero articles, or any other topic we worked on at *Perriodocko*. My only real error, I now realized, had been permissiveness. I should have been stricter with him and less fearful of causing offense to his family. That was my mistake. That and leaving him unattended during a State of Emergency.

I thought to mention this to Uncle, but before I found the will, he continued. "He is not an authorized Information Gatherer, and you and I both know he never will be."

"Well." I shrugged.

His tone became rather rude and aggressive, I thought. "Let me make this clear so none of us has any problems. Listen carefully … TupTup does *chu-chu*. Only *chu-chu*. That is all. Nothing else. No agriculture, no *scrachi*, no National Heroes, no whatever … no diplomacy, no anything. Just *chu-chu*." Uncle paused and made sure I was looking at him. "I just want to make sure I am being crystal clear so there can be no further misunderstandings."

Some tiny part of me wanted to explain to Uncle what happened on a daily basis at our 3rd-floor offices, and perhaps to offer him a brief reminder of my educational background. But I did not think this would be a good idea. So I just said, "Crystal clear, sir. Thank you."

"Very good. Then TupTup can return to work next week, with everyone understanding his future direction."

I attempted to mute my enthusiasm. "Ah, I see. He shall be coming back, then."

"Yes. You can inform your colleagues that he had a family obligation to attend to. Not his father. But, you know. Someone."

I nodded. "I see. Yes."

"And that he is very glad to be back at work, but that he must limit his activities to what?"

"*Chu-chu*," I answered.

Uncle nodded. "Very good."

We drove in silence for what seemed like a long time. I could observe through the window beside me that we had crossed the river, where the streetlights stop, and that we were heading north, into the countryside. I sensed that Uncle had forgiven me, but that perhaps he did not really like me—or that I had unintentionally caused some offense he was too courteous to mention. As a passenger in his *blecky*, I did not want to be impolite. "Uncle, sir, if it is not too private, may I respectfully ask if everything is all right with all of your great and glorious family? TupTup's father, and all the rest of your great and important relatives?"

He looked at me with his eyebrows pinched together. Then he started laughing through his nose again. "You are quite the funny one."

I laughed with him, of course. "Yes. I can be a *vernando*." I thought to add, "Just like your nephew," but did not want to sound too familiar and presumptuous, so I did not say that.

We drove in silence for another minute or so. I saw fewer buildings, and it occurred to me that it was possible the chauffeur was lost. "Uncle, sir," I said pleasantly, "this has been a delightful ride in your delightful vehicle. If you do not mind, sir, may I please ask you where we are going?"

Suddenly we swerved to the right, onto a road made of small stones. At least that is what I assume we were driving upon. I could not see in the dark, but I could hear a dry crunching beneath the *blecky,* like the sound that is made when you grind bones for soup.

The car turned again to the right and stopped beside a low building partially shrouded by overhanging trees.

Uncle said, "Here."

CHAPTER EIGHTEEN

What happened next I will not attempt to analyze. I will simply report. I do not have the audacity to make assumptions without complete information. That is what gets people in trouble.

Uncle escorted me out of the *blecky* and to the front door of the building. The chauffeur stayed in the car.

Uncle produced a key ring from his pocket. It had many keys on it, maybe twenty? I do not know. There were many. He selected one, a silver jagged thing, and unlocked the door, pushing it open. "After you," he said, politely.

I thanked him and stepped inside a hallway, with a wooden floor and electric lights. The walls were painted a light shade of gray. I could hear voices and indeterminate activities, but I did not know where they were coming from. I looked to Uncle for guidance.

"Please," he said, gesturing down the hallway. We began to walk.

After a few steps, I noticed several closed doors on the left. Uncle said, "At the end of the hallway. On the right."

I could hear the clip-clopping of Uncle's shoes behind me. Then I heard him say, "I meant to tell you the other day. You walk very well for someone with a medical disability."

"Oh, it is nothing," I said.

"Really? It certainly was enough to keep you out of military service."

I did not know what to say. "Yes," I agreed. I remember at that moment wishing that I could be back home with my wife, doing nothing in particular. I did not feel comfortable. For some unknown reason, I felt as though something bad might happen. I cannot explain why.

At the end of the hallway, we came to an open door on the right. Inside was a large room, perhaps as large as the Information Gathering section of *Perriodocko*. It probably extended all the way back to where we entered the building. Inside this sprawling space, I saw many men—enough to form several complete football squads, I would estimate—sitting at rows of desks, each of them supporting shiny computer monitors. These men did not seem to be working, or at least not seriously. They talked with each other and joked and laughed in a way that no competent manager would tolerate. I would describe them all as very well-dressed, like Uncle.

Most remarkable, I am compelled to report, was the presence of so many cans of foreign soda drinks, which, I probably do not need to remind you, were prohibited in Year 2, when certain imported products were found to be intentionally poisoning our sacred Homeland's children. Cans were everywhere: on desktops and low tables and in stacks against the wall. I tried not to stare, but it was difficult.

Uncle stepped inside the room and opened a refrigeration unit, retrieving a can, wiping the top of it with his shirtsleeve, and opening it with a startling *crack*. As an afterthought, he asked me, "You want one?"

I sensed this was some kind of test. "No, thank you," I replied. "I am not thirsty," although I actually was. I must confess that I wondered what these outsider versions of soda might taste like compared to our national brand, *Grabvey*, which is quite delicious and known to be copied and consumed in many other places around the world. But I was not brave enough to risk illness. Nor did I want to do anything that was not permitted. I wished to return to Uncle's good graces, as I believe the expression goes. I did not like being thought of as unreliable or unable to follow directions.

He tilted his head back, took a long, hungry slurp and emitted a belch, which he did not excuse, and which, therefore, I did not giggle at.

"Follow me," he said.

Many curiosities crossed my mind, many things I wondered about, but Uncle seemed preoccupied. I have learned in my long career at the National News Service that sometimes it is best to not ask inappropriate questions.

As we walked through the long room, men looked up, seeming to notice us but not making eye contact. They appeared to recognize Uncle, although I did not get the feeling these were necessarily his friends. No one talked to him, or me. I had the natural impulse to greet each of them with a salute and a polite "Hello," but I sensed that no one shared my fraternal feeling.

I could catch fleeting bits of conversation—about *scrachi*, about boxing, about girls—but it was not clear to me what all these men were doing on the night before *Tink*, sitting around guzzling foreign soda drinks and playing with computers.

We came to an unoccupied corner of the room, with several closed doors. Uncle found another key on his extensive ring and opened the one farthest to the right. "Please," he said, motioning for me to step in.

It was a plain little room, painted white. A box, really. There was another door directly across from where we entered. It was closed.

Uncle shut the door behind us and indicated a row of chairs facing the back wall. "Please," he said. "Sit. Anywhere you like."

I took the chair on the end, closest. Uncle stood behind me. Before I could invite him to join me, the back door swung open, toward us.

Another well-dressed man stepped into the room and nodded in our direction. I was not sure what I was expected to do, so I nodded in return. The man peered back toward where he had just entered, snapped his fingers as you might to get a waiter's attention in a fishmeal emporium, and motioned with his hand for someone to come in.

Another man, this one not so well-dressed, entered the room. It took my tired brain a few seconds to process all the new things that were happening to me. I had only seen him one other time, but I knew exactly who he was.

It was Mr. Z, the friendly young fellow who had been at the *U-House* wearing the funny *vernando* shirt, with the letters all mixed up.

"Do you recognize this man?" Uncle asked.

"Yes," I said, a little surprised, a little amused, and very much confused. "I do."

"This is the important question," Uncle said calmly. "Was he in attendance at a certain unlicensed *uchaana* house two nights ago?"

I almost replied immediately. But the young man locked his eyes on mine, as if he were trying to talk to me without using his mouth. He said nothing and never changed his blank expression. But when I looked at Z carefully, his head seemed to be moving subtly, almost imperceptibly, from side-to-side. Tremors, I think you would call it, similar to what one sometimes sees in exceptionally old *flona*.

"It is a simple question," Uncle said, with a hint of exasperation.

"Well," I said, trying to think. "I believe I understand what you are referring to."

"A yes or a no." I could feel Uncle's breath on my neck. Mr. Z said nothing. He merely stared at me, unblinking.

I had no reason not to tell the truth. "Well, in those terms, yes."

I could feel Uncle standing up and away from me. "Thank you," he said.

Young Z closed his eyes. When he opened them, I felt he was disappointed in me, although he had no reason to be. The truth is never something to be ashamed of.

Uncle patted me on the shoulder. I had to bite my lip to avoid crying out. He made a motion with his head toward the door, and I understood that we were leaving. I got up and walked out. I did not look at Z again.

When Uncle and I were out of the room, I asked him, "Is everything OK?"

"Yes," he said. "Everything is OK."

He led me back through the large room. As we passed the refrigeration unit near the doorway, he did not offer me a soda drink.

We walked down the hallway and out the front door and back to the *blecky*, which was idling where we had left it. Uncle opened the back door for me and I got in.

Throughout the return trip, which seemed to retrace the route we had used to arrive, Uncle said very little. I was terribly confused, and perhaps slightly uneasy, about what had just occurred. But I was keenly aware that Uncle was not in the proper mood to provide explanations. He said only, "I am sure I do not have to remind you, but I will anyway. This is all off the record."

"Yes," I said.

"You must obtain your information from authorized sources," he said.

I nodded. "Of course."

The streets of our Capital City came into view, and traffic thickened. The *blecky* slowed. We were nearing the National News Building.

After a series of nifty turns, and without any guidance, the chauffeur arrived at my street and parked directly in front of my apartment building. I was impressed that he could find it without directions. Before I could compliment him, though, Uncle exited the car and seconds later opened the door on my side. "See you tomorrow," he said.

As I stepped out, I looked up at the windows, the ones facing the street. Forgive my *meowkaleet*, but I secretly hoped my wife or my brother might be gazing outside at this moment to witness me emerging from a *blecky*. They would not believe me if I told them my story. They would have to see it with their own eyes.

Without another word, Uncle got into the beautiful car, and it drove away, knocking aside a yelping dog that should not have been in the street.

I suddenly remembered how I had started this strange night, and I thought to call out after the departing *blecky*, to make them stop and retrieve me. It was too late. They could not hear me inside that leathery cocoon. I sighed and told myself I would just have to walk back to the *Go Paja*.

But when I peered into the foyer of my apartment building, I realized I would not have to go anywhere. My bicycle was already home, waiting for me.

CHAPTER NINETEEN

Tink is always a special time of the week, a day of rest and reflection, a day of families and friends. Every citizen in our sacred Homeland looks forward to Tink, whether he is a peasant or a Dedicated Servant, whether he spends the other six days toiling conscientiously or living off the labors of others. Unless you or someone you know possesses an unlicensed generator, the absence of electricity—or hanhkers, or anything else that contributes to noise—allows each of us to concentrate fully on fellowship and self-improvement. We all appreciate Tink.

After the week I had experienced, I appreciated *Tink* more than usual. *Ah bolah,* I could have used three consecutive days of *Tink*!

I awoke with the sun, as is my habit, but instead of rising I tried to go back to sleep. I tell you, I could have slept for twenty hours. But I had previously promised my wife that I would do a stroll with her, and I refused to let fatigue compromise my sense of duty and honor.

My wife had a way of proposing an idea that can sometimes be confusing to me. I think I understand what she is saying, but often it turns out that she actually meant the opposite. She will say, "Dear Husband, I know you are exhausted from work and the late hours you have been forced to keep. We do not have to go on a stroll if it will be too much trouble, although maybe it would be nice to get some fresh air. It is up to you."

Over the years, I have learned that this does not really mean: "It is up to you."

So after some loosening calisthenics and a bath, I put on my comfortable walking shoes and my favorite t-shirt, a white one with the official *Perriodocko* logo on the front and back. My shoulder seemed to be improving, although I had caught a glimpse of a large bruise when I looked in the mirror of the bathroom on our floor. I found that if I refused to muse upon things too frequently, my head did not hurt so much, either.

To be courteous, before we departed I checked to see if my family next door wanted to join us. Perhaps this is unkind to admit, but I was slightly relieved that no one was there. I did not think I could endure any more heated discussions.

My wife and I walked side by side through the subdued streets of our beautiful city. We saw other couples and families strolling, but we observed the custom and did not interrupt them with verbal greetings. We kept to ourselves and had a very pleasant chat about the cool and comfortable weather. But most of the time we said nothing and enjoyed the sights. She was right: it was nice to get some fresh air.

I was careful to not talk about events at the National News Service. For one blissfully unproductive day, I did not want to have to think about work. I did mention, however, that some of my team members were planning on spending *Tink* at the National Park. "That sounds like it could be nice," I said.

"Yes," my wife said. "That might be nice."

"Perhaps—and only if it would be of interest to you—we could possibly stroll there. Although if it is too far we do not have to."

My wife shrugged. "It is up to you, Dear Husband."

I thought about it for a moment. "OK. If you would like to go to the National Park. Sure. Let us go."

My wife tilted her head. "Are you sure?"

I nodded enthusiastically. "Sure. Yes."

My wife smiled. "OK. If you would like to, I would like to."

"OK. Yes."

"Then it is decided," my wife declared.

"It is not too far?" I wondered. The walk would be at least thirty minutes each way.

"I am fine," my wife said. "But will your sore shoulder be OK?"

"It is feeling better," I told her. "No problem."

"Oh, this is very good to hear," my wife said.

"Yes," I agreed.

And then we did not talk very much more. We did not have to. We knew where we were going, and nothing unusual appeared on the avenues to cause comment. We had a very tranquil stroll.

We crossed the river and passed the magnificent National Theater, where the National Song Competition would be held in less than two weeks, and we walked straight through the Fish Market, which normally buzzes with activity but on *Tink* was nothing but shuttered stalls and pavement that smelled vaguely like boiled squid. Just beyond the People's Palace, where our Caring Leaders have their headquarters, sat the National Park, one of our many great civic accomplishments.

I do not intend to dwell on the past, so I will simply say that the enormous space that comprises our National Park was once something else, a foreign-controlled enterprise that really did not do anything positive for regular citizens. In Year 2, it was converted into a splendid green area, with benches and two different ponds and an impressive band shell, the National Park Amphitheatre, at the Park's southern end.

By Year 4, many of the newly planted trees and grassy lawns had died. There was some baseless and unhelpful speculation about the cause of this disappointment. I will not dignify the irresponsible theories by repeating them. Eventually, an official explanation was provided – and announced exclusively in the pages of *Perriodocko*, if you will excuse my *meowkaleet*. Not even NTV-4 was given the proclamation for broadcast until it appeared in our pages.

Now the National Park is mostly a giant dirt field. But it is still a wonderful place to experience the outdoors and to see all different types of citizens enjoying their public birthright.

There was a very brief period of time some years ago when certain people, mostly from a particular ethnic group, it should be noted, tried to usurp the National Park for their selfish purposes. They installed homemade trellises in the ground, along with vegetable seeds, and they brazenly appropriated unauthorized water supplies from the ponds. Everybody knew what they were up to, and a quick and decisive halt was put to the rogue landscaping. This particular ethnic group, it should also be noted, no longer causes trouble in our sacred Homeland, or is seen much anymore.

After that unpleasant incident, the National Park became a symbol of unity. We *all* feel entitled to leave it undisturbed.

It is also a tremendous resource for the housing shortage in our capital. A large number of night-time residents—we call them *blayzoneet* ("fireflies") – erect quaint little shelters in National Park, turning it into a miniature city.

When my wife and I arrived, in late morning, the Park was teeming with visitors. We had not had rain for some time, so the air was somewhat dusty. When children ran their footraces and formed circles for celebration dances, they kicked up brownish clouds that could make you cough if you did not avoid them with a quick sidestep.

The queue for the National Museum and its entertaining educational program was quite long, befitting a spectacular attraction that is presented free of charge to every citizen of our sacred Homeland. We had attended many times previously and found the experience most enjoyable. "Next time," my wife said.

"Yes," I said. "Next time."

We headed toward the Refreshment Center, where authorized hawkers with the necessary permits are allowed to set up booths offering snacks they prepare on the spot. The whole area is smoky and fragrant and quite attractive. Security is very good. Everyone feels safe and confident that what they are getting is what was promised, because you can see it being made right there, as you wait.

I purchased for my wife a special treat, an item that is fried whole and placed on a stick, crunchy and hot. Because of circumstances beyond our control, we may sometimes have rare shortages of certain foods, but these creatures are abundant and nutritious. My wife finds them quite delicious, though people who were not fortunate enough to be born here do not seem to appreciate this delicacy quite as much as the local population.

After the repast, we strolled toward Liberation Pond, the body of water that commemorates our independence from the various regimes that have attempted to enslave us and impose their debased values upon our society. Many years ago, when the National Park was inaugurated, the pond was a brilliant blue that often matched the sky on a cloudless day. But the budget for dye was cut—along with funding for nearly everything else—when the Great Initiative was announced, and it is now more of a brownish color. Most educated citizens will tell you they prefer to have improved missile defense instead of turquoise pools, anyway.

The benches ringing the pond are almost always full, since they afford the most scenic view in the entirety of our National Park. But my wife and I were not in a hurry, so we decided to linger in the area in case anyone left. Dozens of other citizens seemed to have had the same idea: clusters of couples and families and school groups loitered around the pond's circumference, keeping one eye on the calming water and another on the fully occupied benches.

It was in this area that we happened upon an impressively decorated National Hero, in full uniform, including broad-billed cap. Among his many medals, I noticed the Copper Star, one of the most treasured awards in our sacred Homeland, given to National Heroes who have shown extreme bravery in the face of terrorist attacks. Those who confront suicide bombers, or people who are talking about carrying out such a plan, are often candidates for this honor. This National Hero was clearly a great man. I felt a new appreciation for the majesty of my country: How wonderful it was that common citizens could mingle with important ones in a public park open to each and everyone (except convicted criminals).

Indeed, the decorated National Hero was talking with a small group of youngsters, four of them, three boys and a girl, who seemed to be related, or perhaps members of a community club. The youngsters listened politely as the National Hero spoke, nodding and smiling, mostly at each other.

I felt further appreciation: By law, the National Hero could ask any regular citizen to give up his bench seat. But apparently he had waived that privilege and was content to stand, just like the rest of us, even those who had not served our sacred Homeland with distinction and honor. Perhaps this is what people mean when they describe someone as having *character*.

Of course, I did not say this to anyone, including me wife. I did not want to draw attention to myself. But I did want somehow to communicate to this fine man – and the attentive group gathered around him -- that the sterling example he set did not go unnoticed.

As my wife and I approached them, I could hear the National Hero's voice. It was deep and rich. You could not ignore a voice like that! He was saying, "You see, without the security of the state, security that starts from the top down, citizens cannot fulfill their potential."

"Potential for what?" one of the boys asked. I estimated him to be about 16 or 17, probably just starting University or awaiting his National Hero service assignment. "These are *flona* we are speaking about. Not children."

"Potential for being good citizens," the National Hero said.

One of the other boys screwed up his face. "Excuse me, sir," he said. "I want to understand. You are explaining that the reason some of the things that have been happening lately, the reason they are occurring, is because our sacred Homeland is attempting to—"

"Listen to me until I finish, please," the National Hero interjected. "You youngsters get some funny ideas sometimes, and I do not know where they come from. Because everything you need to know is right there in the Guiding Text. That is all you have to read."

The girl clapped her hands together and giggled. "I have read the Guiding Text. Twice, in fact. All the way through."

The National Hero smiled. "See? Very good."

My wife and I smiled and nodded at each other. It was indeed very good—and inspiring in a way. Without children of our own to raise, it gave us a sense of hope that members of the younger generation, such as these nice ones in the National Park, would ensure a bright future for our sacred Homeland.

"Yes," the girl continued. "And I could find nothing in the Guiding Text that addresses the concerns we have been discussing."

The National Hero seemed to be mildly offended, and I did not blame him. "I have also read the Guiding Text, young lady," he reminded her. "I am well aware of its provisions."

Another boy, her brother perhaps, sniggered, which struck me as a bit impertinent and inappropriate. He said, "What the Guiding Text says and what many Dedicated Servants do are two different subjects."

These youngsters seemed to come from good families who had taught them manners and respect. I wondered how properly educated and obviously intelligent youth could be so convinced about matters they could not possibly understand. How did they arrive at their strange and dangerous conclusions? How could they imagine for one moment that every action of our Dedicated Servants—and every action of our Caring Leaders, and all the rest of us, too—was not somehow imbued with the wisdom of our Guiding Text?

The National Hero shared my confusion. "I am not sure what you are attempting to say, but I warn you to be careful with your words."

"We mean no disrespect," the girl said. "But I am certain you have a mother of your own, and perhaps even a grandmother."

The National Hero held a finger to his lips. "Shh. No more."

The youngsters peeked at each other morosely. One of the boys, the brother, looked as though he would speak. But he wisely held his tongue, and they silently shuffled away, looking at the dusty ground.

When they were some distance away, but close enough to be heard without shouting, one of the boys, the brother, turned back and declared, "*Grabvey!* More power to you, sir! *Grabvey!*" He saluted smartly and continued walking with his friends, toward the band shell in the distance.

You could hear the youngsters laughing loudly as they left. A few seconds later, coming from their direction—although I cannot say with certainty that it was one of them who did it, because there were many people in the vicinity and my view was obstructed—someone with a high, youthful voice shouted, "Safety Position! Safety Position!"

My wife immediately dropped to the ground, as did many others around us. Still sore from the last emergency, I was not so fast. I had not yet completely crouched when a large group of men—there must have been at least ten of them—appeared from every direction. They materialized instantly. I tell you, it was like a magic trick, where there is a puff of smoke and suddenly the *scrachi* bird has been replaced by a beautiful assistant. One man leaped up from a bench right beside me and my wife!

The men, nicely dressed and all around my age, I would guess, surrounded a small group of people near the spot where the alarm had been yelled. I could not see clearly what they were doing, but the whole pack of them formed a kind of ring, or blockade, and collectively hustled out of the National Park, a throbbing swarm of insects encasing their hive. They seemed to have some detainees in their midst, but, as I say, I could not really see much.

A man who looked remarkably like Uncle—although I could tell by the sunglasses he wore that it was not actually him—peeled away from the pack and turned back in our direction. "There is no emergency!" he announced. "I repeat: There is no emergency. You may resume whatever you were doing and, you know, please enjoy this beautiful day. *Grabvey!*"

Some people murmured *Grabvey* in response. Everyone who had assumed Safety Position got to their feet, giggling sheepishly, wiping off pants and chiding friends and relatives who did not respond correctly or with appropriate alacrity. My wife said nothing, but I could tell she was somewhat disappointed in me.

"That was interesting," I said.

"Yes," she said. "Very."

I looked toward the band shell. There was supposed to be a concert given later in the afternoon by our Civic Youth Orchestra. I looked toward my wife, who did not seem happy. "Would you like to go home?" I asked.

"Yes," she said, unequivocally.

"We do not have to if you do not want to," I assured her.

"It is up to you, Dear Husband."

I looked at my great-grandfather's watch. It was nearly midday. "We can go home," I said.

My wife nodded. I sensed she might begin to cry, so I said nothing more.

We began walking back. I thought to pay my respect to the decorated National Hero we had almost met, if only with a crisp salute. But when I looked for him he was no longer there.

CHAPTER TWENTY

The day following *Tink* is normally the busiest at the National News Service. We seem to spend most of the day catching up on various Information Reports issued by the most important ministries in our sacred Homeland. After I have reviewed all the fresh directives—and this might consume the entire morning, even when I read rapidly—I make assignments among my staff, outlining our Information Gathering objectives and setting deadlines. Only then may I direct my attention to assembling the necessary materials for that day's edition of *Perriodocko*.

My concentration on this particular day-after-*Tink* was somewhat compromised by the re-appearance of a particular employee, one with a profound affinity for *chu-chu*.

"Good morning, Mr. TupTup," I said when he appeared at my office door, a couple minutes early, just before 8:00 a.m. "I am glad to see you have returned," I said, and I really meant it, despite the extra effort and care I understood I would henceforth need to devote to managing such a special employee.

"Yes," he said, with a subdued voice to which I was not accustomed. He smiled his crazy smile, but it disappeared instantly.

"We have a wonderful new project for you," I announced. "I think you will be most satisfied."

"Hmmmm. Yes," he said, chewing on his bottom lip. I sensed that he wished to say more, but he only stood there, looking around my office distractedly.

"As you are well aware, the National Song Competition is in eleven days."

"Recognizing the very best musical minds. Yes."

"Yes. And we have determined that our coverage of this important event should include an extensive preview supplement, which will be published on the eve of the Competition. And we have determined that you—" I paused for emphasis—"*you* should be one of the Information Gatherers working on this crucial project."

"Yes. Obviously."

I nodded. "Obviously."

TupTup stood in place, unable to maintain eye contact and unable to find the words that might express his happiness.

I tried to help him. "So. This is a good development. Very pleasing."

He tried to smile. "Yes. Hmmmm."

"Do not be too excited," I said. "Just kidding. I am only joking."

TupTup momentarily screwed his face into something resembling mirth. "Yes," he said.

I did not necessarily expect him to be overjoyed. But I thought he would be pleased with his new assignment. "Is everything OK, Mr. TupTup?" I inquired.

"Well, yes. Obviously."

"Good. Good," I said. "Speaking on behalf of our entire team, I can assure you that everyone at *Perriodocko* wishes you to be happy with your work."

He nodded uncomfortably.

"And happy in general," I added.

"Yes."

"OK, then. Very well. Good." I shuffled the papers on my desk. "So. Let us all continue our important work—unless there is something else you wish to discuss."

"Hmmmm. But let me ask you something," TupTup began.

"Yes?" I was ready with all the answers. I was prepared. Our coverage would include charts and helpful Information Boxes, with biographical details and thumbnail photos of the finalists. We would do a sidebar about Boss Bo and Galaxy Records. We would honor past winners. I had it all mapped out.

I waited, but TupTup did not say more.

"You had a question?" I probed gently.

"Yes," he replied—and then he dashed out of my office, without another word.

CHAPTER TWENY-ONE

L ater in the day, after our afternoon water break, when I finally had time to review the page proofs for the week's first edition of *Perriodocko*, I saw that my staff's Information Gathering had been excellent, as always. Our contribution to the National News Service was both useful and helpful. Everything was functioning properly.

On Page One, we had several inspiring stories supplied by the Bureau of Industry and the Ministry of Medicine, all of which suggested that Year 14 harvesting, processing, and healthfulness would show an uptick from Year 13—perhaps as much as a 1.2% increase.

We had our usual profiles in courage about exemplary National Heroes.

The *scrachi* photography was quite vivid, too.

I was proud of each issue of *Perriodocko*, but for some unknown reason this one seemed to me especially good, a perfect balance between education and entertainment, between factual communication and messages of hopefulness. Enormous responsibilities require enormous commitment. Anyone, even a peasant, could tell how much effort and care went into our work. The results, memorialized eternally in print, spoke for themselves.

You can understand, perhaps, my delight—and my pleasant surprise—at discovering my name mentioned in the newspaper.

And not in my capacity as an Information Gatherer, but as a regular citizen!

Yes, there it was, on the bottom of Page 7, in the Capital City "News Briefs" section, a popular feature among busy people. News Briefs are paragraph-length reports, no more than three column *plongi*, summarizing the vital occurrences in our sacred Homeland's most populous metropolitan area. Each item takes only a few seconds to read.

Under a modest headline that read "Insurgents Captured," I saw an unsigned Authorized Report that described the apprehension of a brutal gang of thugs. Quoting a high-ranking National Heroes spokesman, the story did not identify the suspects by name, but it said, "The group was known to be planning a series of unauthorized gatherings for the purpose of recruiting subversives who, if left unchecked, would bring discord and chaos to the peaceful existence of law-abiding citizens."

Authorities credited a "brave and loyal"—these were the words used; I am simply repeating them—member of the National News Service for "providing invaluable assistance" in neutralizing the threat. That person, they said, was me.

I would like to make a confession: deep down I knew I did not deserve the credit. I had done nothing out of the ordinary. Indeed, I did not even know that such a dangerous cell was operating in our midst. The "truth"—and, yes, I know this is a slippery abstract concept that manipulative Europeans like to argue about—well, the truth is I knew I was unworthy of praise.

But I would like to make another confession. *Ah bolah*, this one is difficult to write down on paper, with our without permission … but I must set aside propriety and acknowledge another "truth": I was flattered.

I was thrilled. I was somewhat ecstatic. Something inside me felt very good. I cannot explain why.

All I could think as I sat there at my desk re-reading the article, 91 simple words in total, was: *My wife is going to be so proud of me. And so will my father and my brother. And everyone else I know. They are going to suddenly realize that I am not merely a good provider and a conscientious worker. They will finally know that I am also a role model and, according to people who know about such things, someone who is described as "brave." I have been recognized!*

If I could properly express how ashamed I feel for accepting unearned credit, I would.

At the time, however, my damned *meowkaleet* got the better of me, and I took no corrective action.

I had the chance. As I sat at my desk, peering out the window, imagining how my wife would look at me in the morning, when she found a crisp, fresh copy of *Perriodocko* on her kitchen counter opened to the relevant page, perhaps with the relevant item subtly circled in red ink, a loud knock on my doorframe startled me back to the present.

It was Mr. K. Chief Editor Pops wanted me. Immediately. No time for a formal notice.

I followed Mr. K to the 4th floor, where I was admitted to the Chief Editor's office without delay.

He began talking before I finished saluting and before I could sit down. "Your job is to Gather Information, not *be* the information. We do not pay you what I think anyone would agree is a very generous salary, with *bolo* benefits and all that— we do not pay you to cause sensations or bring attention to yourself."

I bowed my head and said nothing. I could tell that Chief Editor Pops did not wish to be interrupted.

"Now, look. I do not know how you got wrapped up in all this mess. And I do not really want to know. I would like to be left out of your intriguing affairs. All I am saying is that it will be very difficult for me to allow you to continue serving at the National News Service if I get any more Official Releases that link you to unauthorized activity."

I quelled my impulse to respond. Besides, I did not know what to say. Chief Editor Pops was renowned as an exceptionally fair man. It would be absurd for me to say otherwise.

He gazed upon me with pity and a faint aura of disgust. "Your objectives at *Perriodocko* are unmistakably clear. If you wish to be an undercover agent, I suggest you apply for a position with the *Kapaa*. Who knows, maybe they are now accepting old men with disabilities."

I looked at the floor. I concentrated on the pattern of interlocking squares and rectangles. I said nothing.

"Because you have a long record of satisfactory service, we are willing to let this pass. However, it will be noted in your file as an Official Warning. You know the rules: two strikes and you are out."

I thought of a million things I might say, and I very nearly did. I was on the verge of reminding Chief Editor Pops that he might remove or re-write the little article to his satisfaction, that nobody would notice any changes, except possibly the officials at National Heroes Headquarters who had furnished the item. We did this kind of thing all the time, improving grammar and "punching up" the prose. It would be simple. It would take five minutes. Probably less.

I was going to tell him this. I was going to explain and clarify. I was going to "set the record straight," as we used to say in the olden days. But the only words that escaped my lips were, "Yes, sir. Thank you, sir."

Without looking at me, Chief Editor Pops said, "That is all."

I saluted and left his office. Many of the Chief's assistants and secretaries were at their desks, appearing not to be doing much work, at least none that I could discern. But no one looked at me. I felt invisible.

As I walked back downstairs to my office, no longer terribly excited about the next morning's edition of *Perriodocko,* I kept reminding myself that I really could not complain. *A bili en creneckulo.* Some things were simply beyond my control.

CHAPTER TWENTY-TWO

The next morning I did not leave the newspaper open to the relevant page. I am not certain if my wife saw the News Brief extolling my unearned bravery. She never said anything. And she never looked at me any differently.

My father also said nothing, nor did Gurly, who really could not read well enough to understand, anyway.

My brother always slept quite late. I was gone before he awoke. When I came home at night, though, he also said nothing about me.

Of course, I did not bring it up.

All day at work, I was distracted by silly thoughts. I wondered if an acquaintance of my family had mentioned the News Brief to them, and if maybe my family felt a little honored that I was their flesh-and-blood. I wondered if maybe they maybe viewed me a little differently. When I could finally leave the office at the end of the day, I rode home a bit faster than usual. I climbed the stairs with a bit more pep. I suppose I opened the door to our apartment with a bit more verve than usual.

But I could tell immediately that I was not on their minds. They were interested in something else. Was I disappointed? No. They were entitled to their interests.

What everyone in my family wanted to talk about was on the second-to-last page, a section of the paper I tend to skip over because of mild superstition: the obituaries. I used to read the notices carefully, picking out curious details about the victim's demise, but this morbid fascination led me to troubling thoughts and bad dreams, so I stopped.

When I arrived home, I found everyone gathered around the kitchen table, where my wife had placed a large pot of soup and individual bowls and spoons, the good heavy-duty plastic ones. Chattering and eating, my family reminded me of a quartet of crabs, all poking and grabbing and bumping each other sideways.

The obituary they were buzzing about was for a *flona* who, they said, must have been remarkably ancient, maybe even a hundred—although one could never be entirely sure about matters of age, since everyone's official beginning was reset in Year 1.

Employing my best Information Gathering skepticism, I said, "I do not mean to disagree, because you are probably correct. But surely you must be *assuming* that this dear old lady achieved such advanced years. A century of life cannot be proven, it must only be an educated guess." I laughed a little to inject levity. "I am only making an observation."

Boy snorted derisively. "She has a photo, Mr. Observation."

I stifled a gasp. Photos in the obituary section were extremely rare, and only permitted for three types of individuals: Caring Leaders; Dedicated Servants with a minimum of thirty years experience and a file free of demerits; and any regular citizen who attained the age of ninety or more before expiring.

This last category was no guarantee of a photo in *Perriodocko*. It only *qualified* the deceased for a photo obituary.

In order to receive one, the family, if they were so inclined, was required to obtain two separate but related permits, one for Distributing Photographic Material and one for a special Influence Waiver, which indemnified the holder from charges of bribing a member of the National News Service in exchange for favorable coverage.

With the proper documents organized and filed correctly, these permits could be obtained easily at the Ministry of Information. If you got there when they opened the public entrance doors, or perhaps a bit earlier, around sunrise, getting the DPM permit required only four to six hours of waiting time, depending on demand. The IW was known to sometimes take slightly longer, because of the number of forms that needed to be processed. Also, there was a fee involved, which helped to weed the *vernandos* from the serious. Last I heard, the IW had been set at two months of the applicant's annual salary, although it might have since gone up to reflect our sacred Homeland's growing prosperity.

"I stand corrected," I said, humbly. "This *flona* was clearly very old, and she was entitled to have her life commemorated in the newspaper with a photograph." I did not mention that if they looked carefully in another area of the newspaper they would see someone else commemorated, someone they all knew, albeit without a photo.

"Yes," my wife said. "This *flona* seems to have done some nice things."

Everyone around her nodded.

I was intrigued. "Oh, yes?"

"Yes," my wife said.

"Such as?" I wondered aloud.

My father, who knew a bit about such matters, said, "Before the changeover, she was known for feeding members of her community who were not members of her immediate family. That's what it says here. She practiced unauthorized gardening before it was unauthorized."

"A real pioneer," Boy added. They all laughed.

I did not want to be the cause of household tension, especially when everybody seemed to be in cordial spirits. So I did not tell my family that these paid obituaries were written by the deceased's family, and therefore could not be entirely trusted.

I went to the sink to wash my hands with soap substitute. "It is funny," I commented. "The obituaries we remember are about people who die very young or very old."

"Or very strangely," Gurly said.

Everyone murmured their assent.

"That is true," my father said.

"Yes," Boy said, "like the unfortunate sportsman who met his end in a *scrachi* accident, with all the birds going crazy on him."

Everyone made exclamations of horror.

"Yes, that was a good one," my father said. "Or—do you remember? The gluttonous man who got stuck in his toilet? The one who ate his whole family's cooking oil and fishmeal ration?"

They all howled.

"I do not think that was an authentic story," I said.

"What? It was in the newspaper!" my father reminded me.

You had to explain things slowly to my father, as you might to a child. "Yes, yes," I said. "But, you see, sometimes—well, sometimes I think certain stories are published to impart a valuable lesson. It is possible that such stories are somewhat exaggerated."

"Well, you should know," Boy said, enigmatically. He may have been drinking. I did not pursue it any further.

My wife asked, "What is this word, *mulsh*?"

"*Mulsh*?" I scrubbed my hands.

"Yes, I think that is how you say it."

I tittered. "It sounds like something from a certain unauthorized language that began in Britain and was spread around the world through colonization. Can you use it in a sentence?"

"Yes, Dear Husband. It is written here," she began to read, "*The deceased was fond of* chu-chu *and* telastooricks, *and was celebrated in her Central District Community for the fertile* compastee *she maintained with a special homemade* mulsh, *produced from fallen leaves and worm excrement.* Ewww! Distasteful!"

"Ah, yes," I said, drying my hands with our dishrag. "Indeed. I believe *mulsh* is an adapted word, a word of foreign origin that means 'natural fertilizer,' if I am not mistaken."

"I see," my wife said. "Thank you, Dear Husband."

I attempted to be humorous. "So this *flona* had a secret to her old age: worm poop!"

No one laughed. My father said, "You know, they say gardening is good for you, like yoga and walking."

"And *bolo*," Boy added. Everyone laughed.

"Calms the mind, and so forth," father said. "I myself—well, I would like to do it more. But *ah bolah*. It has become too difficult. Quite complicated."

"Father," I reassured him, "you are entitled to garden as much as any other regular citizen."

"Oh, yes, well. *Ah bolah*, I am too old to obtain all the paperwork."

No one said anything. We all knew that father was not too old to get his permits. He simply did not want to follow the necessary procedures, which sometimes involved a little bit of waiting in line—as if that were the most torturous thing in the world.

"I do not mean to cause trouble," father announced, "but I am thinking that perhaps possibly it might not be a bad idea to consider, I mean for our Caring Leaders to consider—for them to make a policy. You know: Once you get to a certain age, maybe you no longer need to obtain a growing permit?"

No one said anything. We all knew that father occasionally got some bizarre ideas, but he forgot about them quickly.

To our collective surprise, it was my wife who spoke. "Like this *flona*, who recently departed our world." I tried to catch her eye, but she avoided my gaze. "This lady, she was one-hundred years old, almost. Perhaps possibly she could have been permitted to tend to her *compastee* without supervision."

Everyone but me nodded in agreement and murmured their assent.

"That sounds very nice," I said, taking care not to insult my wife's education, which was adequate but certainly not advanced. "Let us remember one of our sacred Homeland's most excellent philosophies: *Equality should extend to every person in every way.* Which means, of course, that regular citizens who receive certain privileges are being treated unequally."

No one said anything.

Then, in the silence, Boy said something vulgar, which I did not dignify with a response.

"Look," he continued, seeming rather pleased with himself, "whether or not you think it is unfair for the elderly to get some special treatment -- unequal treatment, whatever you want to call it -- can we at least agree that it is probably not necessary to incarcerate a *flona*?"

"Of course," I said, impatiently.

Boy ranted, "They are not a threat. They do not belong behind bars. You know, assuming they did not kill someone with their unauthorized *filolo*."

"Of course not," I replied. "But this is not what we are talking about."

Boy seethed. "Brother, it is exactly what we are talking about." He pulled the newspaper toward himself with his stump and used his good hand to trace the words as he read. "Here! Listen!" He put his nose close to the page. "*She died in the hospital ward of National Prison, where she was being held for questioning.*"

Before I could protest, Boy shot up from his chair, gripping *Perriodocko* in his fingers and thrusting it in my direction. "Here! Here! You do not believe me? It's in your own damned newspaper! Read it!"

I did not have to read the obituary. The moment I saw the photo of the deceased old woman, I knew. I recognized her immediately—the toothless smile, the laughing eyes. There was the *flona*, staring back at me from the newspaper.

She was the one who winked at me.

CHAPTER TWENTY-THREE

The end of Year 13 was a festive time for our sacred Homeland. So many fun things occurred.

We had our Harvest Celebrations, a vast number of ceremonies that included many encouraging speeches given by many important people. These were happy events attended by many happy citizens, all of whom were appropriately pleased to learn how well our crops had done, especially in light of the past three years, when yields were (very slightly) below the official projections.

We had the annual Citizens Appreciation Event, in National Park, where tens of thousands—maybe hundreds of thousands?—of regular citizens may view our Caring Leaders from a relatively close vantage point and express their collective appreciation in the form of applause. The Year 13 edition had zero trampling deaths and only a few dozen minor injuries. We were having a bit of a drought, so the Park's lawns were not muddy, as they occasionally had been in past years, and most of the park-dwelling fireflies, the *blayzoneet,* were temporarily relocated. The event was an enormous success.

We had our New Start Celebration Day, a national holiday that is observed on the evening before the changing of the calendar. All regular citizens (who do not work for any of the National Services) have the day off from work, staying home smoking *uchaana* and drinking *bolo*. Children make crude paper horns that emit a funny shriek when you blow through them. There was a New Start Celebration Day Parade of National Heroes, in the historic Central District, a grand spectacle that featured our most impressive defense armaments and advanced technological achievements. Everyone, of course, felt a bit emotional, but in a good way.

Another year had passed, but things had not gotten worse. That was worth celebrating.

And then, on the first glorious day of Year 14, we observed two treasured traditions: the National Grand Prix of *Scrachi*, and the Official Processional of National Song Competition Finalists. Shown on NTV-4, each event allowed eager regular citizens to get an intimate glimpse of their favorite entertainers. No matter your preference, sports or music, there was always something for everyone on the first day of the New Year. We are lucky in that way.

I myself felt particularly fortunate. Despite some momentary challenges, I still had my job.

There had been no further incidents at work—nor outside of work. Indeed, I had not spoken with my bosses, or Uncle, or anyone else who might be in a position to express disappointment in me. Even Mr. TupTup seldom appeared in my office. He had taken his assignment at *Perriodocko* seriously at last, and I saw him only at staff meetings and through my window, when I sometimes watched him arrive and depart in his *blecky*.

We managed to produce our annual supplement on the National Song Competition with great professionalism. It was a handsome package, I must say. And educational. Everyone thought it a great success, including the most knowledgeable *chu-chu* observers.

Ah bolah, I was really quite concerned that perhaps our photographs and "juicy bits," as we call our most entertaining *chu-chu* stories, would somehow be a disappointment to Mr. TupTup. For some unknown reason, I got it in my head that he might disapprove of something we had published. For some unknown reason, I got it in my head that if TupTup was disapproving of our *chu-chu* efforts, his illustrious father subsequently would be disappointed. And for some unknown reason, I got it in my head that this series of events could have unpleasant consequences.

So, yes, I took special care in the preparation of our supplement. I suppose now I can reveal something I have not shared with anyone. It is maybe a little funny.

With only a few hours to go before our publishing deadline, at 7:00 p.m. on the night before New Start Day, I was reviewing the biographies of all twelve finalists. I happened to be re-reading the biography of Miss Mae Love, as she was one of the twelve finalists. I noticed an anecdote that I knew—or at least *thought* I knew—to contain a factual error. It said Miss Mae Love had been discovered singing on a bus by Mr. Boss Mike, of Republic Records.

Well, I was quite certain that, in fact, Mr. Boss Bo of Galaxy Records had discovered Miss Mae Love singing on a bus. Obviously.

My source, unfortunately, was someone whose family name was not suitable for quoting in the newspaper. So, being a seasoned Information Gatherer with specialized training, I called Republic Records and attempted to get verification of this vital detail myself.

Mr. Boss Mike was not available. I left a polite message and my National News Service Identification Credentials number.

When he had not called back in fifteen minutes, I phoned again and left another message, also telling the secretary that perhaps I might speak with someone other than Boss Mike, someone with the authority to speak for Republic Records. I was told there was no such person, but that Boss Mike would get right back to me.

When he had not called back after thirty minutes, I went into aggressive mode, what you might call pushy. Some people consider such behavior boorish and overbearing, and I agree with them. But sometimes the job at hand requires a brief lapse in decorum. In this case, I requested that the secretary actually write down, word-for-word, my question for Boss Mike. Then I requested that the message be walked into his office and placed on his desk. Then, if he did not have time to call me back, he could simply relay the message through his subordinates. "But a call would be great!" I said.

When I next looked at my great-grandfather's watch, after reading Mae Love's biographical profile a few more times (searching for other potential errors), I observed that it had been over an hour since I originally phoned Republic Records. No one has ever called me undetermined. I tried once more.

Boss Mike was not available. He *had* received my messages, I was told. He would "get right back" to me.

One hour later, when Boss Mike had still not responded to my query, I understood perfectly. This was their polite and subtle way of saying the item was accurate. No call meant, "There is nothing to discuss."

So we printed the Miss Mae Love biography as written. I previously had been misguided. She was, in fact, discovered singing on a bus by Boss Mike.

When the supplement came out on New Start Celebration Day, no one said anything to the contrary, and in the days following no one mentioned it. I even asked TupTup if he had any comment on the colorful report. But he said nothing—nothing except, "Three of my top-five girlfriends are finalists." I knew I had made the correct decision.

I was feeling good about *Perriodocko*, about my staff, about our productivity, about my ability to conform to the directives I had been given. Controversy and discord really has no place in a healthy workplace environment, or anywhere else. When things go smoothly, everybody is happiest.

If we could simply get through our coverage of the National Song Competition without causing offense of any kind to anyone important, I was confident my troubles would remain behind me, consigned to the past, where they would be eventually be forgotten. I believed the future was bright—for our sacred Homeland, for all regular citizens, and for me. I had stumbled briefly, but I had not fallen down completely—well, figuratively speaking, I mean—and I was determined to show my superiors and everyone who believed in me that their faith was well-placed.

We would handle the National Song Competition in a way that would please everybody. I would see to that.

CHAPTER TWENTY-FOUR

Our sacred Homeland's National Theater is probably one of the most beautiful buildings in the entire world. Anyone who is fortunate enough to attend a performance inside this magnificent and historically significant hall feels a kind of blessing, a special glow. This is not simply because there are only 1,521 seats available for each performance, most of which are reserved for Dedicated Servants and those they choose to honor as guests. It is because the National Theater's very existence reminds every person in attendance that we can accomplish *anything* if we are properly organized.

The full story of the National Theater's humble beginnings are well-known. Any schoolchild can tell you the story. The part I want to emphasize is this: Anyone who claims that structures of architectural merit and aesthetic excellence cannot be constructed by prison laborers has never stepped foot inside the National Theater.

It is genuinely breathtaking—and, no, I am not speaking of the seven flights of stairs that extend to the uppermost balconies. I am referring to the National Theater's immense grandeur, which has no equal anywhere.

It begins with the twin lions standing guard over the entrance. They are carved, not alive, of course. But they seem quite life-like and ferocious. Their fangs are made of real ivory, or something that looks like it but is probably rarer and more dear.

Once inside, past Security Screening and the Voluntary Donation Pots, the soaring lobby, with its floor-to-ceiling murals of our Caring Leaders on one side and the World's Largest Indoor Flag on the other, instantly reminds each visitor that he is an elite witness to an elite gathering in an elite place. This feeling is intensified by the clever color scheme: Everything is painted in royal gold, with sparkling bits that could very well be ground jewels.

Ah bolah, the glittering has just begun. Inside the auditorium, you cannot miss the World's Largest Indoor Chandelier, hovering over the orchestra seats, where the most important people sit. Designed by our best engineers, the WLIC is suspended from sturdy cables that have never once frayed. Imagine the biggest imitation diamond you have ever seen. Now imagine it approximately a million times bigger: *that* is how our chandelier twinkles. It is dazzling.

I can also report from firsthand experience that the seats in the auditorium are the most comfortable and largest found anywhere, especially if you are accustomed to riding a bicycle or a *hahnker*, or if you work in an office. As everybody knows, the chairs are almost big enough to fit two normal-sized people pressed together, as was proved in Year 10, when the annual Charity Gala was somewhat overbooked due to a clerical error. I tell you, these seats are more like miniature sofas, or thrones. The cushions are said to be individually hand-stuffed with feathers from champion *scrachi* birds. It is like sitting on air. Please note: I am speaking only of the seats in the Family Section Balcony, where members of the National News Service are invited to sit (except for the first two rows of the section, which are reserved for VIPs). I have not had the opportunity to test the seats in the lower sections, but based on what I was told by a colleague from National Heroes Headquarters who was once given a Grand Parterre ticket on the lower level, I am confident that those are even better.

Nestled into my beautiful chair, waiting for the National Song Competition to begin, I had time to reflect on how good my life was, how fortunate I was to have arrived at this point in time, at this glorious place. Mathematically speaking, I could have been like millions of others of my fellow citizens, who would see our sacred Homeland's finest *chu-chu* stars only in their most improbable dreams. But, no. Here I was, in person, not more than a very short city block from the stage.

I wondered if the other lucky souls in attendance felt as fortunate as I. It was thrilling: for the first time in the event's glorious history, in honor of our recently implemented Access Initiative, members of the general public were being allowed to attend the National Song Competition. (We had published an Official Directive article in *Perriodocko* about this exciting innovation. It had been properly announced.) There had been some sort of lottery for the tickets, and a number of people had won. Exactly how many is hard to say, since there were different ways of counting that could be somewhat confusing to those not involved in the computations. The point was that some regular citizens were definitely in attendance. That was the important part.

Everybody else who mattered was here—including, of course, my special colleague Mr. TupTup. Without bothering Chief Editor Pops, or anyone else, I had figured out how to fix everything. Instead of assigning a photographer, which really was not necessary since the National Song Competition organizers had agreed to share images of the event, I added some extra Information Gathering manpower, my own squadron of Heroes, armed with notebooks, ready to convey in descriptive words the majesty of the National Song Competition. Including myself, we had three of our most seasoned Information Gatherers in attendance – and one of our least experienced: TupTup was downstairs, with his illustrious father, I assumed.

We had arrived at the National Theater separately—he by *blecky*, I by bicycle—and passed through separate entrances, with different security procedures. Familiar with the protocol at this kind of high-risk event, with so many VVIPs (Very Very Important Persons) expected, I and my colleagues from the National News Service arrived two-and-a-half hours before the performance for the mandatory strip search. Though I didn't see him enter the auditorium, I knew TupTup must have gotten to his seat on the VVIP/VIP Level. Standing at the railing and craning my head over the edge of the balcony, I thought I could make out his distinctive head below. He may have even waved to me.

I imagined TupTup was enjoying the experience, wearing laminated credentials and carrying an official notebook, although lately it seemed that his enthusiasm for *chu-chu* had waned slightly. When I had informed him a few days prior to the big concert that he would be, as promised, an official member of our Information Gathering team, TupTup flashed that peculiar crooked smile and looked as though he might launch into one of his epic monologues about the glamorous contestants, their relative musical merits, and where they stood in his dating hierarchy. But he caught himself and said only, "Yes. That is good. Hmmmm. Very good."

"You are pleased?" I asked. A week earlier, when I had told TupTup he had been assigned to work on our annual supplement, I was surprised that he did not offer a somewhat more effusive reaction. Many, many people at *Perriodocko*—and many, many outside of the newspaper—would consider attending the National Song Competition in person as the crowning achievement of their lives. But that is why expectations really are not worth having; too often they are not met.

I said, "I sincerely hope that you are pleased, Mr. TupTup. Are you?"

TupTup nodded. "Yes. Obviously." For a moment, it looked as though he wished to say more, but he merely nodded again and returned to his work station, where he had made a habit of remaining for eight hours a day, until Uncle came to take him home.

Things got busy in the office, and I did not have the opportunity to mention to TupTup that after the concert he would be permitted to meet his new favorite, Miss Mae Love the Next Great One. All of us working for *Perriodocko* would. It really was no big deal to me. Interacting with very important people was our duty.

With two days to go before the gala night, and then one, and then the arrival of the day itself, you could feel interest and attention growing among our sacred Homeland's regular citizens. People were talking. Everyone had a prediction and a preference. It seemed each person you encountered, no matter how uneducated, whether they hawked *uchaana* on the avenues or sold National Lottery tickets on the sidewalks, had become a self-appointed *chu-chu* expert. If you listened too much to the prognosticating, they could be quite convincing with their theories. *Ah bolah*, it seemed like a compelling case could be made for all twelve finalists, that they *all* deserved the honor and respect (and recording contract) that came from being the champion of our most important artistic competition.

One school of thought held that, in fact, all twelve should indeed be given some sort of prize, because, really, were they not all winners? I suspected my wife believed such nonsense. But she did not say so out loud. She only hinted.

Me, at supper the night before: "Who do you think is the most deserving candidate tomorrow night, at the National Song Competition?"

Her: "I am not in a position to judge. They are all quite talented. The finest musical minds."

Me: "Yes. But only one can be champion."

Her: "That is a pity."

For the record, Gurly was rooting for Miss Angel Lee Diamond the Megastar. My brother also believed that Miss Angel Lee Diamond would be a worthy champion, but she had already won twice, in the inaugural and third years, and maybe someone else should have a chance. "It helps their career, you know," he said, cryptically.

Father was supporting Miss LuLu Lily, who was making her second appearance in the past three years. Perhaps she was not the best singer in the group, father said, bashfully, "but she has the nicest bumps!" He had a point. This was one aspect of singing talent that could not be overlooked.

Almost every member of my staff at *Perriodocko* seemed to have fallen under the influence of one of their more opinionated colleagues and was hoping for a Miss Mae Love the Next Great One victory.

Personally, I did not really care who won. I just wanted everything to go smoothly, without complications. But if pressed, if

I were made to choose, I would say I was secretly rooting for Miss Mae Love—only because I knew that her anointment as the Next Great One would please others.

The auditorium was filling, and with each new wave of arrivals you could feel the excitement building, a kind of electric anticipation. *Ah bolah,* the cameras from NTV-4 posted everywhere, like snipers; the special television lights, so bright they hurt to look at directly; the buzz and hum and trill of conversation and whispering and laughter – I tell you, it was a kind of magic. I could understand why so many regular citizens in our sacred Homeland become *chu-chu* maniacs. It is quite seductive—and I do not mean that in a vulgar way. It draws you in.

I looked to my right, two rows up, on the far aisle. Mr. J, my most trusted Information Gatherer on the *chu-chu* beat, had his nose buried in the Official Commemorative Program. He seemed to be taking notes. "Good man," I thought.

I looked to my left, one row down, four seats over, beside a group of Dedicated Servants. Mr. C, the second most senior Information Gatherer on the *chu-chu* beat, was also busily scribbling notes. He appeared to be interviewing a distinguished lady and gentleman who looked vaguely familiar, a couple that I recalled having some kind of administrative position at the Office of Creation. "Good man," I thought.

Work had officially begun. That reminded me: I checked the ink in my pen and the batteries in my tape recorder. All ready.

I stood and took a last look over the railing to observe the junior member of our Information Gathering team. The crowd downstairs was now too thick. I could not see TupTup. Never mind, I told myself, chuckling, his input was not exactly crucial to our success.

Immediately, I felt bad about thinking such a rude thought, and I promised myself I would make *everyone*, including Mr. TupTup, feel as though his contributions were properly valued and appreciated.

With the house lights still undimmed, a gentleman in a black suit, accented with a Western-style necktie, came on the stage holding a microphone. He offered warm and humble greetings, introduced himself, and said that he was a Production Manager with NTV-4. "Dear exalted ones, please allow me to remind you that tonight's show is going out live on NTV-4. In order to properly convey the excitement and glamour of the National Song Competition, I respectfully ask you to clap loudly when instructed. Laugh when instructed. Show the viewers at home how you feel – you know, within reason. We will have some helpers on the side of the stage to remind you when to clap."

He checked his watch. "Well, I think that's all. We go live all across our sacred Homeland in four minutes."

I checked my great-grandfather's watch. Yes, he was correct. The time was almost upon us.

The TV Manager opened his eyes wide, beaming. "Are you ready?" He turned his head and cupped his ear to listen. I think most of us were concerned about being impolite.

"I cannot hear you," he said in a sing-song way, laughing. "Are you ready?"

"Yes," many of us responded, also laughing.

"Really?" he yelled.

"Yes," we said a little louder, but certainly not in unison.

"OK. Great. Please enjoy." He nervously bowed and dashed into the wings. Some people in the upper levels applauded.

Pretty girls in pretty sparkly dresses appeared in the aisles, bearing placards that said "Clap." A pre-recorded announcement done by the one and only Miss Butterfly Rose came over the loudspeakers humbly requesting that those with cell phones not use them during the performance, except when necessary.

And then the houselights faded to black.

Some people tittered in the dark. If it is possible for the audience to be nervous and not the performers, I would say that those of us lucky enough to be in the National Theater on this grand night were slightly nervous. At least I was, I must report.

The acoustical properties of our National Theater are known to be perfect. Even in the upper reaches of the hall you could hear an un-amplified voice near the stage intoning, "In ten ... in five, four, three, two, one..." And then—*boom*—a big drum, and cymbals crashing, and strings, and the famous golden curtain flew up to the ceiling, and there was our National Youth Symphony Orchestra on stage playing *Yune Leckoolo* ("We Shall Triumph"), our new anthem! I tell you, it was a powerful, patriotic moment.

I wrote in my notebook: *Show begins on time. Excellent punctuality.*

After the anthem's rousing closing stanza—*"We shall triumph! We shall triumph! Oh, yes, by blood and toil we shall triumph!"*—an unseen announcer with a pleasantly deep voice spoke through the loudspeakers. "Distinguished guests, ladies and gentlemen," he said, "welcome to the Year Fourteen National Song Competition, recognizing our sacred Homeland's finest musical minds."

The girls held up their signs. Everyone clapped. I wrote in my notebook: *Nice announcement.*

"Now, distinguished guests, please welcome the honorary host of the National Song Competition and Chairman of the Judging Panel ... Mr. Boss Bo, President of Galaxy Records!"

The girls held up their signs. Everyone clapped. Mr. Boss Bo strode onto the stage, smiling and waving. From where I was sitting, he looked somewhat like the many photos I had seen of him, including the one hanging in the anteroom of the office of Chief Editor Pops: short, round, and gregarious, radiating power and influence. A very impressive man.

When the "alternative" scandal-mongering publications were still around, it was often written that Boss Bo was a world-class *rummee*—a "ladies man." But I had a difficult time understanding why anyone would claim such an obnoxious thing, especially since it was well known that Boss Bo was a large donator to charities, and that he was famously dedicated to his large and celebrated family, many of whom held important jobs at Galaxy Records and in various Ministries.

With all the special TV lights, his bald head gleamed, as though it were a polished ripe plum. His smile was just as bright. I wrote in my notebook: *Boss Bo: charming*.

The great man, who had discovered and launched the careers of so many of our sacred Homeland's most beloved *chu-chu* stars, welcomed attendees and television viewers alike, and helped put the National Song Competition in perspective. "The winner," he reminded us, "is not seeking personal glory. The champion girl represents all our dreams."

Then Boss Bo explained the rules of the National Song Competition, on the slim chance that any among us were not familiar with the procedures, which any schoolchild could explain to you. Each contestant would sing two songs, one from each category: Caring Leaders and Our Sacred Homeland. Then the judges would make a preliminary vote.

At that point, the field of contestants would be cut in half.

Each of the remaining singers, the Spectacular Six, would then sing one additional song, chosen from *either* category. This final song was known as Personal Choice, and if history was any gauge, Boss Bo reminded us, it was this final number that made the strongest impression on the judges.

"Speaking of the judges," Boss Bo said, "we have assembled the greatest panel of musical experts in our sacred Homeland. Please allow me to introduce them to you now."

As Boss Bo announced each judge's name, they walked onstage, smiling and waving, eventually taking their seat at a long Judging Table dressed with pretty gold fabric and positioned on a riser in front of the first row of the auditorium. The sign ladies held up their cards and almost everyone clapped.

I did not, though only because I had my hands full taking notes! I wrote in my notebook:

JUDGES

Jonas "Grampa Joe" Gun, Ministry of Information
Junior Junior, Office of Creation
Bull "Big Boy" Gordon, Office of Creation
General Sam, National Heroes (!)
General Slim, National Heroes (!)
Boss Mike, Republic Records
Miss Baby Sweets (BIG applause; wow wow wow)
Chief Editor Pops, Perriodocko (Surprise!! Very proud)
Mr. ?, Ministry of ???(ask Mr. J; distracted by CE Pops)
Al "Tiger" Tom, Reigning National Scrachi Champion (wow)

After the sustained applause for Tiger Tom subsided, Boss Bo announced, "And the final judge on our distinguished panel, from the Bureau of Industry, Mr. TupTup."

I tell you, I almost fell out of my incredibly comfortable chair.

I looked around in the dark. No one else in the prestigious audience seemed to take note of his inclusion. They just clapped politely, obliviously. I wanted to call out to my colleagues from *Perriodocko*—"*Ah bolah*! Can you believe it? TupTup!"—but they were too far away. They must have been equally dumbstruck.

Ah bolah, bolah, bolah! There was TupTup doing his Tup-Tup Turtle from the wings. The spotlight illuminating him as he ambled onstage seemed to blind him, and he stopped short, shielding his eyes and making strange faces. He was sort of smiling, though, and the audience clapped and laughed.

"*Vernando*!" I heard people chuckling.

Chief Editor Pops waved from the Judging Table and got TupTup's attention. "Over here," it looked like he was saying.

Despite my excellent training, I had stopped writing in my notebook. For some unknown reason, I had the impulse to run downstairs and try to help, although I had no idea what to do. Fortunately, TupTup gave a cheerful wave to the audience—and to the entire National Youth Symphony Orchestra watching from upstage, and then to Boss Bo—and shuffled off toward the Judging Table, where two empty chairs on either end of the dais awaited.

He paused at the closest one, but from the frantic gesturing of the other judges, he was made to understand that the seat was reserved for Boss Bo. TupTup continued down the line, toward the other open chair. But when he got to where Miss Baby Sweets the People's Star was sitting, he stopped.

Ah bolah. Was he pulling out his wallet? Showing her pictures?

He was.

Now he leaned in close. Was he trying to kiss her?

Ah bolah! He was.

The audience roared with delight. How amusing! Miss Baby Sweets, a true professional, played along, as though it had been planned.

TupTup flashed a triumphant smile and a thumbs-up, and ambled to his seat.

The audience howled. I tell you, I could not have imagined such a scene had I drunk one hundred jugs of *bolo*.

If Boss Bo was flustered, he did not show it. He waited for the chattering to die down, cleared his throat, and said, "OK. Well. And now, the moment you have been waiting for … Let us meet our sacred Homeland's finest musical minds. Distinguished guests, ladies and gentlemen, music fans everywhere, please provide a warm greeting to the finalists in the Year Fourteen National Song Competition!"

We rose as one, applauding madly. We did not require cue cards.

I will never in my lifetime acquire enough Information Gathering experience to learn how to adequately describe what it is like to be in the National Theater, to be *right there*, when twelve of our most gloriously talented stars glide onto that magnificent stage. *Ah bolah*, I can only say that it is a wonderful, unforgettable, thrilling, stupendous, awe-inspiring, marvelous, spectacular memory. Many strange things happened to my body, some of which are embarrassing to note. If I have ever been more excited, I cannot recall when. I tell you, it was altogether overwhelming.

But like Miss Baby Sweets the People's Star, I, too, am a professional. I composed myself. I wiped away the moisture on my face. I retrieved my notebook and returned to work.

The finalists stood side-by-side, waving their special permits at us, to the TV cameras, to the judges. Such white teeth! Such nice faces! I wrote down each of their names, and the colors of their dresses, and whether they wore their hair up or down—the details that our readers demanded to know.

They were all so lovely, so very elegant. But I would not be making an accurate report if I failed to mention that the girl farthest to the left side of the stage (my right), the one who looked exactly like her photo but better, the one in a sleeveless white gown, with the straight black hair and long, lean arms, the one who seemed to project calmness and serenity and, I do not know what you would call it, maybe "joy"?—this girl was somehow in another category altogether. I tell you, once I saw Miss Mae Love, I could not take my eyes off her.

Well, that is an exaggeration. I *could*. But I did not want to. I cannot explain why. It was a very odd situation. Maybe because I was accustomed to seeing her in black, her signature color.

For some unknown reason, I lost concentration for a moment, thinking back on my life, on various things that are not worth noting. You could say I was engaged in such as what they call a daydream, but it was not daytime and I was not dreaming. Just remembering. Is it not funny how quickly your life can go? How some things happen and some things do not? Queer and crazy as it sounds, I was thinking about such ridiculous matters there in the National Theater, at the most inappropriate time.

But not for long. I regained my focus when I heard Boss Bo saying, "These beautiful ladies need no introduction. But let us greet them individually."

He pronounced each star's name, and each one stepped forward from the line and made a demure bow. Out of habit and courtesy, I wrote down each name, although, I assure you, everyone in our sacred Homeland already knew who these twelve goddesses of song were.

Based on the volume and intensity of applause, Miss Angel Lee Diamond the Megastar appeared to have the most support-ers. But every contestant was shown the respect they deserved. This was a highly educated audience.

"And now," Boss Bo announced, "let the National Song Competition officially begin!"

While the NYSO played inspiring marching music, the finalists peeled off into two groups. Half went one way and half went the other, into the wings. Boss Bo made his way to the Judging Table, where I noticed TupTup facing the wrong way, toward the audience, looking around as if tracking an escaped bird.

Then the stage lights dimmed to black, and a single spotlight cast a round pool of light, a full moon, on the center of the stage.

Into it walked Miss Lulu Lily, looking quite healthy. It was hard to see the sign girls, but most people understood it was a good time to clap.

The NYSO struck up a swelling wave of sound, and Miss Lulu Lily said, "In honor of our Caring Leaders. This one is called *Slahbouti*." The word is impossible to translate directly, but it sort of means "Warrior King."

I could hear low whispering around me. Almost all National Song Competition contestants began with a number from the Our Sacred Homeland category. This was a bold choice.

I listened to the words of the song. Like everyone else at the National Theater, this was the first time I had heard *Slahbouti*, since every selection at the National Song Competition was a debut. I am no musical expert, but Miss Luly Lily's first song sounded good to me. Upbeat, I think you would call it. Having strong materials was an important part of winning the National Song Competition. Even Miss Angel Lee Diamond admitted in a recent interview that being pretty and having a good voice is not enough to sway the judges. You had to have what she described as "three compelling numbers, three memories that will last a lifetime."

As I say, I do not pretend to know what I am talking about in technical terms, as I never acquired formal musical training or education. But from my limited understanding, Miss Lulu Lily's rendition of *Slahbouti* certainly sounded pretty good.

People clapped warmly when she finished the song, after holding out a long and high note that was really quite impressive.

She curtsied. "Thank you, distinguished guests, ladies and gentlemen. I would now like to sing in honor of our sacred Homeland. This one is called *Natural Wonder*. I hope you enjoy it."

This song also sounded quite all right to me. I would say that Miss Lulu Lily sang almost as beautifully as she looked. But I wrote a note: *Very decent. Probably will not win. Difficult going first.*

The order of performance, I think, was determined by random draw, so you never knew who was appearing next. Each girl was an individual surprise—except the last one, of course, because you knew who was coming out through process of elimination. After Miss Lulu Lily, the next finalist was a very nice-looking lady named Miss Princess Sugar, who I had not previously heard. She was also quite good. She stuck to the more traditional order of songs, and I think the audience appreciated that. They clapped loudly for her. I assumed the judges took notice.

Miss Queenie Glitter was next. She was quite good, also. I really did not know how you could pick. The judges had a difficult challenge ahead of them, I reckoned. But they were well-qualified, and fair. And besides, since all twelve finalists were supremely excellent singers, you could not really make a mistake, no matter who you selected. It was true, I thought. They all were champions. I even wrote that in my notebook.

The fourth contestant was Miss Princess Cookie. *Excellent*, I noted. *But this is obvious!*

The next contestant was Miss Mae Love.

I do not have any notes about her performance. In a moment of weakness, I allowed myself to be distracted by the music, and I failed to make a proper report. At the time, with the sound swirling all around me, I may have told myself that Mr. J or Mr. C would gather all the information we would need, or some other allegedly reasonable equivocation. But I can admit now that I was derelict in my duties, and if I were my supervisor I would place a cautionary note in my file. For some unknown reason, when she began to sing, I stopped writing. I cannot explain why.

Her songs, I believe, were very well-composed, full of native pride and stirring imagery. They made you feel that all our sacrifice and past sorrows were leading to a great conclusion. As I have noted, I do not have any authority to judge musical quality. But to my unsophisticated and untrained ears, Miss Mae Love was more than satisfactory.

Something about her, something I am not able to identify, was unlike the other superb National Song Competition finalists. It may have been the tone of her voice, such as what is called, I believe, the texture. It was dark and smoky. And smooth. Very rich. Perhaps this is foolish, but I remember thinking that Miss Mae Love sounded like melted chocolate, if melted chocolate could sing. I had never heard anyone in our sacred Homeland sound like that. If I closed my eyes, I heard a voice that seemed to come from a land very far away.

But I did not want to close my eyes. It was impossible. The way she gazed out into the darkness, her eyes open and shining, was mesmerizing, hypnotizing, something you had to watch. Miss Mae Love did not make very many gestures with her hands—the upraised fist, the pleading palms, which you saw from other *chu-chu* stars. She expressed feelings with that unusually deep voice, her emotions so undisguised that it was almost embarrassing to witness, like someone's face when he has been informed that his mother has perished.

Though Miss Mae Love was some distance away, standing alone in the milky pool of light, she pulled me in. For some unknown reason, I felt as if I knew her well, although we had never actually met. I suppose you might call it a special kind of intimacy, yet I assure you I do not mean anything immoral. I mean that I felt, perhaps, a closeness. A connection? It was a strange feeling, but also pleasant, in a way. It is hard to explain.

When Miss Mae Love concluded her performance, the entire National Theater was very quiet. It was so quiet I momentarily feared I had gone deaf, that I had suffered a sudden hearing loss because my ears could not adequately process what they had just heard. It is quite funny, I know. But I am not joking.

After some time—it might have been a second, or maybe it was longer; I cannot say with certainty—a collective roar rose from the lower levels, and instantly we were all cheering and screaming and making sure the judges and Miss Mae Love understood that we approved completely of what she had done.

You could tell that TupTup felt the same way. He was standing and applauding and waving his head around, which I was under the impression judges were not supposed to do.

Miss Mae Love held both hands to her chest and bowed her head. When she looked up, she was smiling. I know this will sound odd, but if I am not mistaken, and I do not think I am, for some unknown reason she was smiling right at me.

Maybe her smile was intended for someone else in my particular row of the Family Section balcony, but I do not think so. Even from some distance, our eyes locked.

I tell you, it was quite embarrassing. I felt my face growing hot and moist, and I wondered if everybody in the National Theater could tell that something rather unusual had just transpired.

It was only an instant, but I know what happened.

Then Miss Mae Love clasped her hands beneath her chin, briefly resembling one of those figures commonly seen in the European paintings I studied as a youth, the ones depicting delicate ladies with pink cheeks engaging in Unauthorized Psychic Communication.

Then she nodded twice and walked off the stage, floating away on a raft of applause and adulation.

I heard someone behind me declare, "Now *that* is *chu-chu!*" For the first time in my life, I believe I understood what he meant.

There were many more singers, of course, including Miss Angel Lee Diamond, who must have been quite spectacular, as she always was. But I confess that I did not really hear their songs, not with the attention they surely deserved. I stopped listening after Miss Mae Love. Too many thoughts were raging in my head. I could hardly hear myself think.

What was I thinking? Well, I was thinking I was a stupid goat for forgetting to turn on my tape recorder while Miss Mae Love performed her two songs. I could have. I was permitted. I should have.

I was thinking that I had brought dishonor to my profession, failing to write a single note in my Information Gathering book. I was supposed to be performing a valuable service for my fellow countrymen, not taking a personal holiday. While the contestants sang their hearts out, I had been behaving like a fan, like an invited VIP, not a working member of the National News Service. If any of my subordinates attended the National Song Competition and merely enjoyed the music, I would be compelled to discipline them.

I was also thinking it might be a good idea for me to interview Miss Mae Love the Next Great One, for background purposes. Perhaps directly after the concert.

I was also thinking many other various unimportant thoughts about my life, which are probably not worth noting at this time.

After the last singer, there was a brief musical interlude while the judges tabulated their results. TupTup was hunched low over the Judging Table, his head almost resting on the surface. It looked to me as though he were scribbling furiously, like a schoolchild filling in a coloring book. The NYSO was playing an uplifting medley of familiar favorites at the time, so I do not think many people noticed.

When the NYSO finished, with much exciting crashing and banging of such as what they call percussions, the big golden curtain came raining down.

Boss Bo appeared on the foot of the stage, clutching an envelope wrapped in a gold ribbon.

"Distinguished guests, ladies and gentlemen," he said, "I have in my hands a list of the Spectacular Six!"

I wrote: *Signs, applause, hooting.*

"Let us remember that each National Song Competition finalist is a fine musical mind. Indeed many of them have recordings available on Galaxy Records." He chuckled and looked in the direction of Boss Mike. "And other labels, I am told."

Everyone laughed politely. Boss Bo was quite entertaining.

"Unfortunately, only half the contestants can remain. Those lucky ones are standing right there, behind that curtain." He pointed over his shoulder. "One of them will be your Year Fourteen National Song Competition champion."

Signs, applause, hooting. TupTup had turned his head sideways, as though he was trying to peek beneath the curtain's hem, perhaps hoping to identify the survivors from their shoes.

"Distinguished guests, ladies and gentlemen, it is my great honor to present to you…" Boss Bo paused for what felt like an excruciatingly long time. "The Spectacular Six!"

The curtain flew up, and Boss Bo started announcing all their names. They have all been properly acknowledged in *Perriodocko*, so I do not feel so bad to admit I was not really paying perfect attention to what Boss Bo was saying. I could hear him reading names—"Miss Angel Lee Diamond, Miss Peaches Puff, Miss…"—but I had already determined that the results were correct, that what everybody in the National Theater must have known was inevitable had indeed happened: Miss Mae Love the Next Great One was in the Spectacular Six.

I was pleased by this because it seemed fair to me, and fairness is extremely important. If I were a judge, I probably would have voted for her. She was really very good.

Boss Bo was clapping for the girls, beaming. We all were. They were our sacred Homeland's finest musical minds, and very beautiful.

The Spectacular Six waved and blew kisses—which Tup-Tup caught—and some of them even clapped back at us, the audience. Everybody in our sacred Homeland always feels completely unified in our common purpose, but during this magical moment inside the National Theater, I felt we were all especially close and singularly focused on the concept of *ontongull*. I remember thinking at the time that anyone foolish enough to attempt to colonize us would be in for a big surprise!

Ah bolah. It all seems rather funny now.

The golden curtain started to descend, slowly, eventually eclipsing our *chu-chu* stars. The sign girls put down their signs, and we understood that we should probably stop clapping. Boss Bo was saying, "We will return shortly for the Personal Choice portion of the program. But first, let us enjoy a very brief presentation about the Caring Leaders, Dedicated Servants, and faithful sponsors who make the National Song Competition possible. Unless you are in the VVIP section, please do not use this opportunity to visit the toilet facilities or *bolo* bars. Thank you."

A giant projector screen unfurled over the golden curtain. On it was shown a highly educational presentation about the Office of Creation, and Galaxy Records, and a number of other important entities, including the National News Service and *Perriodocko*, which I was quite proud to see was considered one of the National Song Competition's most essential sponsors. They even showed a little montage of our special preview supplement, and I do not have to tell you that my *meowkaleet* was probably at an all-time high at that moment.

The video presentation was so well-produced and informative that it really did not feel as if thirty-five minutes had passed.

But there was Boss Bo again, clapping with us as the screen rolled up into the ceiling. He was saying, "Wonderful. *Grabvey!*

Grabvey!" and many people in my section of the National Theater replied likewise. "*Grabvey! Grabvey!*"

Boss Bo nodded. Then he said, "Distinguished guests, ladies
and gentlemen, we now return to musical entertainment. This
is it! Get ready. Here we go. Let us now enjoy Personal Choice!"

The NYSO began playing, the golden curtain rose, and
there upon the stage was none other than the great Miss Angel
Lee Diamond.

I must report that from where I was sitting the Megastar
did not appear to be amused, and you really could not blame
her. It was well-known that going first was very difficult. Indeed,
I recalled TupTup informing me at some point during his tenure at the newspaper that no one had ever won the National
Song Competition from Personal Choice first position. Now,
we all understood that the order of appearance was probably
determined by some kind of random draw, that the results were
really just a matter of chance, but if you were a Miss Angel Lee
Diamond supporter, your heart must have sunk a little bit when
the curtain revealed her beautiful presence.

I thought of Gurly back home at the apartment. She would
be perplexed, outraged. Father would probably be somewhat
confused—"Why is a giant star like Miss Angel Lee Diamond
going first?"—but he would try to look on the bright side, real-
izing that perhaps she could inspire and lead those who would
perform later (Miss Lulu Lily, unfortunately, was not among
them). Boy undoubtedly would have something provocative and
unhelpful to say. I was not sure what my wife would think.

Ah bolah, my family. If they could only experience for one
second what I was experiencing on this unforgettable night.

Did I feel guilty for my good fortune? No. In some ways I
knew I had earned this special opportunity. Still, I wished they

could enjoy the unique feeling of being present at the National Theater, with the lights and the VIPs and the VVIPs and the *chu-chu* stars, the thrill of being *right here*, instead of watching the action on a fuzzy black-and-white screen.

Miss Angel Lee Diamond, ravishing in a purple-and-blue gown, flashed her most incandescent smile and said, "Thank you, distinguished guests, ladies and gentlemen, for your kindness. For my Personal Choice, I have selected a song from the category of Our Sacred Homeland. It is called 'Onward.' I hope you enjoy it."

I did enjoy it. We all did. It really was most enjoyable.

Every singer was most enjoyable. Really, just wonderful.

But for some unknown reason that I am not qualified to understand or explain, when Miss Mae Love the Next Great One appeared on the National Theater stage to deliver her PC selection, all the performers who had come before her suddenly seemed to fade from memory. I do not want to suggest that their singing was irrelevant, for that would be too blunt and rude of a way to put it. I only mean to say that when Miss Mae Love stood in that brilliant white light and spoke in song to us, all of us together and each of us individually, with that voice of hers, and the way she stood so proudly, like a champion or a National Hero, but so relaxed and comfortable, as though everyone in the auditorium and everyone at home and everyone in the whole world could be her friend—well, when that happened, the other singers did not seem to matter very much.

I do not think I was the only person who felt this way.

Even a non-expert listener like me knows that the kind of songs that win the National Song Competition have a good beat and a catchy melody, such as what they call the tune. I have never been trained—nor authorized—to write down music in notation on parallel lines, and I do not know the difference between the note sounds and all that. But even I could tell you the way Miss Mae Love's Personal Choice song selection went: four shorts and two longs.

Duh-duh-duh-duh-DAAH-DAAH.

I found my toe involuntarily tapping as she sang.

Duh-duh-duh-duh-DAAH-DAAH.

The words were simple: *Mali golli zeenkey.*

That was the title of her song: *Mali Golli Zeenkey.* It means, "Every single person."

Duh-duh-duh-duh-DAAH-DAAH.

Ma-li-gol-li-ZEEN-KEY.

The lyrics Miss Mae Love sang were so sweet, so inspiring. They captured what you might call the essence of our sacred Homeland. Her poetic verses told of how everybody—"every single person"—was grateful and thankful for the guidance and wisdom given so selflessly by our Caring Leaders. How every single person was grateful and thankful for the licenses and permits given so efficiently by our Dedicated Servants. How every single person was grateful and thankful for the protection and security given so bravely by our National Heroes, and also our *Kapaa.* How truly blessed every single person was to be a regular citizen of our sacred Homeland.

It was a very great song, in my opinion. And I am quite certain I was not the only one who thought so.

If you will permit a small joke: I believe that every single person enjoyed the song.

TupTup showed his appreciation by jumping to his feet during Miss Mae Love's final note, a silver thread of sound, a whisper that could be heard in the rafters. *Ah bolah!* I could not believe it: a few of the other judges abandoned any pretense of objectivity and joined him, applauding and shaking their fists.

People around me were shouting and crying, and I may have momentarily joined them. It was all quite emotional and chaotic. Everybody in the National Theater seemed possessed with some sort of musical fever.

Except Miss Mae Love. She stood still at the end, her eyes open, looking toward the heavens, toward a spot that was very near where I was standing.

She did not seem unduly excited. She seemed calm. Very calm, as though she was not surprised at our reaction, as though she somehow expected it. She had a smile on her lips and a smile in her eyes. You could tell she was very happy. But Miss Mae Love did not seem overwhelmed by our mad applauding and impassioned calls, just pleased.

I reached for my notebook, and I wrote: *Next great one? Yes.*

Another girl sang—poor thing, it must have been quite difficult to go through the motions knowing that it no longer mattered—and then the judges huddled and tabulated their votes, and Boss Bo tried to uphold proper etiquette and act as though the result was not already a foregone conclusion. But I believe nearly everyone in the National Theater was certain who would win. This was clear. It was obvious.

After another brief and informative presentation, this one about the upcoming Charity Gala and all the good things that were being done with our generous donations, the projector screen rolled up and Boss Bo finally returned to the stage, smiling and holding another big envelope.

"Distinguished guests, ladies and gentlemen, thank you for honoring us with your presence tonight. I think we can all agree that this was the best National Song Competition ever, yes?"

Signs, applause. "Before I announce the champion singer of Year Fourteen, please allow me to remind you that whoever the lucky winner is, she will be rewarded by the Office of Creation with a new album of patriotic songs. That will be coming out on Galaxy Records in just a few days, so you will not have to wait long!" *Signs, applause.*

I could not help noticing that TupTup, hunched over the Judging Table, seemed to be writing down everything Boss Bo was uttering, as was I. And for some unknown reason this pleased me.

The next thing Boss Bo said pleased me even more. "More details will be announced soon. Please check *Perriodocko* regularly for updates." Some people, including three people in my section, applauded, even though there were no signs. Very nice.

"I apologize that you will have to wait a few days to acquire this recording," Boss Bo said, graciously. "But you will not have to wait another minute to learn the name of the champion of the Year Fourteen National Song Competition." There was applause, and scattered whistling. I thought I even heard TupTup's voice in the din.

"Distinguished guests, ladies and gentlemen ... the champion of the National Song Competition is…"

He cracked open the envelope and smiled broadly. "Miss … Mae Love!"

I do not have to tell you about the pandemonium that ensued. It has all been well documented. I can assure you, the Authorized Reports were accurate: no one was seriously hurt.

What perhaps is not as well understood was what transpired after Miss Mae Love accepted her trophy and giant (replica) recording contract.

The custom, of course, is for the National Song Competition winner to celebrate her victory with one last song, usually a repeat of her Personal Choice selection, such as what is called a reprise. After the clapping and hooting subsided a little, the NYSO struck up "Every Single Person," and we all sat down to enjoy our new queen of *chu-chu* serenading us with her signature creation. Miss Mae Love stood before the microphone, her arms opened wide, as though she were attempting to hug all of us, every single person in the auditorium.

She started singing the words that had already become familiar and beloved, words that had instantly imprinted themselves on our memory. *Mali golli zeenkey...*

I could not recall exactly how the second line went, the precise wording. But I knew it was about our Caring Leaders. That much I knew.

But what Miss Mae Love the Next Great One was singing now was not about Caring Leaders. Or Dedicated Servants. Or our sacred Homeland.

It was something quite different. That was obvious.

The buzz and hiss of agitated conversation rippled through the audience. People around me were turning to each other, shaking heads in disbelief and with concern.

Miss Mae Love appeared unbothered by the commotion. She was serenely calm. She kept singing.

Then her microphone stopped working, and the stage lights went out.

The electrical power inside the National Theater seemed to have failed. I waited for the familiar sound of emergency generators coughing into action, but they never started. It was too dark to look at my great-grandfather's watch without lighting a match, but even without confirmation from my timepiece, I knew it was not yet *Tink*. Shows in our sacred Homeland tended to run a little late, especially the National Song Competition, which had a reputation for extending past its allotted television time. Whenever that violation occurred, it was well known that the NSC organizers simply paid the necessary fines and started a little earlier the following year. The Year 14 version certainly had gone on a bit longer than anticipated, but unless I had lost all sense of time, there was no way it was yet Midnight. The day had not changed. The power should still have been working.

It was a technical problem. The timing was unfortunate and somewhat embarrassing, especially for the unlucky person who was going to lose his job. But the outage was understandable. These things happen.

The NYSO continued to play for a few seconds, un-amplified. Soon they sputtered to a stop.

I thought I could make out the sound of Miss Mae Love, singing quietly in the dark. It was only a few seconds, but the sound was unmistakable, at least to my ears. Unfortunately, VIPs in the audience were talking loudly—and laughing and shouting and engaging in various distracting behaviors. Eventually I could no longer detect our National Song Competition champion's voice. Maybe I'd only imagined her singing.

The noise and commotion built, rising in volume, such as what is called a crescendo. Then, without warning, the spotlights came back on.

The stage was empty, except for a solitary microphone on a stand. Miss Mae Love was gone.

The houselights flickered to full strength. The curtain came crashing down. The sign girls stood at their posts, smiling and waving, and we understood that the show was over.

The judges stood and shook hands and saluted each other. Miss Baby Sweets and Tiger Tom signed autographs for VIPs in the first row and posed for pictures before being hustled away by Event Security through a door beside the stage. TupTup and Chief Editor Pops and all the other judges were escorted through the same door, which then closed behind them.

No further announcements were given, no explanations provided. I could hear conjecture swirling through the audience: "The lights went out because of a system overload. It happens, you know." "I suspect it could have been a sabotage attack on our power grid." "Probably someone at the Bureau of Energy thought *Tink* had already begun."

It was impossible to say.

But I was not concerned. I would get the Authorized Official Report at the Official Media Conference, which would be conducted backstage in a few minutes, as soon as all accredited members of the National News Service could get down from their lofty perch.

I caught the eye of Mr. C. He gestured toward the stage with an imploring look that I took to mean, "Meet you at the Official Media Conference?"

I nodded, and he nodded back.

I could not find Mr. J. The Family Section balcony of the National Theater was abuzz, everyone talking and shuffling, hurrying for the exits to catch the last *hahnkers* of the night. Everyone around me was chattering about Miss Mae Love's victory song performance, about the unusual, alternate version of "Every Single Person" that many of us thought we had heard.

"It all happened so quickly. Now I am wondering if maybe I misunderstood," one woman told her husband, who shrugged and said, "I cannot recall at this time."

"What did she say?" I overheard someone asking his friend, a Dedicated Servant proudly wearing his Civil Service pin.

"Let us talk about it later," the Dedicated Servant replied.

Someone else, another Dedicated Servant hearing a nice Commendation Medal, shushed his wife when she began to hum the duh-duh-duh-duh-DAAH-DAAH melody, trying to reconstruct the words.

"I think she said 'every single person has a responsibility to uphold the laws of our sacred Homeland,' or something like that," one man announced, filing into the aisle.

"I do not intend disrespect my learned friend," his companion said, with furled brow. "What I heard was 'every single person,' but the rest of her song did not seem to be about our laws. I am sorry to contradict you."

"Well, it is not important. Miss Mae Love is a worthy champion."

"Yes. You are right."

Many of my fellow citizens seemed quite vexed by uncertainty. I got the feeling they were more upset about not knowing the exact words than by the abrupt conclusion of the concert. *Ah bolah*, I even heard one man loudly and rudely announcing that he had been offended, that there was "no place for this kind of reckless improvising at the National Song Competition." But, he allowed, maybe what she had sung was not so bad after all.

Nobody really knew.

But I was not worried. I was a fully certified member of the National News Service. I worked for *Perriodocko*. And this time, when Miss Mae Love sang her victory song, I had not been a stupid goat.

This time I had turned on my tape recorder.

CHAPTER TWENTY-FIVE

Those of us who work at *Perriodocko* are not VIPs. We are regular citizens who fulfill our duties, just like everybody else in our sacred Homeland. But the job we do—well, *that* is very important.

We have VIJs. Do you get my little joke?

As I was ushered by Event Security into the Official Media Conference, held at an impressively decorated space backstage, directly behind where the NYSO had been seated—the Orchestra's music stands and chairs were still in place, on risers—I was reminded of how fortunate I was to be given the tremendous responsibility of gathering information for my fellow citizens. Those of us who have dedicated our lives to the National News Service are perhaps not the highest paid workers in our sacred Homeland. But the rewards of our job, I must say, are impossible to overestimate.

If this seems like *meowkaleet*, I apologize. That is not my intent. I would just like to report that from where I was standing backstage, if I peeked at the correct angle and in the correct direction, I could see the very spot where Miss Mae Love (and all the other amazing superstars) had stood onstage! *Ah bolah*, it made me nervous to look, and I do not even know how to sing.

Also, I must mention that at the Official Media Conference, there was an extensive buffet, with purified water, hot and cold tea, and three different kinds of fishmeal cakes. I do not mean to brag, but if one possessed the proper credentials, one did not have to pay for any of it.

If you have never seen actual VIPs close up, from a very short distance, it is perhaps difficult to understand how impressive they are in person, even more than in photographs, if you can imagine that. They radiate excellence and superior intelligence. Backstage at the National Theater, I was surrounded by so many of them it made me dizzy.

To my right: many of the National Song Competition judges, including General Slim, General Sam, and Big Boy Gordon, all of whom you could instantly tell were very, very important men. To my left: a clutch of high-ranking Dedicated Servants from the Office of Creation, all of them bearing prestigious Award Medals on their chests (and yes, the plural is accurate: medal*s*). Directly in front of me, sipping drinks and chatting amiably with officials and organizers from the National Song Competition, the most attractive VIPs of all: several of the finalists, including Miss Princess Cookie and Miss Queenie Glitter.

All of them, dignitaries and celebrities, right there.

I looked for Mr. J and Mr. C. They were camped at the buffet table consuming fishmeal cakes perhaps a bit too quickly.

I looked for Chief Editor Pops. There he was: in the last row of chairs facing a lectern, in the section reserved for the Media. I made sure I did not have any remnants of the buffet on my clothes before I approached him.

"Good evening, sir," I said, saluting.

"Ah, oh, yes. Hello," he said. He seemed surprised to see me.

I had never really spoken with Chief Editor Pops outside of his office. I did not know the proper thing to say. But I knew I had to say *something*. "What a pleasant surprise it was for me, and for all my colleagues—Mr. J and Mr. C, I mean—and, well, probably for everybody, meaning the people in the audience and the millions watching at home—yes, I must say, sir, it made me very proud to see you selected as one of the judges at the National Song Competition. It is a great honor to know someone—that is to say, to work beneath someone, who is offered such a prestigious position. You must also be very proud, and with good reason, sir."

"Yes," he said, nodding. "But now I have to change hats and go back to work. You know what they say, 'once a newspaper man, always a newspaper man.' Now I am a member of the Media." He chuckled, so I did, too.

"Yes," I said. "That is true."

Chief Editor Pops did not reply. He seemed to be distracted by the arrival of Miss Baby Sweets the People's Star, who, I can assure you, tends to be most distracting. Many people—VIPs, I remind you—formed a kind of disorganized queue, waiting to exchange salutations and maybe, if they were lucky or particularly well-known, shake her hand.

I stood uncomfortably for a few seconds beside my boss. "The concert was quite excellent," I remarked.

Without looking at me, Chief Editor Pops said, "Oh, yes."

I flashed my laminated credential, suspended from a lanyard around my neck, to the Security Attendant guarding the row of seats reserved for Media and I sat down beside Chief Editor Pops. "Sir, I wonder if I may have permission to ask you a question, sir?"

"*Mmph,*" he grumbled, which I took to mean "yes."

"Sir, I was wondering if you could tell me what Mr. Boss Bo is like. In person, I mean. You were at the Judging Table with him. He seems very nice. He is very nice, yes?"

"I am sure you could find out for yourself," Chief Editor Pops said. "Just tell him I said it was OK."

"Oh, that is very kind of you," I replied. "Thank you. But I am afraid I do not see Mr. Boss Bo at this Official Media Conference."

Chief Editor Pops said, "He is in the back. Some kind of meeting. With the, the—" he snapped his finger three times—"the organizers. I am sure he will be out momentarily."

"Ah, I see." Finding my nerve, I said, "And Mr. TupTup? He enjoyed the experience, I am assuming?"

"What? I thought he was with you."

I felt like I was choking. "No. No, sir. I did not—he was, unless I am mistaken, which, of course, that is possible—I thought he was with *you*. At the Judging Table."

"What? TupTup judging the National Song Competition finals? Are you joking me?"

I felt nauseous. "Maybe I did not see clearly."

"Sometimes you cannot trust your eyes. Do they not teach you that during Information Gathering training?"

I nodded.

"So maybe what you thought you saw and what was really there in front of you are two different things," Chief Editor Pops continued.

"Yes," I conceded. That was certainly possible.

Chief Editor Pops burst out laughing, somehow doing it without smiling. "TupTup is in the bathroom. He'll be out any minute."

"*Ah bolah!*" I howled. "*Ah bolah,* Chief Editor Pops, sir, you are quite the *vernando* tonight. *Ah bolah,* I was having a heart attack."

"Have a drink. You will feel better."

"Yes," I said, grinning. "That is a very good idea, sir."

Before I could go to the buffet, the Production Manager from NTV-4 stepped to the lectern. I noticed that his necktie was loosened, and his hair appeared slightly unkempt. He looked tired. "Hello. Hello. Good evening everybody. Distinguished guests, ladies and gentlemen, welcome to the Official Media Conference of the Year Fourteen National Song Competition. May we respectfully request that you take your seats at this time. Media members, you will find your reserved seats over there," he said, gesturing toward me and Chief Editor Pops.

The crowd, perhaps a hundred people (I am estimating), shuffled into rows of chairs, which, for the record, were not as plush as those in the auditorium. Of course, I am speaking only of the chairs in the Media Section. I cannot comment on the seats farther forward.

The NTV-4 Production Manager waited for the entire assembly to come to order, and before he began he seemed to make a final visual check, politely assuring that every credentialed member of the National News Service was properly seated.

I looked around. All eight of us were present: the *Perriodocko* contingent and the NTV-4 contingent.

NTV-4 had sent all three of their Information Reporters— the morning, afternoon, and evening gentlemen—all of whom I acknowledged with a nod. They nodded in return and smiled. We went way back. I saw these guys at all the important events.

"We seem to be missing someone," the Production Manager said, consulting a clipboard. "Someone from *Perriodocko*."

TupTup burst into the room. "Hello. I am here. It is me. Hello, hello! Yes. Hmmmm. Good evening, good evening." I am compelled to note with some regret that his pants were not fully zipped.

"Yes. I am ready for the Official Media Conference of the Year Fourteen National Song Competition, recognizing our sacred Homeland's finest musical minds."

I could hear some of the VIPs snickering. When I looked at my colleagues from the newspaper, they had their heads in their hands, as though they were washing their faces. But not Chief Editor Pops. He was smiling and appeared to be pleasantly amused. So I decided to be, too.

TupTup proudly displayed his laminated credentials to the Security Attendant and sat down right next to me. "Hi, boss!" he said. "National Song Competition finals, recognizing the finest musical minds. I was a judge. But this is obvious. I selected the Spectacular Six. I voted for all the girls. Yes. Hmmmm. But let me ask you something. Would you like to see my top-five girlfriends now?" He was quite excited.

"Later," I whispered.

TupTup flashed his smile-scowl at me and said, "I was a judge. Now I am Media."

"Yes," I whispered, even more softly, making a gentle signal with my finger over my lips. TupTup seemed to understand that this was perhaps not the best time to make a full presentation.

"All right, then," the Production Manager said. "Now we can begin. Well, first of all, on behalf of the Ministry of Information and all my distinguished colleagues at NTV-4, I thank you for being a part of our sacred Homeland's most enduring musical tradition. So, please allow me to give you a hand." He clapped for us, and many of us clapped back. It was very nice.

"As some of you probably know by now, this was a most unusual and remarkable National Song Competition." Many people chuckled. I did not. I was busy transcribing, as were Mr. C and Mr. J.

TupTup was not transcribing. He was looking through his wallet. He pulled out a photo of Miss Baby Sweets and showed it to me.

I nodded enthusiastically. "Yes. Great."

He pointed vigorously and repeatedly to the front row, where she was seated. Then he pointed at his picture. Then he pointed again at the back of Miss Baby Sweets.

I nodded again, somewhat less enthusiastically.

"And as some of you have already been informed, history was made tonight," the Production Manager said.

TupTup was making kissing motions toward his photo.

I shook my head. He flashed me a thumbs-up. I shook my head more.

"So, without further delay, I would like to bring out the Chairman of the Judging Panel and your honorary host, Mr. Boss Bo of Galaxy Records."

Everyone applauded.

Boss Bo smiled and nodded and stepped to the microphone. "Distinguished guests, ladies and gentlemen, that was really an incredible night. *Ah bolah.* Incredible." He patted his shiny head, and we all laughed politely.

"The Authorized Official Report is being compiled as I speak, and it will be made available to you very shortly. It contains all the pertinent details. But for now I can tell those of you who do not yet know—well, like he said, we had history made tonight."

People clapped again.

"There was a very unfortunate mathematical error in our tabulations, which, luckily, was noticed before the Authorized Official Report was certified."

Some people murmured. I just kept writing.

"In the interest of fairness and, you know, fairness, we have reviewed all the ballots, and, as I said—and this is the part we would like to stress—history was made tonight. You see, for the first time in the glorious history of the National Song Competition, we had a tie."

Many people gasped, and I may have been one of them.

Boss Bo nodded and smiled. "I know. It is quite extraordinary and amazing. And it is also quite wonderful, because now we have *two* champions of, you know, equal excellence and popularity."

I glanced at Chief Editor Pops. He was grinning and nodding. He did not seem discomfited in any way. So Mr. J and Mr. C and I knew that we should not be, either.

TupTup looked as though he did not fully understand what was being said. Someone would have to explain it to him later.

"The results have been officially certified as final and complete and accurate, so you can disseminate the information with full confidence," Boss Bo said reassuringly. "And so it gives me great pleasure to introduce to you the co-champions of the Year Fourteen National Song Competition: Miss Mae Love and Miss Angel Lee Diamond."

There was more muted gasping, and this time I am sure I was one of the gaspers. Boss Bo was right: It really was quite extraordinary and amazing.

The assembly started to applaud when Miss Angel Lee Diamond appeared from behind a curtain and sat at a small table facing us. But Boss Bo held up his hand to ask for silence. "Distinguished guests, ladies and gentlemen, unfortunately Miss Mae Love was not feeling well, a little dehydrated maybe from all the excitement, and she will not be able to attend our Official Media Conference. However, we all understand that the

National News Service requires a certified Official Statement from her, and I happen to have that. Copies will be distributed later to properly credentialed Information Gatherers. But for now, I shall read it. Do not worry, it is short."

People chuckled. Boss Bo was funny.

He retrieved a piece of paper from inside his jacket and placed it on the lectern. Then he retrieved a small pair of reading glasses from another pocket and perched them on his nose. "*I am very honored to be co-champion of the Year Fourteen National Song Competition. To be mentioned in the same company as a great superstar like Miss Angel Lee Diamond is a dream come true. This is a wonderful result. A bili en creneckulo. I am the luckiest girl in the whole world.*"

"Miss Mae Love," Boss Bo said, returning the paper to his pocket. Some people clapped.

"And now Miss Angel Lee Diamond is here. She is happy to take your questions."

Hands shot up in front of me. One man, an important Dedicated Servant, did not wait to be acknowledged. He asked, "Miss Angel Lee Diamond, first may I please say that you look quite gorgeous tonight, as you always do. What I am wondering is, could you please describe the color of your gown. Would *lavender* be accurate?"

"Thank you, sir, for your kindness. First, I would just like to give thanks and respect to our Caring Leaders and Dedicated Servants. Without their support, nothing is possible," Miss Angel Lee Diamond declared humbly. "You are very perceptive, sir. I would say *lavender* is a good way to describe my gown. Yes."

Hands shot up again before I—or anyone in my row—had a chance. "Good evening, Miss Angel Lee Diamond," another gentleman near the front said. "I am on the Board of Directors of the National Youth Symphony Orchestra, and I was wondering if in your professional opinion the group was, you know, good. Thank you."

"Tonight, the National Youth Symphony Orchestra showed once more why they are considered the finest musical organization in the entire world," Miss Angel Lee Diamond replied.

A colleague from NTV-4, the afternoon Information Reporter, rose from his seat and began talking. "Was this the most exciting television broadcast that you have ever been involved with during your storied career? And, as a follow-up: If so, why? Thank you."

Miss Angel Lee Diamond appeared to think for a moment, wrinkling her pristine forehead. "I would have to say yes. And—what was the follow-up?"

"Why? Meaning, why was this so exciting?"

"Oh, yes. Well, because everyone was just so great."

As soon as the NTV man sat down, TupTup stood up. "Hello!" he said. "Hello, Miss Angel Lee Diamond!"

She looked startled. "Oh, and I should also mention that the judges were great, too. Let us give a nice hand to the judges." We all clapped.

"Yes. Hmmm. But let me ask you a question."

I held my breath. I really did not know what else to do. It was not my place to interfere. I was just trying to do my job. On the other hand, TupTup was representing *Perriodocko* in some quasi-official capacity, and I did not want our professional excellence compromised. Of course, Chief Editor Pops was sitting right there, right beside me, and he had the ultimate authority on any newspaper-related matters. I was not worried. I knew he would exercise his authority with perfect fairness. My only concern was—well, you just did not know what TupTup might do. He could be somewhat unpredictable.

"You are one of my top-five girlfriends!"

Everyone laughed. Miss Angel Lee Diamond raised her sculpted eyebrows and said, "Oh! Well!" Everyone laughed some more. They turned in their seats and looked back at TupTup, smiling expectantly, as people often do when listening to a *vernando* performance.

"But let me ask you something else. I was one of the judges!"

"Yes," she said, nodding. "And just in case I did not properly acknowledge you and your esteemed colleagues, let me say again what a wonderful job the judges did tonight. Thank you. I am deeply touched."

"Yes. Hmmmm. But let me ask you something. Miss Mae Love was the champion. This is obvious."

Boss Bo interjected. "Well, actually, sir, we had a tie. Co-champions. History was made tonight."

"Yes. Hmmmm. Yes. But let me ask you something else. I voted for Miss Mae Love. You voted for Miss Mae Love." He looked at Chief Editor Pops. "You voted for Miss Mae Love. In fact all the judges voted for Miss Mae Love. She was the best. Miss Mae Love the Next Great One. Champion of the National Song Competition. Obviously."

People were no longer smiling—except for Chief Editor Pops. He was still smiling.

Miss Angel Lee Diamond was definitely not smiling. She looked to me as though she had just discovered a cockroach in her *bolo*.

Boss Bo at least tried to smile, but it would not seem to stick. He cleared his throat and said, "Well, I also was a judge, and, well, I think, sir, with all due respect, that maybe your memory is not exactly clear about this ... this situation, as it were. You know. As we all have been informed, there was a tie. History was made tonight. That has been officially certified, so I guess I am saying that, you know, your recollection is not possible. I am not accusing you of anything. It is an honest mistake, probably. I think maybe perhaps it is just simply possible that there is some potential chance that you do not remember clearly."

That would indeed be possible, I thought—for anyone except TupTup. I was very confused.

"Yes. Hmmmm. But let me ask you something else." TupTup rocked in place, stumped and agitated. There was really nothing more to say. Boss Bo was correct. The results already had been officially certified, and the Authorized Official Report was being compiled for nationwide distribution at this very moment. So there was no use in worrying about things that could not be changed. That was a waste of time.

"Sit down!" someone shouted.

TupTup did not sit down. "But let me ask you something else," he said, his voice rising in a way I had not previously heard. "Miss Mae Love the Next Great One was the best and the champion and the Year Fourteen National Song Competition champion and my number one on my top-five and she was the best and I voted for her and so did you Mr. Boss Bo President of Galaxy Records home to many of our sacred Homeland's most beloved *chu-chu* stars and so did everyone and Miss Mae Love was the best—"

I wanted to evaporate and disappear. I felt personally responsible for TupTup's bizarre outburst. Someone else, of course, someone far more important than I, had decided that TupTup could serve on the Judging Panel. But still, I understood intuitively that I was to blame for this unfortunate and embarrassing situation.

TupTup was going on, like a *chu-chu* record with a skip in it. Event Security Attendants were calling somewhere on their devices.

I turned to Chief Editor Pops for guidance. He shot me a look that I took to mean, "It is best to not get involved," and once again I was reminded of the wisdom and perspective that had gotten Chief Editor Pops to where he was today.

People were talking. All at once. I could only pick out snippets of what was being said: "...father at the Bureau of Industry..."

"Miss Angel Lee Diamond does not deserve this kind of treatment....",

"He is not funny..."

Without thinking, I found words of my own escaping my lips. "Sit down. Please, sit down, Mr. TupTup," I muttered.

He ignored me.

I tried again, louder. But he was in a kind of trance, I suppose. It was really quite upsetting to watch.

I looked around the Official Media Conference. Our Top-100 greatest individuals were here, backstage at the National Theater. The absolute top. I would not know where to begin listing them. Miss Angel Lee Diamond? Boss Bo? General Slim? Where would one start? These were the people who allowed our sacred Homeland to survive. They were our *Slahbouti*. They gave me hope.

I shot to my feet. Somehow finding reserves of courage and resolve I never knew I had, I screamed: "No more questions!"

The room was suddenly silent. TupTup had stopped.

For one indescribable moment, I understood how it must feel to be a Caring Leader.

But I also knew who TupTup was, and who I was. "Please, Mr. TupTup, sir," I said quietly. "Please. Sit down. Sit down with me."

I sat down.

And so did TupTup.

"Thank you," I said.

He looked at me. He had tears in his eyes. "Miss Mae Love the Next Great One is the champion and I would like to make a BABA in the newspaper."

I stared straight ahead, and kept my voice down, not giving in to his nonsense. "You are not entitled to BABA in this case, Mr. TupTup. Now let us enjoy the Official Media Conference. Miss Angel Diamond, top-five girlfriend, taking questions."

He was not placated. "I would like to make a BABA in the newspaper."

Ah bolah, he turned to Chief Editor Pops and insolently repeated, "I would like to make a BABA in the newspaper."

Chief Editor Pops, displaying the restraint and fortitude that has made him a legend in the Information Gathering field, did not dignify TupTup's childish rant with a reply.

Boss Bo attempted to re-start the Official Media Conference, handling the brief interruption with as much grace and dignity as possible. But TupTup grew louder again, repeating over and over his absurd request.

Suddenly, a door swung open and through it dashed Uncle, holding up some sort of credential. I must say I was glad to see him.

He marched straight to the Media Section, guided TupTup onto his feet by the collar of his jacket, and extracted him from the proceedings. It all took about five or six seconds.

People were talking again. Just then, though, several young men carrying stacks of paper entered the Conference. They walked directly to Boss Bo, who announced, "Here is the Authorized Official Report for the Year Fourteen National Song Competition. We will distribute it now. Thank you, distinguished guests, ladies and gentlemen, for being here on a night when history was made."

A few people clapped, and then everyone did, and then we all rose and shook hands and saluted. Chief Editor Pops wagged his head and shot me a look that I took to mean, "What can you do?"

I sent him a look in return that told him, "My thought exactly."

An attendant handed me a copy of the Official Authorized Report. It was very well done. Very thorough. Good photos. Good quotations. Excellent headline: *History Made: Co-Champions at National Song Competition*. It did not need much tinkering.

The night certainly had not been my easiest assignment. *Ah bolah*, no. There had been challenges. But whenever the Ministry of Information provided such outstanding source material, I knew that doing my job at the newspaper was going to be easy.

I walked to my bicycle with a lightness, a levity, that I do not believe I had previously experienced. I may have heard myself involuntarily whistling an increasingly familiar tune. I may have even hummed a line or two under my breath, so no one could hear me.

I was so tired. But I did not want to sleep. I just wanted to go home and tell my dear family that this had probably been the best day of my life.

CHAPTER TWENTY-SIX

I t was very late. There were more dogs on the streets than people. As I pedaled my bicycle toward home from the National Theater, I encountered fewer than a dozen of my fellow citizens, all of whom exchanged pleasant wishes of "*Grabvey!*" with me. I was in such fine spirits. "Yes, and more power to you, sir!" I would say to each one.

The National Song Competition, you see, brings out the nicest parts of our native spirit, reminding the entire population that no matter how hungry some of us may feel at times, no matter how sad some of us may feel at times, we should never forget the most reassuring and inspiring lesson found in our Guiding Text: truly, you are never alone, you just feel alone. We are all brothers and sisters in one gigantic, glorious, amazing and increasingly well-organized and orderly clan.

I felt that wonderful sensation of being part of something bigger than myself. I felt as though everyone—every single person—was my friend.

When I paused at the major intersection of Central Avenue and Hero Memorial Freeway, a nice-looking young couple, a man and his wife, I assumed, crossed in front of me. They might have been somewhat intoxicated, perhaps from *bolo,* or just from the knowledge that they lived in such a wonderful place. They were smoking *uchaana* and giggling and holding hands without any apparent shame. And they were singing.

Out loud—audibly enough, at least, that I could hear them clearly as I straddled my bicycle, waiting for the red light to change.

If the couple had a permit—and I strongly suspect that they did not—they forgot to display it. Indeed, they were so drunk, or giddy, or whatever they were, that they did not lower their voices as they passed me. Quite the contrary. They seemed to sing *louder* when they noticed me, as though they were *chu-chu* stars and I was a National Song Competition judge.

My first impulse, of course, was to reprimand them for their recklessness and disrespect. But I was distracted. I recognized the song they sang, and it is possible I was momentarily unable to stop myself from laughing in amazement.

Mali golli zeenkey …

The song was really quite catchy. For some unknown reason, I found myself squeezing my handbrakes to the beat.

Duh-duh-duh-duh-DAAH-DAAH.

Squeak-squeak-squeak-squeak -SKWAAK-SKWAAK.

A *hahnker* pulled up beside me. The rear compartment was filled with passengers returning home from National Song Competition viewing parties, I gathered. Through the open windows, I could hear laughter and happy yelping and, I must once again report, the unmistakable sound of what I assumed to be unpermitted singing: *Mali golli zeenkey...*

"Every single person..."

I also heard revelers loudly invoking the name Miss Mae Love, as if they knew her personally, as if they were a member of the National News Service who had actually been at the National Theater in person observing first-hand her triumph at the National Song Competition, where history had been made.

I looked around for law enforcement authorities, but none were on duty—and if they were, hiding in the shadows or observing from a secret location, I got the feeling they were purposefully not paying attention. I know this will sound crazy and stupid, but for some unknown reason I got the preposterous idea in my head that even if they *were* witnessing the obvious infractions, they might not necessarily detain the jovial rule-breakers, just as they sometimes allowed *bolo* fiends to get away with only a stern warning.

Willfully ignoring disobedient behavior, of course, is a form of discrimination and should not be tolerated in a civilized society. But it is also true what leading experts say: When handled improperly, music is just like any other drug, and it will sometimes make weak people do horrible things under its influence.

The *hahnker* driver, a rough-looking fellow with a smoldering *uchaana* dangling from his lips, caught my eye and shrugged, telling me without words, "*I know, I know. But what can I do?*"

If I had not been so exhausted, and so eager to get home, I probably would have explained to him exactly what he could do: proceed directly to the nearest National Hero station and make a full report.

Instead, I was an irresponsible citizen, a victim of unchecked *meowkaleet,* a selfish fool who could not wait to brag to his family about all the important people he had seen. I raised my eyebrows at the driver and shrugged back. There is some possibility I may have even inadvertently smiled.

Then the light changed. As the mini-bus pulled away, I swore I could hear the driver adding his voice to the chorus.

I rode on, amusing myself with imaginary conversations I might have had with certain *chu-chu* stars if I had been willing to abuse the privilege of my position at *Perriodocko.* I cannot recall at this time the exact details, but it is maybe possible that I envisioned having a private, one-on-one chat with Miss Mae Love about the excellence of her presentation.

The shortcut that I knew, through alleyways and narrow streets, would be terribly dark at this hour, with more feral canines on the prowl than *flona* hiding vegetables in their aprons. So I remained on Central Avenue, which has the most street-lights of any thoroughfare in the city. My journey home would be slightly longer on this route, but much safer.

At least that was the plan. As I was pedaling, replaying in my head the magnificent performances I had witnessed and the extraordinarily important individuals I had observed, all the lights went out.

It was now officially *Tink*.

Central Avenue was very dark, but not completely black. Candlelight pulsed intermittently from windows on both sides of the street, and a number of buildings outfitted with private generators produced enough reflected light to faintly outline my path. The crescent moon also cast a subtle glow. Still, I must confess I was a little nervous. I cannot explain why. As everyone knows, thanks to various deterrence initiatives, we have reduced our violent crime rate to nearly zero, especially since the major-ity of people on the streets after midnight are there for our pro-tection and security. But I did not see anyone like that. I did not see anyone at all.

Bebudew op en beberoo kap, I reminded myself. *"You will be back in your apartment in ten minutes. Fifteen maximum. Do not be a coward. Do not panic."*

I listened to my breathing. I listened to the rattling and squeaking of my bicycle. I heard dogs fighting and mating. I heard the distant rumble of lorries and the whine of sirens. I reminded myself again that the solitude I felt was artificial, that it was all in my head, that I was never truly alone.

But I felt lonely.

I came to another stoplight at the major intersection of Central Avenue and Industry Way. There was no traffic, no vehicles in any direction. I had the mad impulse to continue riding, to cross the street against the red light, rationalizing and equivocating, telling myself that "it would not hurt anyone" if I failed to wait in the dark for the green signal. Fortunately, I came to my senses, avoiding a potential accident with a car or another bicycle or something else with the legal right-of-way, a vehicle I could not presently see or hear but that possibly might be approaching. In the dim haze of the red bulb, I stood and waited. I tried to check my great-grandfather's watch. I looked in all four directions. I stared at the stoplight.

I knew it was all in my head, but I really did feel alone.

For some unknown reason that I cannot explain, I reached inside my coat pocket and pulled out my tape recorder. Perhaps maybe I was thinking I would feel better if I had some company, another voice in the dark. I do not know what I was thinking.

I held the tape recorder near my eyes, angling it toward the stoplight for illumination, and found the "rewind" button. I pressed it, and the wheels whirred and squealed, piercing the silence. Instinctively, I thrust the machine underneath my overcoat. But then I realized no one could hear what I was doing— and besides, if confronted, I could make a reasonable case that I was not using my tape recorder for unauthorized purposes. All information gathered at the National Song Competition needed to be reviewed at some point. I had a little extra time during my commute. Why not use it productively?

The wheels clicked to a stop. I held the tape recorder near my chin, like the *Go Paja U-House* microphone. And then I pushed "play."

At first, all I heard was brittle static. But when I lowered the volume slightly, I realized it was applause—the applause of an appreciative and wildly enthusiastic audience welcoming their new queen of *chu-chu* to the National Theater Stage.

Then the National Youth Symphony Orchestra began to play, and I was transported back to my plush seat inside the golden auditorium, where only the most beautiful and magical artists shared their gifts.

The stoplight changed to green. But I stayed right there, me and my tape recorder. Me and Miss Mae Love.

Her voice was clear as fresh water. I could hear every word perfectly.

> *Mali golli zeenkey (Every single person)*
> *Ku kolaaku hahnee (Has a special garden)*
> *Ah duwapat mo-loko (Oh, we must believe the truth)*
> *Mali golli zeenkey (Every single person)*
> *Edap wallay nahnay (Growing something lovely)*
> *Edap kosa mokono (Growing gifts from heaven)*
> *Ontongull (Together)*
> *Ontongull (Together)*
> *Mali golli zeenkey, ontongull (Every single person, together)*

Then her singing cut out, replaced by the frantic noise of conversation and conjecture and confusion. Then the NYSO stopped playing. Then there was more static. That was the end of my recording.

I stopped the tape. I paused. I could hear my own breathing, shallow and rapid.

I looked in every direction as far as I could see in the gloomy night. And I started to put the recorder back in my pocket. But I did not.

I rewound the tape to the beginning and played it again.

I suppose I wanted to make sure I understood the words, that I had not misheard the song at the National Theater and that I was not mishearing it now.

No, I was not.

This version of "Every Single Person" was not exactly a tribute to our Caring Leaders. Was it a tribute to our sacred Homeland? Perhaps it was in a backward and indirect way, but it did not mention the words "our sacred Homeland," which you were really supposed to do when you were showing proper respect. I suppose I was not completely sure what this song was about—it was kind of abstract, such is what is called theoretical. But I am an educated person. I understood well enough to know that this encore version of *Mali Golli Zeenkey,* nice as it sounded, was inappropriate material for the reigning co-champion of the National Song Competition. This was obvious.

I felt ashamed for listening to it, just as I had felt when a colleague at *Perriodocko* showed me some objectionable images of unclothed people that he had discovered on his computer. But I am a weak person, with congenital problems that have been duly noted in my unsuccessful application for National Hero service. Sometimes I am not as disciplined as I know I should be. I could not stop myself from looking at the filthy computer photos, and I could not stop myself from listening to Miss Mae Love's song, again and again.

She sang so movingly. Her singing was possibly the most sublime sound I had ever heard. What a shame, I thought, that this magnificent voice was being wasted on inferior material, on irrelevant whimsies instead of something constructive and useful. Something good for everybody.

I cannot say how long I stood there at the intersection listening to "Every Single Person." The light changed back to red, and then green, and I think red again.

Eventually, I started pedaling again toward home, with Miss Mae Love serenading me in the dark the whole way.

At some point on my journey through the deserted streets—I do not recall at this time the precise moment—it is perhaps possible that I began to hum along, to copy the sounds, to sort of in a way partially sing with her (in my head, not out loud). Without trying, without making an effort, I had inadvertently memorized all the words, the whole song. Despite its flaws, I had to admit that "Every Single Person" was somewhat unforgettable.

When I arrived at my street, I saw an orange-yellow glow flickering in the window of my father's apartment. This was splendid: My family was still awake, still eagerly awaiting my return, craving the trusted information that only I could gather, dying to hear my sensational stories.

I clicked off my tape recorder and stowed it in my coat.

I was home.

CHAPTER TWENTY SEVEN

When I walked through the door of our apartment, my entire family was gathered on the floor around several broad candles, slurping soup and excitedly interrupting each other—like children, really. The whole room glowed orange, reminding me of the roasting campfires we used to have at Youth Camp, before the changeover.

My wife rose and skipped across the room to me. "Hello, Dear Husband," she said, cheerfully. Then she gave me a glancing kiss—on the cheek—and giggled shyly.

"Hello, hello," I said. "You all seem to be in a good mood."

"Did you see Miss Mae Love?" Gurly implored.

"Yes, of course I did."

"AAAHHH!" she screamed. "You did not!"

"But of course I did. And Miss Angel Lee Diamond, and Miss Baby Sweets, and Boss Bo. Oh, yes, I saw everyone."

Gurly could not say anything. She was waving her hand near her face and beginning to blubber. Finally she said, "Wow, wow, wow, wow. Wow-wow."

Boy, who I could tell had been enjoying his *bolo*, opened his eyes wide, like a madman, and said, "She is infected. Gurly is infected by that song. Everyone is."

I ignored him. "Hello, father. You are up late! Past midnight. It is already *Tink.*"

"Ah, well. We are having a party. We are celebrating a most entertaining National Song Competition," he said, emphasizing each word with his head. "Most entertaining."

"Yes, I must agree with the accuracy of that statement," I remarked. "That is also how it appeared to me from where I was viewing."

"Tell me *everything*," Gurly said, and everyone laughed.

My wife touched my shoulder. "Pardon me, Dear Husband, but before you begin would you like to have some soup? I have just warmed it for you."

"Oh, I have already eaten," I informed her. "There was an extensive buffet at the Official Media Conference. You know how these things are."

"A buffet?" Gurly wanted to know.

"Yes, with food," I assured her. "Of course, it is free to properly credentialed members of the National News Service."

Boy made an unpleasant snorting sound. "Our taxes hard at work." No one knew if they were supposed to laugh, but Boy did, so then everyone else did, too.

"Yes, I agree, it is hard work. But you know what is said: someone must toil so that others can prosper." I chuckled. "Besides, getting to hear Miss Mae Love the Next Great One live and in person at the National Theater during the finals of the National Song Competition—well, that part is not so bad."

"AAAHHH!" Gurly screamed again. Everyone laughed at her silliness. "What is she like? What is she like?"

I thought for a moment.

"You met her, right?" Gurly asked.

"Yes," I said, silently reviewing all the reasons why that was not really a lie.

"And?"

"Well, I suppose she is like what you saw on the television."

My father nodded. "Quite beautiful. Nice physique."

"Yes, that too," I said, smirking.

The candlelight played across my wife's face. She said, "Beautiful voice, as well. Quite beautiful. Do you not think so, Dear Husband?"

"Yes, I suppose I would have to agree," I said. "That would be an accurate statement. She is pretty good."

Gurly giggled, "You must have the most amazing voice in our entire sacred Homeland to be the champion of the National Song Competition."

"Co-champion," I corrected her.

Gurly winced. "The what?"

"The co-champion. History was made tonight. First time ever. There was a tie."

"Have you been drinking *bolo*?" Gurly said. She cackled, and everyone else laughed, too.

I patiently explained to them what happened, that there had been math errors, and so forth. And I reminded them of the really neat part. "Because this all happened after the NTV-4 broadcast was over, you are just like members of the top one-hundred. You are insiders. Because you know *me*, you know something historical that the rest of our regular citizens will not discover until tomorrow, after *Tink* ends. Is that not remarkable?"

"What are you saying?" father asked, annoyed. "I do not follow what you are saying."

My wife poured me a cup of water, which I drank while I explained it to him all over again. "Year Fourteen co-champions. History was made tonight. And I was there, and now you know."

My father was not a stupid man, just under-educated. He kept insisting that he saw the whole thing on NTV-4. "She was champion, and she did her encore song, and then the show ended."

"*After* the broadcast ended, father. That is when the error was discovered. But, really," I reminded him, "in a way it is even more glorious to have two champions, two great song goddesses. I mean, Miss Angel Lee Diamond, who I also had the pleasure of meeting in person, at the Official Media Conference, is quite superb, also. She is not Miss Mae Love. I can grant you that. But she is certainly not someone to be ashamed of."

"Two-time previous winner," Boy mentioned.

I turned to my brother. "And now three. I must tell you, because I know you have been a long-time supporter of her, that Miss Angel Lee Diamond in person is just as impressive as she is on television. Now, Miss Mae Love—well, now this is a different story altogether. She is probably the most—"

"AAAHHH!" Gurly screamed again. But this time the sound was not enthusiastic. It was terrified.

She had one hand over her mouth and the other pointing at father.

His face was contorted, and he was clutching at his chest. Boy and I both dove to him.

The color drained from his face, and he made whimpering, wheezing sounds, like a dog that has been hit by a *blecky*. It was very difficult to look at.

Gurly and my wife removed his slippers and began the foot massaging treatment that our Health Advisor Experts have determined is the best response to any sort of cardiac event. It did not seem to have an immediate effect.

Boy held father's head in his good hand and rubbed his scalp with his stump. "Father, father, father," he said, repeatedly.

"Father, father, father." But I do not think father could hear us anymore.

The women were crying, getting hysterical. Everything was happening too fast. We could not make it stop.

"Call for a doctor!" Boy yelled at me. "Help! Help!"

I did not have time to explain to him that my phone was at *Perriodocko*, where it was to be used only for official business. I did not know the right thing to do. "Massage his feet!" I cried, dashing for the door.

I did not know where I was going, or who I was looking for. The late hour, the energy restrictions, the widespread intoxication—it was a very unlucky time for this kind of emergency to occur.

Many neighbors had congregated in the dark hallway outside the apartment. When I burst into the crowd, somewhat frantic, they asked, "Is everything all right? We do not mean to pry, but we heard shouting."

"My father," I croaked. "His heart." I tried to say more, but I could not.

"It would probably be a good idea to get him to the hospital," someone proposed. "I am just mentioning this."

Everybody concurred. "Yes. That is probably a good idea."

They looked to me, seeking my approval. The neighbors knew that a hospital visit for a regular citizen such as father would be unimaginably expensive. They probably suspected our family could afford it, but no one had the audacity to make assumptions, or to get involved in our private matters.

"Yes. Yes. Of course," I stammered. "Yes. The hospital." I could not think. I was losing my mind. I was waiting for some sign that this was all a terrible dream from which I would eventually awake.

"We will help," someone offered. "We will take him."

I nodded dumbly. I was having trouble finding words. "Yes," I finally said, "let us take him to the hospital. That is what we shall do. We shall take him to the hospital. Thank you. Thank you. We will carry him to the hospital."

I went back inside the apartment.

But it was too late.

Boy was wailing. "He is not breathing." My wife and Gurly were crying and moaning, hugging father on the floor.

I knelt beside him. His eyes and mouth were open, but he was gone.

"Oh, father," I heard myself saying. "My father."

Everything became blurry and chaotic. The women were weeping and screaming and sobbing. *Ah bolah*, it was terribly upsetting and difficult. I did not want to believe what I was seeing. I wanted to deny it, to find a reasonable explanation. Eventually, however, I understood that the inevitable had occurred, and I could do nothing to change it. At that moment, I had a powerful impulse to lie down beside my father, there on the floor, to go to sleep and never wake.

I did not say this, of course. My family was falling apart, and someone had to take charge, to be a leader. Someone needed to be strong in the face of weakness. I must confess that I was not sure I had the willpower to be that person, but I knew I must try.

I forced myself to avoid tears. I could do that later, in private.

"He was a good man," I said, nodding. "A very good man." I felt many feelings welling in my chest and my voice began to quiver. But I controlled my breathing and concentrated on the candle, on the flame. "Let us give him the proper respect now. Let him rest. Let him be."

I closed his eyelids.

Boy and Gurly and my wife continued to wail. I could not be around them. It was too difficult.

I stood and returned to the neighbors standing in the open doorway. "Thank you. Thank you, all. Thank you for your kindness. I do not think there is anything else to do at the moment. My entire family thanks you."

"I am so sorry. He was a good man," an older gentleman from down the hall replied.

"Yes. Yes, he was," someone else said.

"Yes," the woman next door agreed. "A good man. I am very sorry."

Many neighbors offered their condolences, saluting and shaking my hand, and then retreating back to their apartments. But the crowd at the door did not diminish. As one person left, two more seemed to arrive, many holding small candles. After a while, I did not recognize many of the visitors. They must have lived on other floors. They must have heard the commotion.

There were so many of them, and they were all so nice. Some of them brought little packages of fishmeal cakes, or pots of vegetable soup. "For your family. Please take it in your father's memory. It was an honor to know him."

By now, my wife and Gurly had joined me to receive the visitors and their thoughtful contributions. Boy stayed inside, paralyzed by grief. I was worried about him—even more than usual. Every so often I would excuse myself from the neighbors and check on him. He just stared straight ahead, saying nothing.

An old woman, a *flona*, appeared at our door, with a younger man—her son, I presumed—guiding her by the elbow. "Your father was not a good man," she announced. "He was a *great* man." She handed me a paper bag.

"Thank you, *flona*," I said.

"Open it," she said, looking at the bag.

I unfolded the top and peered inside. It was filled with *sensas*, tiny white onions, the shape and color of fat, oversized pearls.

Before I could properly express my appreciation for this extravagant gift, another *flona,* this one even older, appeared. She thrust a pale green *filolo*, the shape of a wise man's brain, into my hands. "In his honor. Please enjoy."

I tried to show my family's gratitude, to say how unnecessary—but certainly appreciated—it was of them to bring us fresh food, a costly and hard-to-obtain gift. But I was nearly overwhelmed by so many emotions, and all I could manage was, "Thank you. Very kind. Thank you."

Someone else I did not recognize, a man about my age, came next. He said nothing except, "I am sorry," and placed in my hand a firm red fruit such as what is called a tomato, but nearly twice as large as any of those I had seen in pictures. Before I could properly thank him, he left.

The same thing happened with another man, although this man gave me a radish, a plump one.

Then an even younger man, young enough to still be a volunteer National Hero, stood before me, stifling tears and sniffling. Wordlessly, he presented to me the most perfect pepper ever grown, emerald green and voluptuously curved, just as my father would have liked it.

"You knew my father?" I asked, perhaps a bit too skeptically. I had not noticed these neighbors before, not on our floor, not anywhere in the building.

The young man nodded. "He was our hero," he said, his voice trembling.

A girl of the same age stepped forward, holding a platter of gray-brown mushrooms, fragrant of soil. "He helped everyone."

I sighed. "That is very nice of you to say." It really was. Not necessary, of course, yet very nice. How generous, how warm-hearted these youngsters were.

But a horrifying thought crossed my mind. What if all these nice people had come to the wrong apartment, to honor the wrong man? This was my father, after all, not a Dedicated Servant, not even a member of our local Council Advisory Board. Perhaps there had been some mistake, some miscommunication. Perhaps I really *was* dreaming, and all these strangers were inexplicable characters with connections to my father that only my subconscious mind could understand.

I looked down the hallway, now brightened by numerous candles. There must have been a dozen more people waiting to pay their respects. Some were my father's age. Many of them, however, could not have been more than a few years out of University. Most of them were sniffling and weeping. All of them carried gifts.

"Please forgive me if this sounds rude," I said to the girl with the mushrooms. "But could you please tell me how it is that you knew my father?"

The girl placed a small paper packet in my hand and curled my fingers around it. She looked at me, her eyes glistening, and said, "Your father gave us seeds."

CHAPTER TWENTY-EIGHT

By the time the last visitor had departed, it was very late, the middle of the night. I was spent, utterly exhausted. But sleep was out of the question. My father was still lying where he had fallen.

Boy had regained enough of his senses to agree with me that when morning came, when the sun returned, we should arrange for the disposal of the body, which Gurly guarded with a plastic fan, keeping the flies away. He also agreed with my plan to compose an obituary. I would bypass the usual chain of command and give it directly to Chief Editor Pops, who we hoped would grant us an exception and publish the notice in *Perriodocko*.

I sat at my kitchen table staring at a blank sheet of paper, gleaming in the candlelight. I did not know what to write. Other than the most basic details—born; died; resident of—I was uncertain how to describe who my father was.

All around our apartment, on every available space, were donated vegetables. Dozens of them, more than a single family could eat in a week. There were even more next door, on Boy's counter, near the sink. This was not the optimal moment to investigate the particulars, but I was beginning to understand that my father had something to do with this bounty, that he may have done some things, some un-permitted things, our family would not be proud of.

I made a few false starts. When I read my words out loud, nothing sounded honorable, or accurate. I was hopelessly distracted. What other secrets would he take to the crematorium, I wondered? Were there other shameful revelations to come?

There were.

When I went next door to check on Boy, who had returned to his apartment to organize father's few belongings, he was sitting on father's bed, slowly shuffling through a stack of letters and cards and various papers. "He kept this stuff hidden behind her portrait," Boy said, indicating on the wall the large photo of our mother, the picture father had never removed, not even after many years. "He put everything there."

"You knew?" I asked.

Boy shot me a look that said, *You must be the stupidest goat in the whole world.* "We shared a room. Yes."

I had a thousand questions, a million questions. But my mind was not functioning. I was in somewhat of a daze. If you have ever watched your father die, I suppose you would understand.

"I do not know what to say," I informed my brother. "I do not know what to do. I am stuck."

He looked at me, not unkindly.

He nodded.

He looked down at the stack of papers in his lap.

"Here," Boy said, handing me a small rectangular card, yellowed and wrinkled, with handwriting on it. "Now you know.

CHAPTER TWENTY-NINE

The night was cool—pleasantly cool, bracingly cool, but not shockingly so. The night reminded me that I was alive, no matter how empty I felt inside.

I had told my family I needed some fresh air. "This has been a very long and difficult day for me," I reminded them. "Please allow me some time to clear my head."

They had understood.

My wife had offered to accompany me, but I assured her I would be all right, and that I would not be away long, or go far.

I did not really know where I was going. I just needed to walk.

The lights were still out, of course, as they would be for the entire day of *Tink*, until Midnight, another twenty hours or so. Yet my street was not terribly dark. Even at this late hour, long after the last National Song Competition party must have ended, candlelight still flickered in apartment windows. There seemed to be even more people awake than when I had arrived.

I am not a philosophical man, and I do not care to brood on abstract concepts too much. But, I confess, I was having difficulty understanding a world that could make me so happy one hour and so sad the next. I searched my mind for the bad thing I must have done, the transgression I must have committed that made me deserve such sorrow.

There were many. But the one I kept returning to was this: I could have been a better son.

I fingered the crinkled note card in my back pocket, the one Boy had given me. Yes, I could have been a better son.

I could have brought father more treats. I could have listened to his simple opinions with closer attention. I could have tried harder to find him a proper job doing something worthwhile for our sacred Homeland. I could have helped him understand how the system really works.

I should have.

Ah bolah, I could not stand myself. I wanted to disappear, to vanish—like some of my friends, thirteen years ago.

But I kept walking. I figured I would go to the end of our block and turn around. When I got there, the next street was even lighter, with even more candles illuminating the windows. So I continued, aimlessly putting one foot in front of the other and telling myself this was really all I could do at the moment. Just keep going. Do not stop.

For some unknown reason, I feared that if I stopped I might never take another step. It is hard to explain.

I thought about a million things that are probably not worth noting, thoughts about my parents, both of them now gone, and my brother and our sacred Homeland and my fellow citizens, and, I suppose, myself and my damned *meowkaleet*. So many different things.

I got lost in musing too much, and the next time I noticed where I was, where I had walked to, I was rather far from home.

I looked at my great-grandfather's watch, the one he had given to my grandfather, who had given it my father, who had given it me. It was past 5:00 a.m. I had been walking for more than an hour.

I considered turning back, returning to my family—what was left of my family. I had not slept for what seemed like forever. My fatigued brain was probably not working correctly, and I was somewhat distraught about my father, which I think was to be expected under the circumstances. This perhaps explains my very poor decision to continue on my journey to nowhere instead of behaving like a responsible citizen and going to the place I was most needed.

For this I apologize. I am most ashamed of my terrible judgment.

But for some unknown reason, something about the walking and the breathing, the thinking and the remembering, made me feel a little better, a little more enthusiastic about facing another day. I do not know why.

I kept walking.

I cannot say if I consciously decided to go to National Park, or if I was drawn there by accident or some magnetic force, but that is where I found myself. I looked up, and there I was, in the center of the city, not far from the National News Building, strolling beside the impressive iron fence that delineates the Park's perimeter. Without considering the consequences, I wandered inside through the main gate, which remains open year-round except on the occasion of a private function involving our Caring Leaders, and those are increasingly rare. Too many security concerns, it has been reported.

Even with our improved crime situation, some people still believe the National Park is not a safe place to visit at night, that it is somehow dangerous or sinister. But I have always known this to be inaccurate. *Bebudew op en beberoo kap.* How can you be alone when there are hundreds—maybe thousands?—of people sleeping all around you, beside little trash-fueled fires?

The sun had not yet risen, and most of the park's night-time residents, the *blayzoneet*, were still asleep, snoring and grunting as I walked past them and their tattered blankets. Most of these people are from the provinces and are not well-educated. They do not mind the dirt and the bugs. They are used to it.

Two National Heroes on patrol, vigilantly searching for interlopers and permit violators, approached me in the gloom, shining a flashlight. They asked to see my identification, which I handed over with a salute. One of them shined his torch on my papers while the other illuminated my face, hurting my eyes somewhat. "What are you doing here?" one of them asked.

I did not know how to answer this question. "My father," I started to say, but I was unable to find the words to explain everything clearly. I did not know how to make these fine young men understand something that I myself did not fully understand.

"Your father?" the other Hero asked, growing impatient.

"Yes," I said. "My father."

"He is here?"

I shook my head. "He, my father—well, he was a patriot. He wanted me to visit the National Museum to be reminded again why we are all so fortunate to have been born in our sacred Homeland." I looked right into the Hero's blinding white light, and without blinking I said, "I have arrived early to be the first in queue for the educational program."

The Hero holding my papers handed them back to me. "Smart. You know how it gets on *Tink*."

"Yes," I said.

"You are free to go stand in line."

"Thank you," I said. "*Grabvey*." I tried to offer the salutation with energy and passion, but for some unknown reason it came out as a mumble.

"What?"

I cleared my throat. "*Grabvey*," I whispered. I just did not have the strength.

The National Heroes made a somewhat perplexing (and inaccurate) comment about my masculinity and walked away, keeping our National Park safe for everyone.

Assuming they were observing me, I took care to head toward the National Museum, past the Refreshment Center and Liberation Pond, past the children digging for tasty night worms on the banks. I kept walking.

It occurred to me that viewing the multi-media education program at the National Museum might actually be a very fine idea. Unanswerable questions, so many of them, were swirling about in my aching head. Perhaps, I told myself, I would find reassurance and comfort there. Maybe a brief reminder of our shared history and sacrifice would bring me some peace of mind, some solace. Some direction.

Yes, that is what I would do. I would seek inspiration.

The sun was just beginning to appear in the East, gradually changing the blackness to dark grey, and I thought I could make out in the distance a small clutch of my fellow citizens already assembled at the Museum's door. It would not be open for another two hours, but by then the queue would be miles long.

I quickened my pace.

As I neared the Museum's former front lawn, I encountered a group of park dwellers huddled around a modest fire, which, I noticed, was being kept alive with crumpled old copies of *Perri-odocko*—in all likelihood retrieved illegally from "Trash Mountain," our Municipal Dumping Ground. I was so flummoxed by seeing Miss Angel Lee Diamond's smiling face being fed into the flames that I did not summon the appropriate authority or voice my disapproval.

"*Grabvey!*" one of them shouted at me. "Good night. Good morning. Good whatever it is."

I did not want to be rude, but I did not want to tarry. They were an unappealing lot, unclean and foul-smelling, lying around in empty Piko Juice boxes and fishmeal cake wrappers, the rubbishy remains of what looked to have been a grand *bolo* binge. I thought to remind them that if they did not clean up their mess before the Sanitation Inspector arrived they would be cited and placed in the litter lock-up. But I said nothing. They surely were aware of the regulations.

"Have you a spare *uchaana?*" one of the *blayzoneet* asked.

"No. I do not smoke," I grunted.

"That is a shame," someone commented, and they all laughed. "Well, how about some extra wine, then?" They laughed some more.

"Here," I said, pulling out my wallet. "I do not need these." I pinched a wad of unused *bolo* tickets and tossed them on the ground, not too near Miss Angel Lee Diamond's smoldering face.

The men pounced on them like vultures alighting on carrion. "Thank you, sir. Thank you, thank you. You are a great citizen. You are a great man."

I said nothing and continued on. I did not feel great. I did not even feel good.

As I walked away, I could hear the ruffians chortling and joking and brazenly flouting the rules.

I could hear them singing.

Even with their rough voices and awful pronunciation, I recognized the tune. And for some unknown reason, I found myself quietly humming along under my breath.

When I got to National Museum's entrance, about a dozen people, mostly couples, and one enterprising family of four, were already assembled in an orderly queue. They were talking softly amongst themselves, and when I took my place at the back of the line, I could hear the citizens in front of me discussing the National Song Competition and our sacred Homeland's new Year 14 Champion, Miss Mae Love the Next Great One.

I did not bother to correct them. The next day, when NTV-4 came back on the air and *Perriodocko* appeared, they would find out we had been blessed with two winners.

"It is a delightful song," one woman was saying to her husband. "I like it. Miss Mae Love is a worthy champion. I am very happy she triumphed."

"Yes, yes, good singer, good song," he agreed, tapping his foot in the dirt. Very softly, but loudly enough that I could hear, the man began to quote the melody, using nonsense sounds, like a gurgling baby. I do not know if he was being careful to obey all relevant regulations or if he really did not know the words. "*Bah-dop-na-da-ka-ka, boo-pee-doo-pee-loo-pee.*"

I could not stop myself. "I did not mean to be eavesdropping on you, and, no, I am not *Kapaa*," I said, trying to smile reassuringly. "But, in fact, the words are '*mali golli zeenkey.*' That is how it begins. I have reason to be quite sure of this."

"Ah. Yes. I see," the man said, slightly surprised, I think. He nodded. He looked at his wife. He looked at me. "Thank you, sir. *Grabvey.*"

"More power to you, also," I said.

We stood in awkward silence. I wondered if these strangers could tell that I was sad, or if they sensed I was hiding a secret. I wondered if they had living parents. I wondered if they would care to know that the tired-looking man standing behind them in line was a reprehensible weakling who had abandoned those who needed him most. I wondered if the evil I harbored in my private thoughts was as obvious to them as it was to me.

The sun, I noticed, was just beginning to turn the horizon the faintest shade of blue, and the entire majesty of our beautiful National Park was beginning to come into full view in the dawning light. There were more *blayzoneet* congregated on the grounds than I had thought. Some of them had cute little tents constructed from cardboard boxes of dubious origin. Some of them even had pillows made of partially crushed plastic bottles. Although they could not read or write and they would never acquire the necessary education and training to be Dedicated Servants, or anything other than charity collectors, these pioneering campers possessed an enterprising native intelligence that would always be useful to our sacred Homeland's survival and progress, especially if it was harnessed properly. This cheered me somewhat.

Still, I longed for distractions, things to take my mind away from the irreversible, cold facts that could never be fully escaped. But everything I heard, everything I saw, brought me back to the image of my father, my dead father, lying on the floor, desperate for breath, desperate for help. As the sun crept higher into the sky, I remembered how he had liked to go for early-morning walks, before anyone else was awake. Father had always claimed he was simply getting exercise, starting his day fresh. He never mentioned where he went, and I never asked. And now I was not sure if any of that mattered.

I was not sure if *anything* mattered. No, I really could not complain. But I could not be happy, either. Life was too strange for me to understand.

For one ridiculous moment, I thought to say this out loud, to have such as what is called a meaningful conversation with my fellow citizens waiting for the doors to open.

Before a single absurdity escaped my lips, I heard in the distance the unmistakable sound of a motor engine rumbling faintly, getting bigger and closer by the second. In the relative silence of a *Tink* morning, it sounded particularly loud and clamorous. Since *hahnkers* do not run on *Tink*, I initially assumed the vehicle to be an ambulance or fire truck, but there was no accompanying siren, and the sound was weirdly shrill, a mechanical shrieking, as though the engine were stuck in first gear, getting more distressed the faster it went.

Those of us in line fell silent. Along with everyone else in National Park who was awake, we turned in the direction of the noise. We had been warned repeatedly to be vigilant, to be on the lookout for sneak attacks by those who wished to do us harm, to exploit us for their wicked desires, turning our population into their slaves and concubines. I could not help thinking that the fighting machine, or whatever it was roaring through the empty streets, might signal the beginning of our end.

If these were indeed terrorists, they had partially succeeded in their obscene mission. I felt terror.

But I also felt a kind of resignation. Perhaps, I thought, my father, gentle man that he was, had picked a very good time to make his exit.

And I must confess, shameful as it is to admit, that I was almost prepared to join him. *Ah bolah,* that is how confused and tired I had become.

The shriek grew louder. It seemed to be heading right toward us. We frantically surveyed the area. The National Museum was still locked, and there seemed to be no suitable place for sanctuary, except in Liberation Pond, if you were able to hold your breath underwater. Children cried, adults cursed. Frightened *blayzoneet* cowered near their shelters as brave National Heroes, small groups of them from every direction, their weapons drawn and their boots kicking up dirt, ran toward the Park entrance to protect us. Yet for some unknown reason, the sight of them in their proud green uniforms no longer gave me confidence, only a sense of dread. Some things, I had come to realize, were too powerful to stop.

Many of my fellow citizens automatically assumed the Safety Position. I did not. I had lost interest in self-preservation.

As the screaming motor approached the National Park, it sounded as though it might explode. Suddenly, there was a series of crashing, crunching collisions, metal on metal, broken glass, squealing tires.

The noise stopped. The terrorist vehicle had somehow been disabled. Our Heroes had rescued us again. Life as we knew it would go on.

I am sorry, but I did not feel the urge to celebrate.

Then, with a piercing, screaming roar, the machine—or the tank, or whatever indestructible demon this was—resumed its inexorable rampage, breaking everything in its path. I could hear the damage it was causing. There was no doubt: it was headed into National Park, the very heart of our civic pride.

I heard no gunshots. I heard no explosions. Why were our National Heroes not shooting it? Why were they not firebombing it?

Because it was a *blecky*.

Someone very important had to be inside.

I could see it now, lurching and shuddering, swooping one way and then the other, its motor screaming in pain. *Ah bolah,* the car was being driven in reverse!

It was weaving wildly. People abandoned their Safety Position and ran to avoid the swerving sedan. Some people dove into the pond, the closest place to take cover. Others cowered beneath benches. You really could not tell where this out-of-control automobile might go next. It never got close enough to the National Museum to threaten the treasured collection inside, but I was able to get a clear glimpse as it screeched past, leaving dirty clouds in its wake. This *blecky* was badly dented and scraped. Its darkened windows were cracked, and one of the tires was flat. It looked like it was on the verge of disintegration.

But it kept going, tearing through the park as civilians screamed and confused National Heroes gave chase.

I did not have my notebook, and I did not have my pencil. But I had my training. This was quite possibly news. This was quite possibly *front-page* news—assuming there were not more important and enlightening articles that needed to be published. And here I was, the only qualified professional on the scene.

Call it fate. Call it destiny. Call it luck, if you wish. I realized then that I had been brought to this place, this time, for a purpose. A real purpose.

I ran after them. I ran as best I could.

The *blecky* clipped some statues and missed others, avoiding most of the benches and cardboard tents and, miraculously, all of the obedient citizens grabbing their knees and staring at the ground. Those who dared, those who could not quell their foolish impulse to get involved, followed the car, their hands full of *scrachi* rocks, ready to defend and attack if called upon.

All of us in pursuit were careful not to get between the juggernaut and our National Heroes, who did not seem to know if they should command the *blecky* to stop, or if they should escort it to wherever it wanted to go. No one had ever encountered such a situation before. No one was sure who was in charge.

The car retreated in the general direction of National Park's far end. There was no place else to go, really. It was running out of room to maneuver—and I was running out of breath.

I could not keep up. My legs refused to move. I stopped, wheezing and huffing, cursing my short leg, cursing the few precious *plongi* that had made all the difference in the course of my life. And as I stood there, it suddenly became obvious what the battered *blecky* was targeting: with a booming, sickening explosion of metal meeting stone, the car crashed into the National Amphitheatre band shell.

National Heroes, careful not to get too close, surrounded the vehicle, its trunk end smashed and folded into the back seats, completely wrecked.

The band shell had been damaged slightly, a whole chunk of the stage-front lying in pieces on the ground. But it was still standing, undefeated.

I willed myself to be a man, to be a winner, not a quitter. I made myself put one foot in front of the other, and then again, and again, and again. I made myself keep going.

I was gasping, limping, suffering. But I was alive. I was present. I was there.

I was right there when the driver's door cracked open.

I saw it with my own eyes. I was there.

As the door swung out, with a pronounced creak, all the bystanders jumped back, including the National Heroes. "Safety Position!" the Heroes yelled at the onlookers. "Safety Position!"

Everyone dropped, cowering behind their protectors. I did not.

The National Heroes seemed unsure of where to point their guns. No one was giving clear orders.

Then the top of a head appeared, a puff of black hair. And then a pair of nervous eyes, peering over the door frame. Then the whole face.

It was TupTup.

He was bloodied, with cuts on his chin and his hands. One of his legs seemed to be injured, for he could not stand straight without great difficulty.

But he was smiling.

"Hello. Hello. Good morning. Hello," he called out, waving to everyone, as though he had just arrived at an office party. "My name—well, that is a different story altogether. I am called TupTup."

A clutch of National Heroes approached him.

"Wait!" he cried out, bending into the car.

They froze. I feared they would shoot him. I feared they would assume he had a bomb.

TupTup reemerged with a stack of papers, which he began distributing to each of the startled National Heroes. "Here. Here. Yes. Here you are. I am TupTup. I am the celebrated son of a distinguished man. I am a distinguished man. Yes! But let me ask you something. You can read it for yourself."

Even from the back of the crowd, I could see what TupTup was handing out to the confused National Heroes. It was an old copy of the newspaper. I could make out the headline: *Celebrated Son Joins* Perriodocko *Staff.*

"I will read to you if you cannot read it," TupTup cheerfully announced. "It says, 'We are honored and humbled to welcome such a distinguished man, the offspring of an equally distinguished man, to our humble enterprise.' Yes! That is what Chief Editor Pops of *Perriodocko*, published by the National News Service daily, except on *Tink*—that is what has been said about me. I Immmm. Yes. I am a distinguished man. I work at *Perridocko*. I am an expert on *chu-chu*. But this is obvious."

National Heroes were making calls on their radios. Nobody knew what to do. Where were the *Kapaa?* Where were the backups?

"This is my *blecky*," TupTup said. "My father runs the Bureau of Industry. He is also a distinguished man. Yes. Hmmmm. But let me ask you something. I can show you my top-five girlfriends."

To anyone who did not know and understand TupTup, it would be plainly apparent that this man had lost his mind and was probably a danger to himself and others. Two National Heroes stepped forward to apprehend him.

"Safety position!" TupTup screamed at them. "Safety position!"

I had never in my entire life heard someone yell so loudly.

"Safety position! Now!"

The National Heroes hesitated.

"This is my *blecky*! I am a very important person!" TupTup raved. "I was a judge at the National Song Competition, on NTV-4! With Miss Baby Sweets! I am very, very important! Now do it! Make the Safety Position! Now! All of you!"

The National Heroes looked at each other. No one knew which rule took precedence.

TupTup seethed, "If you do not make the Safety Position, there will be consequences. I am giving you a warning. I am being nice. But let me ask you something else. The warning time is now finished." He pointed his fingers outward, as though they had death-rays coming out of them. He pointed at every National Hero. "Safety position!"

They squatted on the ground. All of them.

I was the only one still standing.

"Hello! Hello, Boss! Hello. Good morning. Hmmmm. I was not expecting to see you this morning of *Tink* in the Year Fourteen—but this is a different story altogether. I would like to talk about something else. Hello! Good morning. Hello."

"Hello, TupTup," I groaned, walking toward him through the maze of squatting people.

TupTup flashed his unique smile-scowl at me. "Hello. Let me ask you something." He seemed to be angry at me.

"Look," I said, calmly, "I am very sorry that I raised my voice at you last night—this night—at the Media Conference. That was wrong."

A crowd of onlookers had gathered, perhaps a hundred or so. They wanted to gawk, but they did not want to risk getting involved. They squatted behind the National Heroes. "But I really must say, TupTup, and I do not mean to be rude, but, Mr. TupTup, you could have hurt these people," I said. "The car. That is not how one drives it, I believe."

"Yes. Hmmmm. But let me ask you something else."

"You need medical attention," I informed him. I had lost my patience. "Enough of this foolishness. You have caused great harm."

"Obviously," he said, avoiding my gaze. "However…" He frowned and breathed rapidly through his nose. I thought he was about to start crying. "However. Yes, obviously. *However*, I am supposed to have a BABA."

I threw up my hands and shook my head. Was *this* how he explained his outrageous behavior? It was despicable. And I was going to tell TupTup this. I was going to say it right there, in front of everyone. A rather large group was continuing to assemble around the scene of the crash, encircling us. They had come from every section of National Park hoping to see blood, to witness a kind of human *scrachi* match. But the world had turned upside down. Now they were confronted with National Heroes in Safety Position and an injured lunatic blabbering utter nonsense. Right in front of everyone, all of them, I was going to summon my courage and tell TupTup to his face that even though he was indeed a Very Very Important Person, I was under the impression that he still was required to obey our laws and our regulations, because they are for the good of all of us, from Caring Leaders down to charity collectors.

I was also going to mention what had happened to my father, and that I would personally appreciate it if he might not make the day any more difficult than it had already been.

I was going to say all this. I was going to put a stop to this unbecoming spectacle. But before I could say a word, TupTup genuinely lost his mind.

I am paraphrasing slightly. He went on at length. "I get a BABA because—and now I think it would be nice if you would listen, boss. Thank you. Thank you for listening. Now. Well. The most important thing is that Miss Mae Love is now my number one girlfriend. Number *one*. And I was a judge, and I know that she was the only champion of the Year Fourteen National Song Competition, and she had the best song, and she was the best, and also she is very extremely beautiful sexy, sexy, sexy, and she was the winner by the voting of the judges and I was one of them and also you were there also as well so it is obvious to everyone that Miss Mae Love the Next Great One was the greatest one, and she is my Number One, my Number *One*, and I am going to marry her because she is the Number One *chu-chu* star, and I am loving her because she is so beautiful and also sexy sexy, and she was the winner of the National Song Competition, but—*but!*—I know what you are going to say in the newspaper where I work, just like you: you are going to *not* accept my report because I am a very important celebrated son but, you see, I am also a special junior Information Gatherer working on *chu-chu*, and you do not, you *never* accept my report because you think I am *DipDip*, but I am *not DipDip*, I am TupTup and I want my BABA, because when they detained the *flona* and they sprayed gas on everyone you said it was a terrorist attack and not what really happened, because I was there and I had my official notebook and I saw old old old ladies who did something wrong with their gardening permits, because probably they are old old old old ladies, and so they did something wrong and so they had to go to jail, which is what happened—and I mentioned, when I mentioned, I *said this* to Uncle and he gave me punishment and hurt me, and he said I was bad and I could not be a worker on *chu-chu* at the newspaper, so *I* said—Ha! Ha!—I said *you* would explain to him everything and then everything would be better and nobody would get in trouble or go to jail, which is where bad criminals go, obviously."

He pointed at me, forcefully, punching the air with his finger. "*You* were supposed to make everything better."

I looked around. The crowd had grown quite large, squatting in crescent arcs around us. I felt as though I were back at the National Theater. But this audience was maybe even larger.

"I am a Deputy Supervisor at *Perriodocko*, our sacred Homeland's newspaper," I announced. "I work for the National News Service. I can be trusted."

TupTup turned his back on me and started to climb upon the plaster rubble and boulders that had been blasted from the band shell in the crash. "Mr. TupTup is in fact a very important person, and we all respect that," I said, certain of what I must do. "But he does not have a license to drive this vehicle. He does not have a permit to perform Public Oration. And he most definitely does not have any authority to give orders to our National Heroes!"

I tried to make eye contact with one of them, but they were all looking down, in classic Safety Position, just as you are taught in school.

I never felt more certain of why I had been placed on this planet. And I never felt happier or sadder in my whole life. I said, "Please, arrest this man."

Nobody moved. TupTup was now standing on the foot of what remained of the stage. "Him," I said, pointing. "The cause of all this trouble."

A single National Hero started to rise.

Then I heard, "*Mali golli zeenkey, ku kolaaku hahnee.*"

TupTup was singing. *Ah bolah,* he was *singing.* The National Hero hesitated, hopelessly confused. He had not been trained to deal with this kind of situation.

"*Ah duwapat mo-loko!*"

TupTup was singing. He was singing Miss Mae Love's encore song. He was singing the words—the other words, the alternate words.

My father's words.

I pulled the wrinkled yellow card from my pocket and followed along. "*Mali golli zeenkey, edap wallay nahnay. Edap kosa mokono.*"

I must say he was not bad. TupTup could carry a tune somewhat.

"*Ontongul. Ontongull. Mali golli zeenkey, ontongull.*"

An elderly *blayzoneet*, his face streaked with grime, his hair matted beneath a goat-hair cap, and his intelligence robbed by *bolo* abuse, rose to his feet. "That was pretty good," he said. And he started to applaud. Others near him rose to their feet, clapping.

"Thank you. Thank you," TupTup called from the stage. "This is a song made famous in Year Fourteen by Miss Mae Love. It does not fit into a category of approved National Song Competition selections. It is called 'Every Single Person.' And she is my number one girlfriend."

A *flona* rose gingerly from the dirt. She had few teeth, and her eyes were rheumy. "I cannot sit any more," she announced.

TupTup began to sing again. "*Mali golli zeenkey...*"

And then, I am compelled to report, with a frail ribbon of a voice, the *flona* joined him. "*Ku kolaaku hahnee.*"

The old *blayzoneet* did a kind of dance, a little jig. "*Ah duwapat mo-loko,*" he croaked.

The three of them sang in rough unison. "*Mali golli zeenkey, edap wallay nahnay, Edap kosa mokono.*"

They were perfectly aware of what would happen next, but TupTup apparently did not care. This was how he wanted things to end, with innocent seniors drawn into his madness.

"*Ontongull!*"

The National Heroes finally came to their senses and moved to apprehend TupTup. He did not run.

He continued singing.

And then, so did everyone else.

As the National Heroes clambered onto the stage, leaving those on the ground unattended, everyone began to sing.

Mali golli zeenkey (Every single person)
Ku kolaaku hahnee (Has a special garden)
Ah duwupat mo-loko (Oh, we must believe the truth)

All the bystanders were abandoning their Safety Position. Everywhere I looked I saw people rising up from the ground, singing.

Mali golli zeenkey (Every single person)
Edap wallay nahnay (Growing something lovely)
Edap kosa mokono (Growing gifts from heaven)

The *blayzoneet* nearest me, a hideously unappealing fellow with black grit beneath his fingernails, turned to me and shouted, "I do not know the words."

One million replies came to my mind, but not one of them seemed to matter. "Here," I said. "This will help." I gave him father's card.

National Heroes had surrounded Tup'Tup. They were pulling out handcuffs.

Hobbling to her feet, a *flona* yelled, "Take me first!"

"You must also arrest me!" an uneducated woman cried out, jumping up.

"I do not have a permit to sing!" a dirty man yelled at a National Hero.

Ontongull (Together)
Ontongull (Together)
Mali golli zeenkey, ontongull (Every single person, together)

There must have been a hundred or even two hundred regular citizens for every National Hero on the scene. They were overwhelmed, and I think I understood how they felt at this moment: You know you are correct and in the right, that you only want the best, but for some unknown reason nobody seems to care anymore.

One brave young National Hero called out to the crowd below, "You must all stop. All of you, every single person, is in violation! *Mali golli zeenkey!* All of you!"

The mob took this as their cue to start the song again. Even louder.

The National Heroes attempted to silence the grotesque and growing choir, to restore order, but it was impossible to hear the authorities. They were drowned out by the sound of a thousand voices, all of them singing.

> *Every single person*
> *Has a special garden*
> *Oh, we must believe the truth*

I knew that reinforcements would arrive soon and all the foolish people and their insane ringleader would face the consequences of their stupidity. I knew that this embarrassing charade would pass. I knew that things would eventually go back to normal.

But I also knew that the sound of all their voices in the morning air, the whole National Park of them, was unlike anything I had ever heard.

As any schoolchild can tell you, we have been taught from the start in our sacred Homeland that many great civilizations have been ruined by an internal cancer, by a sickness that eats away at human minds. This disease causes potentially worthwhile citizens to become distracted by absurd fantasies involving some imaginary deity, a powerful force such as what is called God. The delusion makes people believe that some mythic creature will take responsibility for them.

We have come to understand that this God concept is a lie that was invented to rob of us of our land and our pride.

Da-da-da-da-DAAH-DAAH. I heard my fellow citizens singing, individually and *ontongull,* out of tune and perfectly, and at that moment I knew that everything I had been taught was perhaps possibly somewhat of a mistake. That maybe possibly it was, well … untrue.

Because now I knew. I could hear this. There *was* a God, and he was in every single person. Singing.

This God was in every single person, singing a song. I could *hear* this! And I must say that it was glorious.

It was divine.

Please, I beg your understanding. I am sorry if I have caused offense, and I am sorry that I cannot explain things better. I am sorry to mention certain unpleasant facts that we would all like to ignore. I am very sorry.

But, you see, I have expert training, and, *meowkaleet* be damned, I am proud of that training. It has gotten me to where I am. Therefore, I cannot make a proper Report—Authorized or not—without putting down here on paper exactly what happened. I may be quite wrong about this, but I do feel it is necessary.

I hope I can be forgiven.

When the massive chorus came to the end of "Every Single Person," someone would yell out, "Everybody sing!" and the whole congregation would begin again, with even more singers joining in.

I am sorry to note that I observed several National Heroes who had abandoned all sense of duty. They were singing, too.

The last glimpse I got of TupTup, he was singing with his mouth wide open and tears streaming down his face, in some sort of ecstatic fit.

I never spoke to him again. But I can still hear his voice.

An arm wrapped around my neck and shoulders, putting me in a reverse headlock, and I collapsed backwards into the assailant.

"You are under arrest!" he hissed in my ear, dragging me away from the crash site.

I looked down past my chin and saw an arm and a leg dressed in the familiar emerald green of our National Heroes, and for some unknown reason I immediately relaxed. "Yes, yes," I said. "OK. OK. I am not resisting."

"Keep your head down and keep walking," he ordered, shouting at the back of my head. "Say nothing!" I could barely hear him, but I understood.

The crowd parted for me as I was pushed out. I saw children, little ones. They were singing. I saw *flona*. I saw men my age. I saw men who reminded me of my father. They were all singing.

Mali golli zeenkey, ontongull!

Nobody was stopping them.

"The tanks will arrive soon," I heard my captor say. And although the singing was vibrating in my ears, I thought I recognized his voice.

"Boy?"

He loosened his grip and leaned into me, his lips beside my ear. "If you want to live, keep walking."

"How did you—"

"I have a friend. Please, brother. Walk."

He guided me through the multitudes of singers, thousands of them, of every description. It would be hard to blame one group for this disaster. Which is why, perhaps, no one seemed scared. Everyone was smiling.

We stumbled past Liberation Pond and came to a secret exit that I had not known existed, a small unmarked portion of the iron fence that swung open if you pushed on it the right way, which Boy did. The next second, we were standing on the sidewalk, beside Central Avenue.

"*Ah bolah!*" Boy gasped. He saw it first.

"*Ah bolah!*" I also saw it.

The street was jammed as far as you could see, covered by *hahnkers* parked on the road blocking traffic in every direction. There must have been a million of them, every *hahnker* in the city. It would take you a week to ticket them all.

Each one broadcast the song from their loudspeaker.

It was the National Song Competition version. Someone had obtained an unauthorized recording of the encore performance, and now it was too late. The culprit would be punished, of course. But the music was already out in the air and could never be taken back.

All the windows in the buildings along the avenue were cracking open. Heads emerged, and voices poured out into the dawn. Below, on the sidewalks, people streamed out of the apartment buildings, holding their neighbor's hand, and singing. Little girls made rings around their parents, dancing and giggling and singing. Old ladies in their wheelchairs tapped their armrests in rhythm. Old men in robes and slippers danced with each other, singing. Everyone was oblivious to the seriousness of the situation. Everyone was singing.

My brother was singing. He looked so smart in his National Hero uniform, so dignified. He held his good hand beside his heart, just below his Valor Award, and he sang.

I tried to say, "I am proud of you," but I do not think he heard me. He was crying.

Many other people were crying, too. But they did not appear to be unhappy.

I looked everywhere, as far as I could see. It seemed like every single person in our sacred Homeland was awake now, and alive. And singing.

You could have heard the sound across the ocean. Everybody singing.

Then the shooting started.

CHAPTER THIRTY

I was taken to a safe place. And another one. I have been here at my present location for one night, and I do not know when I will leave, if ever.

I survived. Many did not.

I am a survivor. I suppose I should be grateful for that, and I am, because I am writing this—and if you are reading this then something good has happened. This story, our story, has also survived.

I confess, I did not sing that day. I did the right thing.

But I am singing now, in a way.

I am singing for my sacred Homeland. I am singing for all my fellow citizens, and for my father, and my brother. And for TupTup.

And I am singing for Miss Mae Love.

I am very sorry to say this, and I do not mean to cause offense to anyone. But after talking with people who are experts on such matters, I must also confess that for some unknown reason I think it is perhaps somewhat possible that I am what is called in love with her.

It is a very strange feeling. I cannot explain it. But what they say is true: She is different. And now everything is different, and it always will be.

Now we know a different version. In this one, every single person has a special garden.

There. I have written it.

And I will do it again: *Every single person has a special garden.*

No, I did not sing that day. But I am singing now.

And I hope that you are singing, too.

Every Single Person
By Miss Mae Love & My Father

Mali golli zeenkey (Every single person)
Ku kolaaku hahnee (Has a special garden)
Ah duwapat mo-loko (Oh, we must believe the truth)
Mali golli zeenkey (Every single person)
Edap wallay nahnay (Growing something lovely)
Edap kosa mokono (Growing gifts from heaven)
Ontongull (Together)
Ontongull (Together)
Mali golli zeenkey, ontongull (Every single person, together)

Final Notes

A Note From the Editor

It's always rubs me the wrong way when editors talk about "discovering" writers. I'm sure from time to time it happens that a smart editor finds a promising writer—at a reading; in an issue of a little magazine like Barrelhouse—and then nurtures his or her talent over many years. But more often than not, at least in my experience, "discovering" a writer means learning about someone who's been there all along. It means opening up the electronic submission queue and reading through a slush pile of submissions. When you happen upon the right submission, the feeling can be one of discovery—but less like a scientist discovering a new element in the lab, and more like the "where have you been all my life?" moment when you meet someone you suspect you'll be friends with for years to come.

It was in the slush pile that I first encountered Michael Konik's novel, *Year 14*, in pretty much the form in which it exists here. Given that you've just read the book, I don't need to explain to you why I wanted to publish it. The decision felt pretty obvious. In fact that's one reason I wanted to put this note at the book's end, instead of at the beginning: Michael's novel speaks for itself; it doesn't need my help.

So why include this note at all? Only so I can say a few things about the circumstances under which I read Michael's book the first time, and how those circumstances changed before I read it again, and how they've continued to change over the months in which we've worked at turning his book into the physical object you're holding right now.

The first time I read Michael's manuscript was in the summer of 2016. The second time was in the fall of that year, just a few months later. I don't suppose I need to tell you what changed in the interim.

I mention this context for a couple reasons. The first is to emphasize that the book wasn't written with any explicit political axe to grind. It wasn't written to take down a particular politician, or a particular set of politicians, and while I could certainly recognize certain strands of current American politics in its authoritarian vision, I didn't read the book as any sort of partisan screed. And I still don't, despite everything that's happened since I first decided to accept the book for publication.

Though the book does feel especially relevant right now. And while the events of the last year or so have left me pretty disheartened about the state of American politics—hell, about the state of American culture—re-reading this book while helping to shepherd it to publication has been something of a balm. I've felt really lucky to have had it in my life.

I love books, and I'll always advocate for their importance, but I'm not someone who thinks literature will save us. If literature were going to save us, given the sheer number of great books that exist in the world, we would've been saved a long time ago. But I do believe books can change our lives, even if they do so in small, difficult-to-articulate ways. They can remind us what it means to be human. They can briefly restore our sense of justice, and shared decency. They might not have the answers to our problems, but they can remind us that our struggle toward those answers is worthwhile, and perpetual.

I hope you enjoyed this book, and I hope it did some of that stuff for you. It certainly did for me. And so I guess this note is really just a long-winded way of saying thank you to Michael, for sharing his work with me, and Barrelhouse Books, and letting us put it out into the world. I can only hope we do right by it.

—Mike Ingram
Editor, Barrelhouse Books

Acknowledgments

I completed the first draft of Year 14 in 2009. (It was originally called "Everybody Sing"). For more than three years, my tenacious literary agent Uwe Stender shared the book you're reading now with every publisher in New York you've ever heard of and some maybe you haven't. Although I've never received such loving and reluctant rejection notes, eventually I lost track of how many houses turned it down. Somewhere around 2014, I started to think *Year 14* would remain an unpublished but treasured family heirloom.

So you will please forgive my unchecked meowkaleet if I tell you that when Chief Editor Mike Ingram picked *Year 14* out of all the manuscripts cluttering his desk—well, I was possibly the happiest writer in the world.

I love *Year 14,* and I love the folks at Barrelhouse. They're a righteous crew. Their fighting literary spirit supports countless writers and small publishers, re-affirming the transformative power of stories. Chief Editor Mike not only has tremendous taste in fiction, he's a fine, unobtrusive line editor, with an elegant touch. Adam Robinson's book design and Shanna Compton's cover design (and original illustration) present the work beautifully, poetically. I'm honored to collaborate with such talented people.

I feared I wouldn't get to share my favorite book with the world, that *Year 14* would remain unpublished. My inspiring and encouraging wife Charmaine Clamor periodically and consistently assured me I was mistaken. How grateful I am that she was right.

And if you've gotten this far, if you've honored our creation by reading and living it, I thank you for receiving our love.

Michael Konik
Los Angeles

MICHAEL KONIK is the author of many books of fiction,
non-fiction and poetry. He lives in Los Angeles, where he serves
as poet laureate of Vista Street Community Library and tends
an organic vegetable garden.